"Zaca is one great ride. It serves up everything I need for a page-turning read...settings that make the story come alive, great characters, an intriguing mystery and a dash of paranormal."
Fiction Author Barbara M Hodges

ZACA

R Lawson Gamble

This is a work of fiction. Although the author has
described some actual locations any resemblance to events
or persons living or dead is entirely coincidental.

First Paperback Printing 2015
Rich Gamble Associates
Cover Design Copyright ©2015 By Digital Donna
Photo of Author by Jeffrey Bloom
ISBN-13: 978-1514149430
ISBN-10: 1514149435

FOR ANN

Special thanks to neighbors Pamela and Craig, and to Word Wizards benign dictator Barbara.

FORWARD

There is a place where the mountains tumble one upon the other off into the far distance, peak after treeless peak. Steep ridges connect them and deep canyons slash them apart. The grassy summits are wreathed with black sage. No roads intrude upon this jumble of oak-filled canyons and steep-sided hills, only the ambling trails made by deer, coyotes, and bears. The local Indians believe the spirits of the ancients still travel these trails.

These are not the high ranges of California's Sierra Nevada, towering and snow laden. These mountains are less than five thousand feet high. Little snow falls here, only in the rainy season, and then only on the highest peaks. The rest of the year it is dry. The meadow grasses turn brown, the creek beds fill with dust, and fallen oak leaves are crackly and brittle underfoot. The cattle here have never known the lariat or the branding iron. Bear fatten up on acorns, mountain lions prowl the ridges, and coyotes scout the dry slopes in search of ground squirrels.

The San Rafael Wilderness is fifty miles deep and a hundred miles long, a barely penetrable refuge for wildlife––and for men who wish not to be found. Those who do venture here, to hike or to hunt, keep to the known trails and camps. No gold or other precious minerals were ever found in these mountains. The trees are sparse, only a few fit for lumber. There is water, deep in the hollows, for those who know where to look.

Hundreds of years ago, these hostile hills provided a way for the Chumash Indians to travel around the Santa Ynez Valley and the mission, away from the zealous Spanish priests and the stern discipline of the soldiers. The sacred pyramid summit of Zaca Mountain, and in its shadow the black, bottomless waters of Zaca Lake have special meaning to the Chumash. Some say the lake's unsounded depths contain a passage used by their ancestors to migrate from the Channel Islands to their mainland home. In the old days, the Indians returned each year to the shores of Zaca Lake to perform ceremonies and to absorb the strong currents of energy they found there.

There are legends about this mountain wilderness, stories about strange beings with powers beyond those of the strongest warrior, spirits that roam freely in the dark of night. Before venturing there, the Chumash always appeased the mountain spirits with gifts of bear meat, venison and fruit. Even today they don't tarry in these mountains. When they must travel there, they hurry. No one wishes to be caught beyond the shores of Zaca Lake, past the familiar shoulder of Zaca Mountain after the sun has set.

CHAPTER ONE

A horsefly buzzed him. He swatted at it. The distraction justified a stop, a momentary rest to wipe the sweat from his face with a silk bandana. The sun was unforgiving, the mountainside slope relentless, the prickly brush hostile.

He adjusted the heavy holster where it draped against his damp chest, a clumsy pendulum that swung across his polyester wife-beater undershirt with each labored step. The Glock 22 pistol added little weight, even loaded. The true culprit was his embossed leather holster, a source of pride under most circumstances.

Pedro the Pacifier was a freelance contract killer. The Mexican cartels kept him employed on a regular basis——one or another of them, it didn't matter which to him. His office was an untraceable post office box served for negotiations, a disposable cell phone for all other business. The writhing humanity of the inner city was his usual hunting ground.

Not this, though. Not these dry mountains.

Dust puffed with each footfall. The new Nikes were coated in it, ruined, encased in sweat-moistened adobe. No matter. His fee was generous enough to compel him to cross the border, the first time in his professional career. It would pay for a new pair of sneaks, and much more.

He came to a temporary shelter. It surprised him. There had been no prior indication of its presence. Ahead, the leafy green of marijuana plants confirmed he was in the right place. He pulled out the Glock, checked the load, holstered it. The lean-to was empty; a rifle leaned against it.

A dirt path led up among the young plants. The leaves brushed his shoulders as he walked. Their lush, skunky smell filled his nostrils. He saw movement up ahead among the plants.

Pedro set his hat at a jaunty angle. "¡*Hola,*" he said.

A head popped up above the plants, the face a caricature of surprise.

"Don't be alarmed. I am Pedro. I work for the cartel."

The face stared.

"I have been sent to learn how you progress." Pedro stepped forward.

The face showed alarm. "Who sent you? What is his name?

Pedro advanced another step. He was about three meters from his target. Perfect. "His name is"—in one swift motion Pedro pulled the Glock and fired—"*Señor Muchos Pesos.*"

A round hole appeared in the forehead of the face, a slight surprised look, and the head disappeared.

Pedro went no closer; there was no need. He holstered the Glock, searched among the marijuana stalks for the shell casing. It was gone. Frustrating, not serious.

The walk back through the marijuana plants was pleasant. At the lean-to, Pedro picked up the rifle, a Henry. It looked like a replica. Nice weapon. He put it under his arm.

Time to go. A smile teased his lips. One more arduous trek, a ride to the airport, and he'd be home for supper.

What he saw next had no resemblance to anything in his experience. A creature blocked his path: bipedal, powerful rounded shoulders, ropelike musculature under translucent mahogany skin, lizard-like talons on large leathery hands, hate-filled red eyes in a reptilian face with a long snout and prominent nostrils. It exuded a moldering smell.

Despite his shock, Pedro the Pacifier's instincts kicked in. It took two seconds to raise the rifle. The creature was on him in one.

Pedro felt surprise—nothing more.

CHAPTER TWO

Jesus shivered. The night air sagged around him like a damp cloak. His lips tasted of brine and chafe burned his inner thighs. His whole body ached as if he'd been beaten in a back alley by thugs.

The panga rode gently up and over the swells and water slapped a hollow beat against the wooden hull. Jesus couldn't hear it—he heard only the thunder of the twin 250 horsepower outboard engines that roared on in his ears.

Jesus Hermenegildo Romano did not notice his discomfort. His focus was on the black landmass before him, this coast of Central California. His dreams, his hopes for his family rested there.

Jesus brought the blue glow of his watch close to his eyes. Two A.M. He was on the GPS marker. The signal must come soon, four quick flashes from a truck's headlights somewhere in that darkness. It would come once. If he missed it, it was over. He could not find the secluded rendezvous on his own. His choices then would be few, all unthinkable.

The stillness felt strange after the relentless pounding of the waves against his tough little boat, hour after hour, all the way from Mexico. Few would attempt such a journey, but Jesus was a seasoned sailor, a fisherman accustomed to discomfort in rough seas. He fought waves and weather every day of his life to feed and clothe his family, even as his father and his father's father had done before him.

Jesus had never before ventured on such a long journey in the little panga. Still, it was the perfect boat for the purpose—twenty-two foot long and deep hulled with room for nearly three short tons of cargo, narrow beamed for speeds over thirty-five knots, high bowed with a floatation bulge at the gunwale to minimize spray and increase buoyancy. The small boat rode low in the water and left almost no radar footprint. Best of all, he could drive it right up onto the beach.

He waited. It was difficult to be still. Panic rose and he suppressed it. Time passed. Why hadn't they signaled? They would not desert him; they would not abandon this rich cargo. They would do all they could to preserve their investment.

His mind wandered despite his anxiety. Images of his tear-cheeked Isabella, her brave smile, and his two little girls Juana and Ana Dominga flashed into his mind. His heart ached. They were his life and loves and he would do anything for them, even this sea voyage of five hundred nautical miles all alone in a small boat in the dark of night.

There was no choice. The seas were warming where Jesus fished in Playa San Pedrito. The fish had migrated to cooler waters. More and more often his days ended with an empty boat. Without money from the sale of fish, his family could not survive.

Raul's timing was perfect when he came to him from the Sonora Cartel and offered him work with enough money to support his family for many years to come. Jesus listened. Who would not?

Now the wind picked up and the swells grew and the slender boat rode deep into a wave trough. The wall of water erased the smudge of land for several seconds and when the boat raised again a pinpoint of light twinkled and vanished. Jesus stared. How many had there been? Then another winked and another and still another in rapid succession: four in all...and then darkness. It was the signal. It would not repeat, but it didn't matter. Jesus had his bearings now. He turned the key and the outboard motors roared to life. The propellers thrust the small boat across the tops of the swells.

By the time he saw the white phosphorescent breakers they were all around him. He down-throttled and the little boat tried to pivot sideways but he gave it just enough gas to skim the wave tops. He thought the beach must be close but had no way to know in the darkness, was not prepared when the bow dug deep into the sand and stuck. He flew forward like a rag doll. The soft cargo cushioned his landing but his right knee slammed against the gunwale with cracking pain. The motors roared on, the propellers flailed. He struggled to rise but then the motors went silent and he felt strong hands pull him upright. A whispered voice said, "*Beinvenidos a los Estados Unidos, amigo.*"

Dark shapes moved around the boat. Hands helped him over the gunwale. As his feet touched sand, he saw a shadow lift a bale and pass it to another shadow that moved away. He looked up. An outline of cliffs loomed above him. He breathed in and smelled the smell of a strange land and grew excited.

A heavy bale was thrust into his arms and someone turned him and pushed him toward the cliffs. When he put weight on his knee, pain came in a wave and he gasped, but the knee held. He lurched forward, his legs not yet steady, his knee painful. He followed the silhouette in front of him. The sand underfoot felt dry and loose, then it was the firm footing of a beaten path, and steepness. He saw an area of lighter sky above and then he was ascending a narrow trail alongside an arroyo. The way seemed endless. Jesus was tired, his injured knee nagged. He slowed. He felt a poke from behind.

"Keep moving, *amigo*," came an urgent whisper. "If we are seen the sheriffs will come and we will all go to jail and be deported."

They emerged from the arroyo and came out of the shadows. Bright moonlight illuminated a pickup truck backed to the path. A man stood next to it and took the bales one by one and passed them to a second man who stacked them in the truck bed. Jesus handed off his own bundle and turned to go. A hand gripped his arm.

"No, Señor, your work is done. Get into the truck."

"But my boat..."

"You can not return to your boat. Don't worry. Soon you will be able to buy many more boats. Hurry." The man turned away and took another bale.

His mind fogged with wonder, Jesus climbed into the rear of the large cab. He sank into a soft seat that smelled of leather. He saw the glint of polished chrome. He marveled. He was conscious of his wet clothing, stiff with salt, and the smell of his unwashed body.

Jesus had nothing to wear but the clothes on his back, no possessions, no money, no identification. He was a non-person in a foreign country. There was nothing to do but trust the men who brought him here.

CHAPTER THREE

The planting platform never slowed its steady, relentless pace. It threatened to creep beyond his reach at every step. On either side of him, workers moved as if choreographed: reach up, take the young plant, bend to the earth, scoop a hole, place the plant, pack it, step forward...repeat.

Jesus' back ached. His knee stabbed at each bend. He longed for the end of the row, for the merciful pause while the tractor turned around. The sun bore down. Jesus was thankful for the hooded sweatshirt Jorge had loaned him. It was rank, stiff with dirt and sweat, but its shell-like outer skin deflected the sun's rays. It provided insulation from the cold of the early morning, yet vented the heat from his body during the day.

Jesus was exhausted.

The previous night, once the bales were loaded, the men had concealed the truck's cargo with crates of strawberries before melting away. Only Jesus and two other men were left in the vehicle. They drove to a storage facility somewhere in a sleeping city. A large *Americano* met them with a key. They unloaded the bales into the unit. They stacked cartons labeled Pesticides in front of the bales. The Americano locked it and left. The men got back in the truck, drove out of the city and into the night. They passed wide, flat moonlit fields. On they drove, and on, then turned off the main road into a tunnel of trees. The driver turned off the headlights and slowed the truck. They crunched up a gravel drive to a long narrow building lit by a single bulb alive with moths. A man led Jesus from the truck into the building. They went down a long corridor with many doors. The man opened one of them and ushered Jesus into a small room with a chair and bunk beds.

"I am Jorge," he said. "Give me all your clothing. You can wear this tonight. It is all you will need until morning." He handed Jesus a long woolen nightshirt, pointed to the upper bunk.

Jesus climbed up, crawled beneath the blanket. He went right to sleep.

Too soon it was morning. Every muscle ached when Jesus tried to move. His knee was stiff and painful. None of it mattered to Jorge. Merciless, he pulled Jesus down from the bunk, gave him a pair of baggy trousers, sandals, gloves, a bandana and a sweatshirt, then led him to a large room at the end of the corridor. Food steamed on a long table. It smelled wonderful. It tasted wonderful, the best breakfast Jesus ever had, but no time to savor it. A horn sounded. All the men rose from the tables, shuffled outside, and packed into the back of a flatbed truck. There were women in it. They rode to the fields together.

At the side of the field, pickup trucks and SUVs drove up and the workers climbed out. Did they own their own cars? Jesus gaped. Another horn sounded. Jorge took his arm and tugged him toward a platform on wheels towed by a tractor. He showed Jesus what to do. The platform jerked and started forward. Soon Jesus was in an agony of soreness.

There was no time to think so long as the platform moved. The only rest came in the five minutes it took the tractor to turn and face the next row, when Jesus could close his eyes and stand still. At last the tractor motor went silent. Everyone scattered toward the porta-potties and a shaded table that held drinks and snacks. Jesus stood numb, immobile. He felt a nudge, looked down into flashing brown eyes beneath a sweatshirt hood.

"Come with me," the girl said. "We have only a short time to eat something and rest. You'll need the food for energy. It's a long day."

Jesus went with her as a log moves down stream with the current. At the snack table, he took the cup of juice and tortilla she offered him. After several bites, he said bluntly, "Who are you?"

The girl laughed. "It is I who should ask, who are you? After all, you are the stranger here."

Jesus stumbled over his words. "I am from Mexico..."

She burst into a merry peal of laughter. "And here I thought you were from Sweden." She laughed again, stopped at his look of confusion. "Look around you. We are all from Mexico or South America somewhere. We don't talk about our home, or how we came here."

"I'm sorry..."

"Don't be. I know you are new and I think I can figure out the rest."

The girl pushed her hood back. She was young, perhaps eighteen or nineteen. Her dark hair was lustrous and full, her face was broad with dimpled cheeks.

"Thank you," Jesus said, flustered.

She smiled at him. "We look out for one another here. We become like family."

Jesus gazed at the workers crowded together in the shade.

"We are lucky to work here," the girl explained. "The owner, Señor Reyes, treats us well. Most of us remain here through the year, form friendships. I'm told on other farms it is not this way."

Jesus wanted to ask more questions but the air horn sounded.

"Back to work," the girl said. She tugged her colorful bandana up over her nose.

"Wait! What is your name?"

"I am Candida." Her voice came muffled. She laughed and turned away.

He called after her. "I am Jesus."

She waved.

Jesus trudged back to the platform.

The day was long as any Jesus ever spent, and more taxing. They had an hour for lunch. A shaded table awaited them with drinks, sandwiches and the ever-present tortillas. He didn't see Candida but his new workmates were friendly and made him feel welcome. Toward the end of the lunch hour he saw her arrive in a car with other workers. They had gone elsewhere to eat their lunch. He was filled with wonder at the money and opportunities these workers enjoyed.

When the day was over and the platform cleared and made ready for the next day, Jesus followed the others from the field. Many scattered to their own cars. Jorge found him and guided him to a truck for the ride back to the barracks. The people near him chattered eagerly about their plans for the evening. Jesus dropped his head to his chest and dozed.

After showering—all that hot water—Jesus caught a second breath. Jorge supplied him with clean clothes. After he dressed, Jesus wandered outside and around the building. A dirt drive stretched along an avenue of trees, the way to the women's housing, he guessed. Beyond the barracks with its protector grove of oak trees, an ocean of green fields lay flat as a tabletop to the distant swell of golden hills. The sky was as blue as the sky back home, without a single cloud. Vultures circled in the distance, tiny dark spots. Jesus stood transported by the wonder of it all.

A touch on his shoulder startled him. He turned. It was Jorge.

"It is different from Mexico, yes?"

"Yes, it is very different. Everything is so...perfect. It's all so clean, so tidy and bright."

"Here in the United States, people are not so poor," Jorge said. "They take pride in their possessions. They can afford to keep them up."

"There is so much of everything." Jesus said. "Even these clothes." He looked down at the pressed shirt and trousers Jorge had given him. "I have no money to pay for these."

"You don't need to worry," Jorge said. "Those clothes belonged to Manuel, a worker who went away. He will not be back. He left a closet full of clothing. It is fortunate he was close to your size."

"Why did he leave all his clothing?"

Jorge shrugged. "Why do people do anything? Around here, people come and go. We don't question it." He smiled.

Jesus was drawn to Jorge. The man was relaxed, confident. He had a sincere manner. Jesus thought he could trust him.

"That reminds me," Jorge said. "We need to talk. But it is time for dinner right now. You must eat to keep your energy up. After that, we can talk in our room.

CHAPTER FOUR

Jorge stretched out on his bunk, crossed his arms behind his head. "Make no mistake, you owe much to our business friends in Mexico. They ask little in return. A large payment was sent to your wife so that you need not worry about your family."

Jesus sat on the edge of a produce crate that served as a table, rubbing his knee. He nodded.

"I think you know the business of the Sonora Family," Jorge said. "They are wealthy and powerful but they are also generous to their employees and friends. Their import business is against the law here in the United States. If we are caught, the product is lost, we are sent to jail, maybe even deported. This is a risky business. The family can lose a large amount of money from the loss of a shipment. If they cannot pay the *sembrador*, the grower, he in turn cannot pay the *campesinos*, those who plant the seeds. Of course, the *burro* is lost and another must be found to replace him. The entire system breaks down." Jorge sighed. "It is a very difficult business for the *financiero*, yet the family is ever generous."

Jesus lowered his head. "I am grateful."

Jorge watched him. "Do you like to work in the fields?"

Jesus paused. "It is difficult," he admitted. "But I will soon grow accustomed to it, like the others."

"Perhaps you will not always work in the fields," Jorge said. "Perhaps, if you continue to work hard and remain loyal to the Sonora Family, there will be other work for you, less difficult work. You must understand, it will not be without risk." Jorge's head fell back on his pillow and he yawned. "We will see."

Jesus slept well that night, with pleasant dreams of his wife and daughters. He felt better after Jorge's assurances that his family would receive the promised money. If they lived in comfort until his return, he could face almost anything.

He awakened to the warm touch of the sun's fingers on his cheeks. He sat up in panic. He'd overslept. Jorge was gone. Jesus looked at his watch. He might just be in time for breakfast. He threw on his borrowed clothing and ran down the corridor.

He entered the dining room; the sound of female voices woven with the men's low murmurs surprised him. The women wore their work clothes, their hair already covered by scarves. Only the flash of dark eyes and softer lines of the face gave them away.

Jesus stood with his loaded tray, looked for a space at the crowded tables. He saw an arm wave at the back of the room. It was Candida. He went there. She squeezed out a space next to her.

"Why are you here?" Jesus said. He put his tray down and stepped into the space.

18

"My, you are direct." She giggled. "I work here, remember?"

The space was tight. Jesus was aware of the warmth of Candida's thigh pressed against his. He was flustered; he wasn't ready for morning yet.

"Today is meeting day," Candida said, with a smile. "Men and women always eat together on meeting day so that Señor Reyes can give us news and instructions."

"This way, the time does not come out of our work," said the woman across the table. She looked Jesus up and down with raised brows. "Who is your new friend?"

"Don't get excited," Candida said. "He is married and has children."

The woman pretended to pout and ate her beans.

Jesus' fork paused mid-journey. "How did you know that?"

"I asked Jorge," Candida said. "Do you think me forward?"

Before Jesus could respond, a spoon chimed against glass. He saw an older man of stocky build walk to the front of the room. Pale blue eyes searched from face to face. He held his hat by the brim in both hands, turning it bit by bit as he spoke.

"I don't thank all of you enough for what you do," he said, in Spanish. "I will now. Thank you." His voice was deep and rumbled low in his chest, which made it hard for Jesus to understand.

"That is Señor Reyes," Candida whispered.

19

Señor Reyes waited for the murmur of voices to pass. "We're going to keep planting squash this week," he said, "as we have been. We're right on schedule and the weather has held steady for us. We need some rain soon, though." He gave a wry grin. "I do not understand why God doesn't adjust His weather to fit our schedule."

There was laughter.

Reyes paused, and his face became grim. "It is my duty to tell you that a man we all know, Manuel Ortega, a man who worked side by side with us every day...is dead."

The room grew silent. All eyes fixed on Señor Reyes's face.

"I try to provide good working conditions for you. I know the work is hard, I know the pay could be better, but the market controls that." He looked around the room. "The market controls everything. So what I do, I diversify the crops. I plant different crops for different markets. If the bean market fails, we got the peppers, if that market fails, we got the squash." Reyes paused to look around the room. "That's how I can keep you employed all year round. I diversify my crops and you diversify your skills. It works."

He glared. "I know you can earn more money in other ways, but those ways are risky. So long as you stay here on my farm, and work hard, I can—I will help you. But once you leave to go out there" —Reyes waved an arm in a general direction— "I can do nothin' for you."

He paused again, and his face drooped. "I'm sorry for our loss." He stared down at his hat for a few long moments. His head came up. "Rafael will give you instructions for the day." Reyes shuffled over to the door and left.

A large man with prominent cheekbones and sun-blackened features stood before them. His bristly mustache framed yellow teeth.

"He is Rafael Rodriguez, the supervisor," Candida whispered to Jesus. "He—". She went silent as he began to speak.

"My friends," said Rodriquez, "it is a good day for work. The Lagunas Field must be finished before we are done tonight." He flashed a gapped smile. "We lost a hard worker." His eyes found Jesus. "We must work hard to make up for it."

Rodriguez turned and walked out. The workers all stood as on a signal and cleaned their places, the clatter of utensils on plates followed them. Jesus dumped his unfinished food into the trash and hurried to catch up to Candida.

"What were you going to say?" he said.

Candida's facemask was over her mouth now but brown eyes rolled toward him. "It is not important." She hurried off to the waiting truck.

At the field, Jesus climbed down. The dank smell of the rich soil comforted him. He stretched and walked toward the planting platform where others took their positions. The tractor hummed, ready to begin.

His elbow was seized in a harsh grip. A voice spoke in his ear. Jesus turned and stared into the supervisor's contorted countenance.

"I watch you yesterday, new man," Rodriguez said. "You work too slow and the planter must wait for you. "

"I'm sorry. I—"

"You earned only half your pay yesterday because of your slow work. If you do not work faster you will lose more pay today." The grip grew harder. "Listen, *amigo*. You leave Candida alone, you understand?"

Jesus felt a last painful squeeze. Rodriguez walked away.

CHAPTER FIVE

Dear Isabella,

    I am safe and well in California. The boat trip was long and difficult but there were no problems. The meeting with my new business partners was good.

    I hope you have received the money they promised. Please write me at once if you have not. Please write me soon anyway. I miss you!

    How are Juanita and little Ana Dominga? Please tell them I miss them greatly and will return as soon as I have finished my work here.

    California is everything they say it is. None of the land here is wasted. Every hectare that does not have a building on it is used to grow food, raise cattle, or grow grapes.

    I live in a barracks with many men. We have a large shower room, and hot water every day, a dining room with many large tables, even a room for relaxation—with a pool table! And so much food! Senor Reyes insists that we always have as much to eat as we wish. We eat the same food as Senor Reyes. He told us so.

    The work is hard, but not so hard as fishing in the bay all day, although I prefer that. Today we planted summer squash. We follow a large platform called a transplanter pulled by a tractor. The platform holds the young plants, which we take out of the plastic and place in a hole in the ground we make with our hands in the soft earth. This work is easy but reaching up and bending down all day is painful for the back.

I have good news! Jorge, my new roommate and associate in the organization told me that I might soon have a change in work. He says my new work will be much easier and I will have greater responsibility. I don't know what this is or when it will be, but I think I will like the change.

There has been just one small unpleasantness. My supervisor has taken a dislike to me, I do not know why. He has made threats. But Jorge tells me not to worry about him.

I wish I could be there with you. Jorge says my contract with the business will be over in just one year. That is not so long! And by then I will have earned a lot of money for us and we will live better than we ever have before. So I must be patient.

I must sleep now, for the work is very tiring and breakfast comes early.

But it is important that I know that you have received the money they promised. Please write and tell me as soon as you finish reading this.

I miss you very much.

Te Quiero Mucho, Jesus

CHAPTER SIX

Zack looked down at his hands. They rested palm up in his lap. He thought he must seem about to catch a watermelon and crossed his arms instead. It occurred to him the students in front could see his nervousness. He felt uncomfortable here on this little chair up on the stage, nothing between him and a hall full of curious faces. He wondered about his legs—should he cross them, or would that be too casual? With his legs slightly apart he felt vulnerable, but with them tight together he felt prissy. Zack squirmed.

At the lectern Susan swung into high gear, her pretty face pinched with intensity. Zack felt envy. This was her arena; this was the environment where she was most comfortable. Her slender good looks belied a fabled list of academic accomplishments. Susan knew her craft.

Zack looked at the upturned faces. Susan was deep into her presentation yet she held every eye and connected with every young mind. The students were absorbed, drawn in by every word. Soon it would be Zack's turn. He was not a skilled public speaker and not as comfortable in these academic surroundings. His anxiety grew. The bright collegiate minds before him could swing from idealism to cynicism, from support to derision in an instant. Like sharks in the water, they would sense his fear, probe his vulnerabilities, and attack, laying waste to Susan's hard work in the process. Zack shuddered at the thought.

When Dr. Susan Apgar first approached Zack to help present her lecture at the Criminal Justice Department at Allen Hancock College, he refused. He offered the usual arguments: lack of comfort with public speaking, a busy schedule, and not least, his ineffectiveness. But Susan trumped all of that with a single point. Her topic supported his work, after all. In her lecture she proposes the possibility that creatures from an undiscovered branch of the human evolutionary tree might theoretically exist today in our society, yet unknown to us, possessing extraordinary powers, posing unknown dangers, with us but not of us. She was after all speaking to Zack's area of experience. She could present the subject effectively as a theorist, but only Zack, the FBI agent, could introduce the missing sense of reality.

Zack couldn't turn her down.

"A quick glance along this timeline suggests that at the time fire became a tool for human beings, our species had already exited Africa and were spread around the globe," Susan was saying. "Of course we all recognize the so called discovery of fire could not have been a single incident, but rather a period of time when humans experimented and gradually learned to nurture this life-changing tool. Nor could the discovery of fire have happened simultaneously within every society on earth."

She absently pushed back a strand of blonde hair from her eye. "We must therefore conclude there was a period of time when some of our predecessors had fire, and some did not. Those with fire would have had an enormous advantage. They would hold dominion over those without. So you see, our inevitable conclusion must be that humans without fire capitulated to those with it, or else concealed themselves in some way."

Susan peered over her glasses, made eye contact. "It is therefore possible some fireless humans remain hidden after all these centuries They may well have evolved along different lines, may look different, perhaps with different skill sets and unknown capabilities. What strengths might they have developed? Think about recently discovered tribes hidden deep in the forests of Papua New Guinea, or of DNA evidence that proves the existence of an unknown species of bear in Nepal. Might not a divergent species of human beings have survived all these centuries in the same way, in environments that modern people seldom frequent, such as the deep forests or the high mountains, and emerge only after the sun goes down?"

Susan paused for dramatic effect, her eyebrows raised above her glasses rims. "I leave you with this simple question: Why not?"

There was a moment of pin-drop silence and then applause roared through the hall. Susan nodded and smiled and stepped back from the lectern, waited for it to ebb. She stepped forward, held up her palm.

"Thank you. Thank you." She beamed a charming smile. "It is my good fortune--or perhaps I should say our

good fortune--to have with us this morning FBI
Supervisory Agent Zachary Tolliver. Agent Tolliver
worked as FBI liaison with the Navajo Nation Police on
the Navajo Reservation in the Tuba City region for over a
decade. In that time he became familiar with the myths and
legends of the Navajo People, including some that have a
direct bearing on our subject this morning. I give
you...Agent Zack Tolliver."

Zack rose to his feet to a smattering of polite
applause. As he walked forward he sensed the anticipation
of the audience. His chest tightened. Then he was in front
of the lectern with his wrinkled notes spread out before
him. He stared back at the hall full of students and
teachers for a few seconds while he tried to collect his
thoughts, and his courage.

Zack was a careful person, overly deliberate to
some, perhaps. To others his sun-bronzed face and
unfaltering blue eyes came across as honest and
trustworthy. He would have been surprised to know the
audience saw him as poised and confident.

"I'm honored by this opportunity to address your
Criminal Justice classes," he said. "I once sat where you sit
now."

There were a few polite grins.

Zack swallowed and began. "In my life among the
Navajo, I learned never to dismiss out of hand long held
cultural beliefs, no matter how outlandish they might
appear to me. Myths, traditions, stories—they all have a
purpose, or they wouldn't exist." He flicked a bead of

sweat from his nose. "Most of these stories are harmless and reflect a different way to think about things. Yet some myths and legends touch upon darker places most of us prefer not to visit. Unlike us, the Navajo give credence to their spiritual side. There is a place for it in their culture. They look such things square in the eye.

"Consider for a moment how you and I deal with mysteries. For instance, is it possible any among us have not heard a ghost story? How many of us believe ghosts exist? How do those of us who do believe explain them in terms of established physical science, or in terms of religion for that matter? Yet ghosts and spirits have been with us as long as there have been humans, and judging from recent TV shows they are no less important to us today.

"Now consider how we deal with the subject of ghosts as a society. The fact is, we don't. When we deal with it, we do so in secret, as individuals. We follow our own path and keep our cards close to our chests. Our personal beliefs about ghosts come from our own experiences. Indigenous people, on the other hand, face the subject of spirits together as a society, head on, not obliquely."

Zack paused. He felt he still had the audience. He charged ahead. "When I began my work as FBI liaison in support of the very modern and effective Navajo Nation Police, I had my own prejudices. The agents who held this position before me didn't stay long. It was more than just the heat and isolation, it had to do with an inability to accept the Navajo way of thinking."

Zack raised an eyebrow. "My job wasn't considered a dream posting." There were a few chuckles.

Zack was encouraged. "I was lucky. I made a friend on the reservation who taught me to reserve judgment; to listen. It was an important lesson. That advice kept me involved—and alive. Over time, I became privy to the more guarded thoughts of the Navajo people. I came to know something about their view of the paranormal.

"In their culture, the shaman wields great power. He has the ability to see beyond the veil. He understands all things natural and supernatural. He can use this knowledge to heal or to hurt.

"Not all shamans have equal capabilities. They have graduated levels of experience and potential for good or for evil. A holy man can lose his way, just like any other man. An evil man of such power can become an evil entity indeed. That is the origin of the Skinwalker, the legendary Navajo witch who assumes the shape of animals to achieve his ends."

Zack reached for the water glass in the lectern. As he sipped, he watched the audience. He thought they looked intrigued but skeptical.

"I see by your looks I may have lost some of you here. It is an idea people of science have trouble getting their heads around. I know I did. Is such a thing possible? When assisting the Navajo police, you are confronted by such possibilities almost every night. The policemen regularly receive complaints about Skinwalkers. They handle them as a matter of fact, investigate them, and write reports about them. Sometimes the evidence is difficult if not impossible to refute.

"No doubt you'd like to hear some of the cases." Zack felt the rising anticipation of the audience. He looked at his watch. "There is insufficient time to relate all the situations that have strained my belief. Suffice to say, I have seen animals butchered during the night by beasts that don't exist. I have seen the glow of eyes shine red in impossible places. I have followed blood trails of wounded fugitives and at their end found dead animals with the same wounds. I have seen animal tracks that turn to human prints and then back to animal. I have heard tales of manlike figures running alongside speeding cars. I have glimpsed creatures that simply don't exist in our every-day world."

Zack wiped his forehead. The room had grown silent. "I'm not here to tell campfire stories. There is an old saw that says once you've eliminated all other possibilities, whatever remains, however improbable, must be the truth. Our culture tends to limit the possible far more than other cultures. My friend and mentor taught me to avoid such limitations. If all my senses, experience, and knowledge lead me to the impossible, I must alter the shape of the possible in my own mind. Once you close your mind to anything, it ceases to exist for you. But for others, it may still be there."

Zack smiled and looked around the room. "Thanks for listening. I'll be happy to take questions."

There was a thunderous round of applause.

A young professor rose from an aisle seat. "Agent Tolliver, as a law enforcement agent, you deal in tangible evidence. Yet you have presented scenarios to us today for which you have not presented proof. Do you have real evidence to convince us of what you have seen?" As the man sat, he sent a meaningful glance at the students near him.

Zack waited, aware of the sea of intent faces. "Let me ask you a question in return. What evidence would you require in order to believe? When I tell you, as a federal agent, that I have seen such things, do you consider that sufficient evidence?"

There was a hush as everyone waited.

The professor stood again. "To answer your question, no. I would require hard evidence, such as corroborating witnesses or a photograph."

Zack moved to the side of the podium and leaned against it. "Have you ever been shown a picture of a ghost, or of a Bigfoot?"

"Uh, yes, certainly."

"Do you now believe they exist?"

"Well...no."

Zack pushed further. "Have you ever known of corroborating witnesses to a Bigfoot sighting, or an alien craft sighting?"

"Well, yes, but..."

"Do you now believe in them?"

The man shook his head and smiled sheepishly.

"That is our problem in a nutshell," Zack said. "The suspension of belief. When dealing with uncommon events such as these, it is a human tendency not to believe in them even when we've seen them with our own eyes.

"I return to my earlier point. Advanced societies such as our own, centuries removed from the fundamental concern of surviving the night, tend not to support belief in anything beyond the conceived reality of our present world. When confronted by an unnatural entity, we tend not to believe.

"In cultures where the night still holds unpleasant possibilities, however, people who are vulnerable to their physical surroundings tend to believe in such entities until they are proven false. It is a survival instinct."

* * * * *

After the presentation Susan and Zack stood together in the reception area, sipped coffee and nibbled cookies. The young professor who had challenged Zack approached them. With him was a middle-aged man, his face browned and weathered. The man's hair bore the imprint of his hat, as if he rarely removed it. He held the hat by the rim and slowly spun it with his fingers.

The young instructor stuck out his hand to Zack. "I'm Jack Burns, one of the course teachers here." He flashed a row of perfect white teeth. "I want you to know it was not my intention to give you a hard time back there. The lesson on the nature of evidence was too good an opportunity to miss. I appreciate your response. These students need to understand the determining factor for sufficient evidence often varies, depending upon economics, cultures, environment, and last but not least, the brain of the presiding judge." He turned to Susan. "May I say, Dr. Apgar, your presentation was brilliant. Your reputation appears well deserved."

Susan nodded her appreciation.

Burns turned to the man next to him. "Allow me to introduce Rufus Reyes. Mr. Reyes owns a ranch near Santa Lupita, just a few miles west. He's an old friend of mine. When he learned about your lecture today he asked to come along. He wanted to meet you in particular, Agent Tolliver."

Mr. Reyes's leathery face creased into a grimace of a smile. He shook hands with Zack, nodded to Susan, and went back to turning his hat brim.

He stood, looked uncertain. "It's more of a farm, really." The man's voice appeared to rumble direct from his chest. His eyes were a pale blue, as if bleached by the sun. "I run some cattle on the south hills, but mostly I grow peppers, squash and beets in the river bottom." He paused, clearly uncomfortable. He looked at Zack. "Agent Tolliver, I'll come right to the point. I was lookin' for a little advice."

Zack was caught by surprise. "Advice? I don't know anything about farming."

"Nothin' to do with farming. It's more along your line of work." Again he paused. "Listen, what I got to say needs more space than this." He waved at the crowded room. "Can we go get a sandwich, and talk?"

"Well, I..." Zack looked at Susan. "Do you need...?"

"You go ahead," Susan said. "I've got nothing more planned for you today. We can meet later back at the Inn." She leaned in toward Zack, put a hand on his arm. "I think it went well today, don't you?" she said, just to him. "Thanks for the help."

She turned, beamed a bright smile at Professor Burns. "It's been a long time since I've been on this campus, Jack. Have you time to give me a quick tour?"

The young professor seemed more than willing to accommodate her.

Susan took his arm and they melted into the crowd.

CHAPTER SEVEN

Mr. Rufus Reyes led the way out the double doors of the Allan Hancock College Library across the large parking lot to a white Chevy Silverado. The dents and scratches on the truck's body suggested it was for work, not show. Zack noticed the Reyes Ranch logo painted on the door, a longhorn cow under an oak tree.

Reyes got behind the wheel. He reached over to knock an old newspaper off the passenger seat.

Zack sat, his feet straddling a coil of rope.

"Didn't take time to dandy things up," Reyes said. "Don't often have passengers." He grinned. "Other than my dog Duke, that is, and he don't much care how it looks."

Reyes maneuvered the truck out of the parking lot. He glanced at Zack. "Just for the record," he said, "I don't believe any of that bullshit you spooned out in there."

Zack smiled. "Most people don't. As I explained, we're all in our own cozy worlds, and if we don't have to disturb them, why do it?"

"Well, my cozy world's been disturbed. That's why I want to talk to you, but only informal-like." Reyes paused to make a turn. Once they were safely in the stream of traffic he resumed. "I especially wanted to talk to an FBI guy who's good at mysteries. I got one for you."

"Is it criminal activity, Mr. Reyes? If not, you'd be wasting my time and yours."

"Call me Rufus. An' I guess if I knew the answer to that question I wouldn't need you no more."

They crossed over route 101, then turned left into the dirt parking area of a timeworn brick-faced restaurant. The sign read "Pappy's".

"They got a good tri-tip sandwich in here," Rufus said.

"Tri-tip?"

Rufus stared at Zack in consternation. "It's a cut of beef, son. It comes from the bottom half of the sirloin." He climbed out of the truck, shaking his head.

Zack followed him into a dark and narrow entrance hall.

A woman with curly grey hair and a large bosom greeted them with a smile. She wiped her hands on a stained apron. "I thought I saw your truck pull up, Rufus." She grabbed a couple of menus. "Usual place?" Without waiting for a response she breezed away.

The men followed her along a row of booths to a large corner table. Light from frosted windows set the polished wood aglow.

"How's your place out to Santa Lupita?" She slapped down the menus as the men found chairs.

"Just fine." Rufus gave a long, dramatic sigh. "Dorothy, I need your help here. Would you explain to this poor fella from Arizona what tri-tip is, and why it's so special?"

Dorothy's face took on a look of mock horror. "I hope you didn't make any disparaging remarks about tri-tip in front of Rufus. He gets all discombobulated."

"I..."

"Never mind, Sweetie. I'll tell you. Tri-tip steak is to Santa Maria what coals are to Newcastle. It's who we are." She thought for a moment. "Excepting for strawberries, maybe. We're known for them, too. Anyway, we invented our own style tri-tip barbeque right here in Santa Maria. A tri-tip steak is the most flavorful, low fat, low cost beef you can get. But you have to do it right. And we do it right."

Rufus jumped in. "I'll tell ya the right way. Dorothy, correct me if I'm wrong. " His face showed real excitement. "First, ya rub it with salt, three different peppers, fresh garlic, paprika, and a secret seasoning made with—what was it again, Dorothy?"

Dorothy swatted his shoulder. "You keep trying to wheedle that out of me, Rufus."

Rufus grinned. "Next you gotta barbecue it skewered on steel rods over red oak wood—gotta be red oak, nothin' else. Then ya gradually lower the rods as it cooks. Cook it to medium rare and prepare yourself for a treat."

Rufus looked up at Dorothy. "For the second half of this lesson, would you bring us two tri-tip sandwiches and two Firestone DBA's, please, ma'am."

Dorothy hustled off.

Rufus' smile went away. "I'll get right to it," he said. "Here's the thing. I'm not sure if I got a missing person's complaint, an immigration problem, or if I'm just plain goin' crazy." He leaned forward over the table. "I told you I got a ranch and I grow vegetables. I can't get it done without help. I need workers.

"I don't have a real big place, so I don't hire as many as most. I try to keep 'em on beyond one growing season, though, so if they are *tomateros* for instance, I'll retrain 'em as onion pickers. Another thing I can do 'cause my place is small, I house these folks right there on the property. The other, bigger ranches can't do that. An' I feed 'em—I feed 'em good. I make an effort to get to know my people better than most, even if they don't speak no English." Rufus smiled wryly at Zack. "Which they don't, 'cause most of them have just crossed the river."

"Undocumented?"

"Yeah, but—" He lifted both hands. "I got no way a' knowin' that."

Dorothy appeared with beer bottles and glasses, placed them in front of the men. Rufus took a pull directly from his bottle.

"You don't ask for their papers?" Zack said, after she'd gone.

"Sure, and I get 'em. And most of what I see probably wouldn't float at Immigration."

"Yet you..."

"Look, before you climb on your high horse, this is the way it works. If you want to enjoy your veggies at a reasonable price, I can't spend all my days takin' documents up to Sacramento. And don't think you're on some moral high ground. I wonder how many underpaid, overworked Chinese kids it took to make your sneakers there."

"Okay, okay. I'm a federal agent—I got to ask these questions." Zack sipped his beer. "I still don't know how I can advise you."

Rufus calmed down. "Well, here's the thing. Some of my people have gone missing."

"Missing?"

"Yeah. Every so often my major domo tells me a worker is gone. I ask the others about him. You know, is he sick or somethin'? I check where he lives, I check the infirmary, but *nada*."

"So he ran off."

"But a few days later, he's back."

Zack sighed. "You didn't bring me out here just to tell me your workers sometimes take an unofficial vacation...?"

Rufus glared at Zack. "You don't get it. When one of 'em disappears like that, I still got the same number of workers. When he's back, the number still doesn't change."

Rufus took another swig of his beer while Zack's brain caught up.

"Another thing," Rufus said, "when the guy is back, he's pretty much useless. He's wiped out. Whatever he's been doing, it ain't no vacation."

Dorothy returned with two steaming platters. Zack stared at an enormous sandwich of hot juicy meat piled high on crusted bread with a mountain of French fries.

"Git goin' while it's hot," Rufus said. He picked up his own sandwich, unmindful of the dripping juice.

Zack looked at his sandwich but his thoughts went to what Rufus said. "Let me get this straight. You say sometimes a worker disappears for days at a time, and during that time a stranger replaces him. Then that stranger goes away and the original worker returns?"

Rufus put down his sandwich and wiped his hands on his napkin. "Not quite. Sometimes the stranger stays on and another worker disappears. But there's always the right number of workers. Here's another funny thing. I got real good workers, they work hard. I try to make their lives comfortable. Every once in a while, though, maybe once every couple of months, I get just half the work outa' them. It's like a bunch of 'em came to work exhausted on the very same day. I see they're trying hard—they just haven't got the energy."

Zack chased a bite of his sandwich with a sip of beer. "I still don't see why you need an FBI agent."

"What if I told you the last time my crew came to work all worn out like that, the cops found an empty Panga boat that same day?"

Zack's head came up.

"Ah, that got your attention. But this last bit concerns me most. A couple a' days ago my numbers came up short again. Manuel, a good worker, one I know well, was missing. He's not been replaced yet, an' he's not been back. Manuel has a family, a wife and two kids. When my major domo and I spoke to his wife, she couldn't, or wouldn't, tell us anything. She was real upset, though. I tried talkin' to some of the other workers; they just got scared and clammed up." Rufus glared at Zack. "I think something bad happened to that fella, maybe somethin' to do with drugs. I ain't gonna sit around an' let somethin' like this happen on my ranch." Rufus slapped the table for emphasis.

"Why don't you just report it to the local police?" Zack said. "Let them deal with it."

"You still don't get it. If I report Manuel missing, they start askin' questions about who he is an' where he came from. One thing leads to another and first thing you know I got no workers."

"I still—"

"I think it all ties together somehow," Rufus said. "A worker gone, another in his place, a whole batch of 'em real tired one day—it feels like some kind 'a plan goin' on. I'm real worried about Manuel. I know you can't do nothin', I'm just lookin' for advice."

Zack sighed. He looked at his phone and brought up his schedule. "Tell you what. I don't leave until tomorrow. Dr. Apgar said she didn't need me any more. Suppose I pay a casual visit to the police in—where did you say? Santa Lupita? I'll pose a hypothetical scenario; see what they say. Give me a telephone number so I can call you and tell you what I learn. Fair enough?"

"Hell, yeah. That's more'n I expected. Don't mention no names, though. George Barnard—he's the Chief over there—he knows me pretty well. If he finds out it's me he'll feel obligated to come down to the farm and start checkin' papers."

CHAPTER EIGHT

Zack used the GPS in his rental to find the Santa Lupita Police Station. It was on the corner of 10th and Obispo Street. He parked along the curb, followed the concrete walkway through a well-watered emerald lawn to a heavy hardwood door.

Inside, the patrolman working dispatch checked his notes and nodded Zack right into the Chief's office. It took the man behind the desk a long time to raise his 6'4" frame to his feet to greet him. The Chief was an older man, maybe late fifties. Despite a bit of middle-body spread, he looked strong and capable.

Chief George Barnard frowned at Zack. "Hello, FBI Special Agent Zack Tolliver. What brings you to my little town all the way from Arizona? It's been my experience when an FBI agent from some other state ends up in my office, I got a boatload more work ahead of me."

Zack grinned. "You can relax. I'm not here on official business."

Barnard traded his frown for a smile and offered his hand. "In that case, have a seat. What can I do you out of?" He gestured toward a chair.

Zack sat. His eye roved the room. He saw a framed series of black and white photos of historic town buildings on one wall. On another was a diploma from the police academy and a certificate for distinguished marksmanship. A large map of Santa Lupita hung behind the desk.

"In a way, I guess I'm on a mission to help out a local man," Zack said. "Just some questions, a fact-finding sort of thing."

Barnard dropped into his chair. "Go on."

"My questions concern farm workers."

Barnard's chin came up. "You're not one of those bleeding hearts come to cure the migrant worker situation, are you?"

Zack put up a palm. "I've got no agenda. It would help me to know how you handle workers out here."

"How who handles workers? Each farm is a little different from the next. Everyone does it his own way."

"Is there a standard in terms of pay or hours or benefits?

"Benefits? You mean like health insurance and stuff?"

"For a start."

Barnard laughed. "For a guy without an agenda, you go right for the jugular." He stood and walked to a file cabinet. "As it happens, I've got some recent numbers from a survey authorized out of Sacramento." He removed a thin booklet from a file. "I can tell you one thing before I even look. The answers to your question will differ. It depends on one factor: are the workers documented or undocumented. Here, for instance, it says 30% of documented male workers have some form of health insurance but only 15% of undocumented male workers have it. Only 17% of documented workers have employer-provided insurance."

"So what do they do if—"

"What do they do if they get sick? They can visit a clinic provided by California's Emergency Medi-Cal program or a program called WIC, a federally funded health and nutrition program. They'll take the undocumented ones, too."

"Why don't employers have to cover all the workers?"

"Because most of 'em work part time. The farms hire them for one specific job, say picking tomatoes. That job might last three months, if they're lucky. Then they move on to the next farm, the next crop, the next job, if there is one. Each employer hires them as part-time workers, so they aren't required to provide health insurance."

"But 17% of them get it?"

"Like I said, you got good bosses and you got not so good bosses. Some of the good ones work extra hard to re-train workers and keep 'em on for another crop or another job around the farm. Those bosses cover their health."

"What about pay?"

Barnard slapped the folder shut and returned it to the cabinet. "Well, most farms contract workers one of two ways: either by the hour or by the number of buckets or bags or whatever they pick that day."

"Is there a minimum wage?"

"Sure, but the worker seldom sees it. Say an onion producer offers eighty cents a person per sack. Working hard, a family of three can earn maybe sixty bucks a day. Divide that by three, its only twenty bucks a person. That's way below minimum wage, but the workers contract to do it that way, thinkin' they can make more money. They seldom do."

Zack was mystified. "Are these owners just cruel? How can they do this to people?"

Barnard walked to his chair, sank into it with a sigh. "It's the system. You try to keep the costs low to maintain or increase consumption so you can compete abroad. The costs to a farmer are set. They're consistent across the board, all except one— the workers. They're the weak link in the chain. The lower the farmers can keep those wages, the lower the selling price, the better their chance to sell their product."

"The workers don't protest? They don't strike?"

Barnard's laugh was bitter. "Most of them don't speak English and half of them aren't educated beyond fourth grade. If you're undocumented, you don't want to draw attention to yourself. I'll guarantee you half of 'em don't even know who Cesar Chavez was or what he did." He glared at Zack. "So tell me, why this interest in farm workers?"

Zack smiled. "I met a farmer this morning with a curious complaint. On the basis of what you just told me, I'd say he's one of the good bosses. At any rate, he knows his workers and cares for them. That's why he knows when things aren't right, and right now they're not. "

"What do you mean, not right?"

"He's noticed that a worker disappears occasionally for a short time, yet the overall number of workers stays the same. No explanation, no reason. They seem to think the farmer won't notice."

"Most farmers wouldn't."

"Yeah, that's what this guy implied. He lets it go because no one wants to explain it. He also said he has days when several of the workers arrive dead on their feet, again no explanation."

Barnard jotted something down. He nodded for Zack to continue.

"What's got him worried, a worker disappeared for a couple of weeks now. He happens to be a guy this farmer knows better than most. The man's wife is real upset. This farmer doesn't know why his workers disappear like they do but worries it's some kind of risky business. He thinks Manuel—that's the missing guy—may have come to harm."

Chief Barnard glanced at his notes. "So what does Rufus think you can do about it?"

Zack looked sheepish. "Guess I gave it away, didn't I? In answer to your question, I don't think he knows. I guess he hopes I'll come up with something."

"And here you are."

"Here I am."

Barnard stood up behind his desk. "I know very well why Rufus didn't want his name mentioned. First, he doesn't want me rounding up his illegals. Second, he knows what's going on."

ZACA

Zack lifted an eyebrow.

"He's set you up. This is his way to get me to work on his problem." Barnard turned to the map on the wall. "Look. This is Santa Lupita, where we are right now. Over here are hills with deep canyons and steep cliffs leading down to the sea. Nobody goes there much, which makes it a good place to land a panga full of drugs from Mexico. I'll bet a year's wages that's where his workers go at night. They unload a boat and move the drugs to a safe place. No wonder they're tired in the morning."

"And the missing guys?"

"My best guess they may work as couriers or the like."

Barnard's finger slid east across the map. "Say a Mex national comes up from Mexico in a panga. Now you got an illegal you got to hide. Where do you hide him? You hide him in plain sight, in the field with all the other Mexicans. Who's to know? At the same time, you pull one of the other workers to do other jobs for you."

Zack whistled soundlessly. "That's impressive. Rufus noticed only because he's small and concerned about his workers."

"You got it."

"Now he's worried about Manuel, so he sets me up to report it to you."

"Right again."

"What will you do?"

"Nothin'." Barnard shrugged at Zack's look. "It's outside my jurisdiction and Rufus damn well knows it.

Even if it weren't, I wouldn't find anything. Nobody would talk to me. They know they could expect swift retribution from the cartels."

"The county sheriff?"

"Got more important things to do than beat the woods for missing illegals." Barnard had a head of steam up.

Time to go, Zack thought. He stood and offered his hand. "Thanks, Chief Barnard. I've taken a lot of your time. You've been straight with me, and I appreciate it."

"What're you gonna do?" Barnard demanded.

Zack laughed. "If all this is outside your jurisdiction, it's way, way outside mine. I'll just poke around a little in an informal way. I'm scheduled to fly home to Arizona tomorrow, so I can't do much. I just want Rufus to know I did what I could."

CHAPTER NINE

Zack accepted Susan's invitation to dinner at the Inn. The weather was warm and the patio was open. They lingered over drinks before ordering. Zack was scheduled to fly to Las Vegas at nine the following morning. He'd left his truck in long-term parking at the airport there. He would drive several hours to his home near Page, Arizona.

Susan would stay on. Her next lecture was at the University of California, Santa Barbara.

"I wish you would help me with one or two more lectures," she said with a small beguiling pout. "You add reality to my abstract presentation."

Zack smiled. "You don't need me. All I do is add a note of controversy."

"It's important to move beyond the theoretical. These students have heads stuffed with theory; they simply snooze through mine."

"I watched those kids today," Zack said. "They sure as hell weren't snoozing."

Susan looked amused. "You are a sweet man, but transparent. Yes, I know how much you want to get back to your family. How is Libby, by the way? And the little one?"

Zack's expression warmed. "They're both fine. Libby would love to be out here with me, but little Bernie keeps her busy."

"That's wonderful," Susan said. "You must be very happy."

"Oh, I am. Libby's had her own kids before, but this is my first."

Zack was about to say more when his cell phone rang. He glanced at it.

"Sorry, Susan, I should take this."

Zack was glad for the interruption. He felt awkward when Susan asked after his child, as she always did. Susan and Libby had become pregnant within months of each other. For Susan, the news seemed miraculous, a gift from her murdered lover, a final expression of his love from beyond the veil. But it didn't last—Susan miscarried in her third month.

Zack stood and walked to the foyer. "Hello."

Chief Barnard's brusque voice sounded in his ear. "Thought you'd like to know they think they found the missing Mexican worker, Manuel."

"Oh, that's good."

"Well no, it's not. They found him dead."

"Where?"

"Some hikers stumbled over his body in Los Padres National Forest. They reported it."

"How did he die?"

"He was shot."

"Was it drug related, do you think?"

"Yeah," Barnard said. "I'd say so. They found him in the middle of a marijuana grow."

"I'm sorry for the man's family," Zack said. "But at least they know what happened now. Thanks for the info." Zack prepared to sign off.

"Whoa there, partner," Chief Barnard said. "There's more."

"Yeah?"

"There's other blood near the scene. A lot of blood, but in a different place—so much blood that whoever left it couldn't have walked away."

"No body?" Zack was fully engaged now.

"If there is one, they can't find it."

A dark memory stirred in far regions of Zack's mind, he pushed it away. "Sounds like you boys have your work cut out."

"Agent Tolliver, when we met this afternoon you neglected to tell me the reason you came out here. I've done some back checking. I know what your, uh...specialties are."

"Oh?"

"I thought this case might interest you."

Zack hesitated. "It does sound interesting, but there are a number of reasons a body might be missing."

"Zack, here's the thing. Rick—that's Rick Malden, the forest ranger—knows his stuff. He found one set of tracks, the ones he followed to the blood pool. That's it."

A distant warning bell sounded again in Zack's mind.

"Agent Tolliver, you still there?"

"Yeah, I'm still here. What does the ranger think happened?"

"He's got no idea. It doesn't make sense to him." Barnard hesitated for a moment. "I know you got a flight in the morning. I'm headed up there right now. I could swing by the hotel and pick you up if you like..."

"Uh, sure, why not? How soon?"

"See you in twenty minutes." Barnard hung up.

Zack grew excited despite himself. His mind buzzed with possibilities as he walked back to the table. When he reached it, Susan's chair was empty. He found a short note:

"Sorry, Zack, I must prepare my presentation for tomorrow. Thanks for dinner. Please come by my room later tonight, I'd like to discuss more cooperative presentations.
XXX Susan"

Back in his room, Zack changed into a pair of jeans and trail shoes. He threw a jacket, water bottle and flashlight into a pack and went out front to wait for Barnard. Five minutes later a patrol car with a City of Santa Lupita shield on the door pulled up. The car window rolled down.

"Get in," commanded Barnard.

Zack climbed into the seat and at once the cruiser accelerated. Chief Barnard flipped on the flasher lights.

54

"We'll have no more'n a couple hours of daylight left," he explained. "Once it's dark, we can't do much."

"No work lights at the crime scene?" Zack said.

"Not where we're going. We'll have to walk the last half mile just to get there." He glanced at Zack. "Got a jacket with you?"

"It's in my pack."

"Good. It's 80 degrees now, but in another hour and three thousand feet higher it's gonna be a whole lot cooler."

Zack leaned back in the comfortable seat. "Tell the truth, Chief," he said. "If I hadn't come to talk to you today, would you go to this crime scene?"

Barnard gave a tight smile. "No. I got plenty to do in Santa Lupita. After our chat today, I feel it's important you understand where the illegal immigrant and drug trafficking problems meet." He gave a sidelong look at Zack. "That's not to say we don't help each other out around here. With cutbacks and all, there're not enough of us to do our jobs. No one's gonna be surprised when I show up." He grinned across at Zack. "You might surprise them, though."

The patrol car roared over a highway bridge and at once the city streets evaporated, replaced by endless fields.

"What happened to the city?"

"Without these fields, there's no city," Barnard said. "You're looking at the life breath of the region, agriculture. This is Betteravia Road. It runs the length of the Santa Maria River valley, from Santa Lupita through

Santa Maria and up the valley there. Betteravia Road may look like a city street in Santa Maria, but two thirds of it passes through AG fields."

Barnard turned off the flashers. There were no cars here. "You know anything about this region?"

"No," Zack said.

"Not to bore you, but here's what you should know. We live and die by the moods of the Pacific Ocean. Where the Santa Maria River meets the sea, cool, damp air flows up the valley. Fog—we call it the marine layer—rolls in like smoke in the mornings and evenings, sometimes all the way up this valley and round the corner into the Sisquoc River valley. Yeah, we're in a semi-arid region, but the ocean keeps it more like a Mediterranean climate. There's nothin' won't grow here."

Zack stared, took it all in. The beauty of his Arizona home was in the raw red cliffs and barren flat-topped mesas, rainbow hued sandstone, great jumbled rock formations—all bone dry. Here it was mile after mile of wide bottomland, green with produce. Ahead were naked mountain ridges sharp-edged with shadow from a sinking sun.

Zack glanced over at the speedometer—eighty miles per hour. Barnard was a good driver. He alternated brake with accelerator smoothly when avoiding potholes, yet maintained his speed. The road ran arrow straight. When it seemed they must finally reach the mountains the road curved and followed the valley south. Here it

56

narrowed; gold crested round hills encroached from the west.

"These are the Solomon hills," Chief Barnard explained, "named for the Zorro bandit, Salomon Pico."

"Speaking of criminals, what do you know about this crime scene?"

Barnard grunted. "Not much. From the ranger's description, I'd guess a typical fall-out among cartels over marijuana grow. Happens too often."

Barnard braked and they turned off on a side road, across the width of the valley, over a dry riverbed, and up a river bench. The road entered a narrow valley among steep hills, carved its way along the hillside. Treeless slopes above them glinted gold in the late sun, cottonwoods guarded a tortuous creek below.

"This is Tepusquet Canyon," Barnard said. "We've got just a few miles to go, but it gets rougher."

They turned off onto a forestry road. Pavement gave way to rutted hard pack. Barnard barely slowed. The car launched from rut to rut. The grating sound of rock against metal came often.

The arroyo narrowed to the width of the car, then climbed the side of a bluff. The earth fell away on the driver's side. The front wheel drive patrol car spun its tires often on the steep grade. The corners were tight and blind. Barnard never slowed.

"Is this a one way road?"

"No."

"Just asking."

The slope eased and the road straightened out.
They entered a grove of trees, darker now. Red strobe
lights flashed up ahead. Barnard skidded to a stop. A
California Highway Patrol SUV blocked the road. Beyond
it was a gate.

As dust settled around their car, a state trooper
unraveled himself from the front seat of the SUV. He
stood, taller than Zack expected, big boned, long legged.
He walked unhurried to the car and leaned down to peer in
Barnard's window. Two huge hands rested on the sill. An
opal pinkie ring glittered in the flashing red lights.

"Hello, Chief."

"Hey yourself, Dom."

A craggy face dropped into view and hard eyes
came to rest on Zack.

"Any new developments?" Barnard said.

"Not since we notified you." The eyes stayed on
Zack. "We got a whirlybird on the way with the crime
boys. Rick Malden is at the scene—you'll want to talk to
him."

"Malden. That's good." Barnard nodded toward the
SUV. "We'll head on up, then."

Dom kept his grip on the windowsill. "Who's
this?"

"Dominic Antonio, meet FBI Agent Zack Tolliver.
He's in town to talk to the college kids. I'm showing him
how we work out here."

"This ain't no FBI case."

"He's just a guest, Dom, just a guest. Nothin' official."

The face moved out of Zack's sight, but the hands still didn't move. Barnard's gaze stayed on the trooper, there seemed to be a silent exchange.

"Okay, then," Dom said, after a minute.

The hands disappeared from the window and Dom walked back to the SUV. Wheels spun, dust kicked up, and the vehicle moved out of the way. Dom climbed out, walked to the gate, pulled it open. He gave them a mock salute as they passed.

"Dom didn't approve of me, seems like," Zack said, as they drove on.

"Just doing his job," Barnard said. "Dom's a good man."

The road clawed out of the basin along a rivulet, up a narrow twisty gorge. Then it leveled out and they were in a meadow of waving grasses studded with white and gold flowers. They encountered stately pines in scattered groves. As they passed among them Zack breathed in their fresh smell. The road climbed on—not so steep now.

"Almost there," Barnard said.

They wound around a large sweeping turn and the road vanished. They were at the top of the ridge where the road ahead dropped back down the other side. To the left was a dirt track guarded by a metal forestry gate. On the right loomed a high bluff. Several vehicles were logjammed into the small space. There was even a horse trailer.

Chief Barnard nosed the patrol car in behind the trailer. They scrambled out. The cooler fan for the engine sounded loud in the forest stillness.

"Let's go. It's Shank's Mare from here," Barnard said. He opened the back door and hoisted out a backpack.

Zack had started up the dirt track to the left.

"Whoa!" the police chief called. "We're not going that way. Over there's our trail." He gestured toward the steep bluff.

Zack turned to look. A tiny path edged its way up the near vertical face. "You're kidding me."

Barnard laughed. "Wish I was. But that's the only way to get where we're goin'."

Zack looked at the path, then the horse trailer. "They took a horse up there?"

"Not a horse—a mule." The Chief bounced his backpack up onto his shoulders and walked to the trailhead. "We're both gonna know exactly how that mule felt in about ten minutes."

The way was steep, but not as bad as it looked from below. Switchbacks at critical spots made all the difference. The men reached the ridgeline in the ten minutes that Barnard had prophesied. They paused there to catch their breath and look out over the valley.

"That there is Rattlesnake Canyon," Barnard said, and swept his arm toward the void. "From here you can see how the old road hugs the far canyon wall all the way down. The only way to get anywhere on this side of the canyon, unless you drop off the cliff, is drive part way down that road and walk across on an old burro path." He grinned at Zack. "If you can find it, that is." Barnard stood, hitched up his pack. "A marijuana grower down there can see you coming a long way off."

"Is there a grow down there?"

"Probably." Barnard gave a tight smile. "There's a new one starts up here every year. We know they're down there somewhere, but it's a lot of land to cover."

Zack peered down. A vertical cliff fell away a hundred feet to a slope blanketed with oak trees and chaparral. It was wild and desolate country. No wonder the marijuana growers felt safe.

"The only way to surprise 'em is to drop a rope down the cliff from this side, but you gotta know where the grow is to know where to drop it," Barnard said.

The path led them along a narrow ridge crest. Zack felt on top of the world, with a jumble of ridge tops and valleys spread below him to one side and the cliff edge to the other.

"Is that how we'll get down there?" Zack said. "On a rope?"

"Yep."

A sudden whop-whop startled Zack. A helicopter rose from nowhere and hung above the ridge. Dust kicked up, grit stung Zack's cheeks, he covered his face with his hands. In a moment the copter moved beyond the ridge and hovered over the chasm. Zack could hear the tinny squawk of a radio over the roar of the rotors.

Barnard dropped his pack and walked to the cliff edge. "This'll do," he said. He pulled a coiled rope from his pack and a mesh bag of gear. He passed a belt harness to Zack.

"You know what to do with that, I'm sure."

Zack reached for it. "If I don't, the US Government wasted a lot of your tax dollars."

The policeman doubled a long sling around a sturdy sapling and set up a rappel. After a final check of his setup, he backed off the edge. "See you below."

Zack waited and watched the rope stretch and jerk at the cliff edge. It slackened and he heard a faint call. Zack took a bight of rope, looped it through the rappel device, set up and backed off. It was a short rappel of less than 80 feet, only a dozen feet of it came free. He landed softly on low underbrush next to Barnard.

The chief gave him a wry smile. "Bit of a surprise, that undercut?"

Zack nodded, grinned back. The rotor noise was louder now. The helicopter settled lower, 100 yards beyond them.

Barnard clipped the mesh bag to the rope. "Leave the gear," he shouted. "If we can't hitch a ride up with the helicopter, this is how we'll get out."

They dropped their harnesses and Barnard led the way down the slope to a well-worn path, easy to follow along the cliff face.

CHAPTER TEN

The body was a dark mound in the center of a circle of trampled marijuana plants. The area was a maelstrom of activity. Zack saw figures move among the trees. Above him a man dangled from the helicopter while another man knelt in the open bay door and guided his descent. Still another man knelt by the body. The whomp of whirling blades smothered the men's words and the whoosh of blasted air bent the slender marijuana plants around the victim.

Zack followed Barnard over to the body. The kneeling man saw them and stood. He was tall and gaunt, with weather-wrinkled features. The National Forest emblem on his dark green jacket identified him. The ranger stuck a hand out to Barnard.

"Glad to see you, George," he said, shouting over the rotor noise.

Barnard nodded and shook the hand. He leaned toward Malden's ear. "This here is FBI Agent Zack Tolliver," he said. "Zack, Rick Malden."

"FBI here already?" Malden said, and reached for Zack's hand.

"Not what you think," Zack hollered.

Malden broke away to go help a man out of the copter lift harness.

Zack took the moment to study the victim. A short stocky man, he lay on his back. He wore jeans, huaraches, a soiled brown sweatshirt with a hood fallen away to reveal black curly hair and a deeply bronzed face. His eyes were open, staring up with that look of surprise Zack often saw in men who met death unexpectedly, small gashes where birds had been to work. There was a single round hole in his forehead.

Malden came back leading the other man. The helicopter began to move away, conversation became easier.

"This here is Bruce Darby, from the state trooper crime unit. Bruce, you know George. This here is a friend of George, FBI Agent Tolliver."

"Call me Zack."

They shook hands all around.

Darby scanned the area around the body and set down his case. "Another cartel blowup?"

"Seems like it," Malden said.

"The wildlife has been at him," Darby said. "Been here a while."

The men looked at the face and at rents in the sweatshirt around the abdomen, and nodded.

"We think he's been here a couple of days," Malden said.

Darby nodded his agreement. "Without a closer look, I'd say overnight, probably most of yesterday. Who found him?"

"A couple of hikers." Malden smiled at their reactions. 'Yeah, they were way off course."

"Not much question what killed him," Barnard said.

"Small caliber." Zack looked around at the green plants stretched down the slope. "Quite the operation here."

Malden grunted. "This is nothing. Sometimes the size of grows up here can rival the vineyards down below."

Zack knelt among the flattened plants. He saw droplets of dried blood here and there on leaves. His eye moved along and came to a small pool of blood, now tacky and black like tar on the brown earth.

"He was shot right here where he lies," Malden said. "No signs of a struggle. Execution style."

Zack nodded in agreement. "I'd say the amount of blood is consistent with a single gunshot wound to the head with a small caliber weapon."

Barnard walked a wide circle around the body. He stopped on the downslope side and bent to study the ground. "I see footprints coming and going," he said. "Looks like some kind of sneaker."

"The victim is wearing sandals," Malden said. He peered at the soles. "Not much tread on 'em."

Barnard nodded. "These prints must belong to the killer."

Zack went to Barnard and knelt to study the footprints.

"The victim was shot from close range, maybe eight to ten feet," Darby said, back at the body. "We might find the shell casing around here."

Zack stood and walked away along the prints another yard. Then he turned, faced the body, made a mental calculation. He came forward a foot and a half, turned, and walked straight out to his right, eyes to the ground. Six feet away he bent down and picked up something shiny, held it up. It was a shell casing.

The men stared.

"How the hell did you find that?" Malden said.

"From the size of the bullet hole in Manuel's head, I guessed he might have been shot by a Glock," Zack said. "It's a handgun easily obtained and in general use." Zack shrugged. "Anyone who knows a Glock knows they eject to the right somewhere between six to ten feet, depending on the recoil."

Malden just stared.

Barnard grinned. "That's why I brought the man along."

"The killer approached Manuel to about here—" Zack stepped forward and stopped "—then shot him, like you said, execution style. The victim never moved from that spot. It's as if he knew his killer and had no fear of him."

"That's the way I read it," Malden said.

"Then the killer walks back the way he came...this way."

Zack turned and followed the footprints among the marijuana plants. Everyone but Darby followed him. No one seemed to notice that Zack had taken over.

They emerged from the plants at a perimeter path, trampled hard from use. Zack squatted, studied the ground in both directions, made his decision and turned right. Ten yards along the path brought them to a pair of tarps slung between trees, disguised from above with black netting. More of the netting lay in a pile nearby and rolls of thin black irrigation tubing were stacked among the trees. Beneath the shelter of the tarp they found a sleeping bag, partially unrolled. A duffle bag erupted with unwashed clothing. The rear of the shelter must have been the kitchen—a small gas camp stove on a crate, a cooking pot next to it. Food packages, drink boxes, cans, matchboxes littered the area. A crate held fertilizers, bug and rodent repellents, Miracle Gro, and tins of chemicals. Beyond the tarp's shelter they saw the tools of the grower trade piled on the ground—a rake, hoe, shovel, ax and pruning shears. The men studied the camp and the ground around it.

"Just the one guard, do you think?" Barnard said.

"Double duty, guard and grower," Malden said.

"A guard without a firearm?"

"Oh, he had a firearm." Zack pointed to a box of shells next to the crate of chemicals.

Barnard read the label. "Twenty-two Long Rounds. He had a rifle."

They glanced around. No rifle.

"The killer came here first, maybe checked the shelter, then went to the grow to find Manuel," Malden said. "He could have come up the path over there."

They started that way, but Zack put up his hand. "Just a second." He squatted to look at the ground at the base of a tree next to the shelter fly. "The rifle stood right here against the tree." He pointed out a small indent in the dry dirt made by the stock.

Barnard put his hands on his hips. "Okay, so how'd you spot that little dent in the ground?"

Zack grinned. "I didn't. I looked for a likely place to stand a rifle, then looked closer."

"Well, it's gone now. Maybe the killer grabbed it and took it with him." Malden waved them to follow. "The other blood is down here."

They followed him down the slope. Where the dirt was less packed they saw the killer's footprints, headed in both directions.

The path led out of the clearing through shoulder high chamise. It grabbed at their clothing as they passed through it. They came to another open area shaded by a large oak. The killer's footprints vanished in a large pool of a black viscous substance. Zack had no doubt it was blood. He saw more coating the tree trunk. Whoever lost all this didn't walk away. His bad feeling came again.

"Jesus!" Barnard said. "It's like someone walked into a shredder."

"When I saw this, I turned right around," Malden said. "The crime boys need to handle this."

They faced the scene of the carnage, took it all in.

Zack walked a slow perimeter around the blood. Barnard followed. At the far side of the blood spill they found the rifle, a lever action Henry replica.

"Better leave that for the lab boys." Zack hunkered down to study the scene.

Malden looked at the sun, ready to dip behind the ridge above them. "We're almost out of daylight. Darby sent for lights. He'll want to take a close look."

Zack was reluctant. His eyes went over the scene one last time. He stood, looked at Barnard. "That rifle should yield blood samples and DNA, if not fingerprints."

Barnard nodded.

"I see the footprints where Manuel's killer came up the path," Zack said. "I don't see any others."

"Where'd the body go?" Barnard asked what was on everybody's mind.

"Like I told the state guys, there's nothing here but blood," Malden said.

Barnard stared at the blood pool. "What the hell could have happened to the body?"

"What gets me, there's no turf dug up, nothing disturbed on the ground like you'd expect from a struggle," Malden said. "It's as if the guy's blood drained out and his body drifted away like a balloon."

The sun was almost gone behind the ridge. The strange bends in the oak branches and shadows in the dense chaparral, cloaked in dusk, took on new meaning.

"It's too dark to do more," Barnard said.

Zack nodded.

They took a last look around, aware of a new stillness in the woods. No helicopter noise, the men's voices up the slope had ceased for the moment.

It was dead quiet.

Zack felt the hair on the back of his neck prickle.

Malden spoke for the three of them. "Let's get the hell out of here."

CHAPTER ELEVEN

High noon is a good time of day for vultures, when the heat simmers over the fields and smells borne on the warm breezes are strong and pungent. Decay is more rapid when the sun is hottest.

The vulture spread his wings wide and lifted lazily with the thermal. He waited, his nose ready to catch the tiniest scent that could mean his next meal. In the field below, the humans drifted away to eat and talk. The unplowed far reaches were abandoned to the ground squirrels, lizards, and snakes—and the dead and the dying.

The vulture saw two humans break away from the larger group, walk toward a grove of trees. One pulled the other along by the arm. As the bird watched idly, he saw the female grow agitated, wave her arms, the male grab her and throw her to the ground. The female struggled but she was no match for the big male. The vulture's interest grew. There might be a meal in the aftermath.

The struggle slowed, became less frantic. There was no smell of blood. The vulture heard cries from the female but he knew this was not a kill. Disappointed, he stretched his wings full and allowed the thermal to lift him back to his former height. His search for food resumed, the humans forgotten.

* * * * *

Jesus watched Rafael Rodriguez lead Candida away across the field. She seemed to go freely. He wondered what she had started to say to him that morning. He thought it had something to do with this man Rodriguez, something that worried her. Mind your own business, he told himself. The last thing you need is trouble.

The remainder of his lunchtime he thought of home. At the end of lunch he saw Rafael come back across the field alone. It occurred to Jesus to ask Rafael about the girl, but again thought better of it. It was not good that he was already in disfavor with his supervisor; don't make it worse. Jesus pulled on his gloves. To his relief he saw Candida come running across the field toward the platform.

There, you see—you worry for nothing.

Jesus walked back to his position, his sandals in his hands, enjoying the feel of the rich damp soil beneath his bare feet. No expense was spared to treat this soil— fertilizer, nutrients, insecticides, irrigation, all of the things to make vegetables practically leap out of the ground, all the things the farmers in Mexico could never afford for their dry, dusty fields.

When he saw Candida approach he waved her to an open station at the planter next to him, but she turned away down the line to a place next to some of the women. From her brief glance he saw she was crying.

He thought about her during the afternoon. His worry gnawed at him. He decided to approach Candida at the next break. He walked toward her but she turned her back on him. Candida's friend from breakfast came to stand between them. She shook her head at him with her finger on her lips. Jesus hung his head and turned away.

When the horn sounded to end the day Jesus cleaned his station, removed his gloves, and walked over to the transport truck. His mind was made up to confront Rodriguez when he came in from the field.

The foreman came last, urging the straggling workers before him.

Jesus stood in his path.

"What do you want, new boy?"

"What is wrong with Candida?"

Rodriguez put his palm against Jesus's chest and pushed him back. "How do I know?" he said. He tried to walk by but Jesus stood his ground.

"You left with her at lunch time but came back alone. When she came back she was crying." Jesus looked Rodriguez in the eye.

The big man glared back. "You need to learn to mind your business," he snarled. "Now get out of my way, *mojone*."

Jesus felt a strong hand grip his arm from behind and pull him out of the way. It was Jorge. Rodriguez passed on with a glare.

"You must not call attention to yourself in this way," Jorge said. "If he turns you in to ICE, you will be sent home. The payments to your family will stop."

Jesus took a deep breath. He thought what that would mean to Isabel and the girls. He nodded, choked down his anger. Jorge patted his arm and moved away.

By now the truck was gone. He sat on the bench to wait for the next one. To his surprise, Candida's friend came and sat next to him.

"I know that you are concerned for Candida," she said. "But you must not risk your job or your welfare. There is nothing you can do."

"About what?"

She looked at him, shrugged. "About things."

Jesus was puzzled.

The woman's look was sympathetic. She extended her hand. "I am Marcella," she said. "My husband works at another farm nearby."

"I am Jesus Hermenegildo Moreno," he said.

"I know. You left a wife and two children in Mexico."

Jesus's eyes widened.

Marcella smiled sadly. "This is a small place. Word moves quickly. But we must be careful. Always, the fact that we are illegal hangs over us. It is what people like Rafael Rodriguez use to get their way."

Jesus looked at her. "What do you mean?"

"I mean if he wants something, you must give it to him or risk deportation."

All at once Jesus went from puzzlement to sudden understanding and horror. "You mean he...she..."

"You have never heard of the green motel then," she said. "It is a name we give the fields because people like Rafael Rodriguez take advantage of us. They know there is nowhere to turn. One word to the authorities, and all our dreams are done." She looked away.

Jesus struggled with the impact of her words.

"So today, he...she..."

"Yes, he raped her. She can feel only shame. There is nothing to be done."

"But Señor Reyes, wouldn't he—"

"Oh, yes," she said. "He is a kind man. If he knew, he would fire Rafael, or worse. But that would not help Candida, or any of the rest of us he has abused. If Señor Reyes learns of his criminal act, you may be sure the authorities will learn of our illegal status. We will be deported, no matter. Our families will suffer." She sighed. "We must preserve our opportunity here above all things. Scum like Rafael know this."

The transport truck arrived. They joined the line to board it.

"You must say nothing of this to anyone," Marcella cautioned before she turned away.

Jesus was stiff with anger. He masked it only with great difficulty. On the short ride back to the barracks he kept to himself, ignoring the light-hearted banter around him. At the barracks, he went directly to his room, his mind roiling with the injustice of the situation. Jorge had not returned, which was not so unusual, for he often had impromptu meetings with some of the workers. Jesus wished he were here so that he could talk to him about this. Finally, he went to shower and change for dinner. He felt a bit better when he was clean.

At dinner he understood why Candida surrounded herself with her girl friends and did not invite him to sit with her. But his anger still festered. He spoke little during the meal and left the dining hall at the first possible moment. He took a walk outside.

It was dusk and brilliantly clear, as it often is when daylight, about to relinquish its dominance, tries to illuminate everything in one last sparkling effort. It felt discordant that the evil personified by Rafael's actions existed in such a setting. He thought of his own Isabella. If such a thing should happen to her, he wondered, how would he react? Just thinking about it, his anger returned.

Jesus took a turn around the building, along the windowless western side where the setting sun reflected off the whitewashed building. His ruminating was interrupted by a sound behind him. He felt his neck grabbed in a powerful grip.

"I should wrench your head off your neck, you little turd," Rodriguez said.

Jesus became blind with a fury that rose without warning from his depths. He grabbed Rafael's wrists with his own powerful hands, tough and strong from a lifetime of hauling nets full of fish. He pulled with all the adrenaline-powered strength of his rage. He felt Rafael's grip give. When the man tried to shift to a better position, Jesus held his wrists with an iron grip and spun around, causing the man's arms to cross and twist painfully. In one motion, he lifted Rafael's crossed arms high, kicked him hard between his legs. Rodriguez fell to his knees. Still crazed with anger, Jesus pushed the helpless man's upstretched arms over his head, down behind him hard. He put his foot in the middle of the man's back, forced his arms down until the tendons in his shoulders cracked.

Rafael screamed in pain.

Jesus released his grip.

The man's arms fell uselessly to his side. Pain contorted his face. "You are a dead man," he screamed.

Jesus realized he had gone too far. He stared at Rodriguez, confused. The enormity of what he had done overwhelmed him. Not knowing what else to do, he walked away. A steady stream of curses followed him. He went directly to his room and went to bed.

CHAPTER TWELVE

Jesus swam to the surface from an anxiety filled dream. The rough grip by ugly, angry Rafael Rodriguez slowly morphed from dream to the reality of an insistent tug at his shoulder.

"Wake up, Jesus, wake up," Jorge whispered. "It is time for you to go."

Jesus opened his eyes to darkness. "Go where? What time is it?"

"It is time for your new job. You forced us to move our timetable up. We must go now. Come, get dressed. Quiet, now."

Jesus climbed groggily from his bunk and groped for his clothing. The night was chilly; he pulled his clothes on quickly, grateful for the warmth of the hooded sweatshirt. After he slipped into his sandals he started toward his closet.

"Where are you going?" Jorge hissed. "We must go."

"But my things..."

"Forget them. You will not need them. Everything you need will be supplied. You can't stay here any longer."

Still befuddled, Jesus followed Jorge out the door and down the corridor, dark but for a safety light at each end. His sandals made a scuffing sound along the floor.

Jorge turned and glared at him, his finger to his lips. Outside, the moon cast a phosphorescent glow on the gravel and the stars were a million laser points. It was easy to see the way and their movement was swift and quiet. A pickup truck waited for them part way down the drive, its motor a soft idle, lights off. Jorge pushed Jesus up into the warm cab and closed the door. He waved the truck away. Jorge was gone. The truck crunched snail-like down the drive to the main road.

The driver put on his headlights and powered along the macadam. Jesus's brain was in turmoil. He tried to bring order to his thoughts. The driver seemed disinclined toward conversation, the truck hummed along the dark road like a silent shadow. They avoided the well-lit parts of town, a distant glow. They went on a highway. Huge trailer trucks outlined with brightly colored lights like carnival booths roared by. A minute later the driver left the highway. They purred along a single lane road, nothing but blackness around them, their headlights stabbing into the unknown.

Jesus did not realize they were deep into the mountains until the driver stopped to engage the four-wheel drive. The road grew rough and the headlights glowed on rock ledge and high brush. On sharp turns the lights pierced into space and he realized a gorge ran beside the road. Jesus held back the questions that came to his mind; it was not the time to disturb the driver. He felt sudden panic when the driver turned off the headlights, plunging the truck into darkness. The vehicle slowed. Jesus' eyes gradually adjusted to the moonlit road.

The driver spoke for the first time on the trip. "The Forest Rangers patrol up here," he said, his eyes on the road. "They come here and park at the side of the road in the dark and look for headlights. But we don't need them; the moon is bright tonight. I know this road well."

The driver lapsed back into silent concentration. The bottom of the truck occasionally grated and scraped along rocks and there were spring-testing lurches into ruts. They crept along. Jesus lost his sense of space and time in the dark. He had a feel of where they traveled only when the truck passed close enough to the cliff side for him to momentarily see protruding rocks and twisted roots. Once a sinewy shape crossed the road at the outer reaches of his vision.

" *Un león de montaña*" the driver muttered. "A mountain lion."

The truck finally creaked to a stop. Jesus had no sense of how long the grinding uphill journey had been. The driver stepped out; Jesus did the same. The glow of the moon was surprisingly bright, the air smelled sweet from pines. Jesus stumbled in the darkness, his perception of depth and distance altered.

The driver came to him with a large pack and thrust it into his arms. "Put it on."

Jesus slid it over his shoulders and adjusted the buckles; this, at least, was familiar territory.

The driver handed him a flashlight, its beam pencil narrow. "Aim it at your feet," he whispered. "Never into the air, even if you fall." He disappeared in the darkness.

Jesus followed.

The next hour was an ordeal of steep scrambles, stumbles, toes against roots and rocks, knee pain, sweat and shoulder ache from the weight of the pack. Once Jesus dislodged a rock. It rolled down the slope and thumped into a tree. His guide spun around in anger.

The terrain leveled, the path smoothed, they picked up the pace. The only chance to catch a breath came when his guide stopped, listened. At those moments the night was still as a tomb, for Jesus a foreign world with no beginning, no end, yet strangely peaceful. They moved on.

At one of those pauses the driver stopped, whistled, whistled again. A soft whistle answered. They went toward the sound. A shadow formed among the trees, approached them.

The driver hugged the stranger. "This is Javier," he said. "You will replace him. He will instruct you for the next two days. After that, you are on your own."

His guide, whose name Jesus never learned, whose face he never saw clearly, turned and vanished.

CHAPTER THIRTEEN

It was late, after ten when Zack returned to the hotel. He paused at his room just long enough to drop off the pack, then went to Susan's room and knocked lightly.

The door opened at his second knock. Susan was wrapped up in a fuzzy hotel robe, her blonde hair pulled back. Blue eyes glimmered behind glasses.

"Hi, there. Have you had an interesting day?" She opened the door wide and stepped back.

"You might say so," Zack said, and entered. Notebooks, clothing, papers were scattered around the room. Chaotic surroundings for such a tidy mind, he thought.

"Would you like a drink?"

"No, no thanks. It's late for me. I wasn't sure you'd be up." Zack moved a sweater and slumped down in an armchair.

"Well, as you can see..." Susan grinned and spread her palms. She sat on the bed and tucked her legs beneath her. "Well, c'mon. Tell me about it."

"Susan, I'm worried."

She frowned. "About what?"

"About..." Zack paused. "Look, let me tell you about it, then you can see what you think. I'd like you to tell me I'm concerned about nothing."

Susan looked puzzled. "Okay. Go on."

Zack told her all about the night's events from the moment he left her in the dining room to answer his phone to his arrival at the crime scene.

"You certainly do have a way of getting involved."

"Yeah, sure seems that way," Zack said. "But here's where it gets interesting." He described the dead worker, the evidence that suggested an execution style murder, how they backtracked the killer. "Susan, all that was left of this guy at the end of his prints was a huge pool of blood. We found the missing rifle a few feet away. That's all—no clothing, body parts, not even a watch. Nothing."

Susan stared. "What do you think it's about?" A thought came; her face fell. "You don't think it's..."

"I don't know. To be fair, it grew dark so quick we didn't have time to study the ground well. I could have missed something."

Zack watched Susan's face. Her eyes leveled on him, but he knew her brain was racing.

"This man, a cartel rival presumably, shoots Manuel," she said. "He walks away and disappears without a trace except for most of his blood."

"That's about the size of it."

Susan shuddered. "So you think..."

"I don't know what to think."

"When I hypothesized this killer creature with Jim Snyder a lifetime ago back in San Francisco, watched it come to life on paper from the evidence, I didn't really believe it. It was an exercise, inference from data, just a design on a blackboard. It's another matter to know these things exist..." She looked hard at Zack. "Do you really think this could be one of them? There must be another explanation."

"I don't know. All we saw was the blood. Maybe tomorrow, in the light of day, they'll find something to explain it. But tonight, in the dusk, well, warning bells went off."

"Will you catch your plane tomorrow?"

"Of course. I got spooked out there but there's not enough to keep me here. That ranger's a good tracker and Barnard knows a thing or two. There isn't enough reason to call my boss and tell him I want to take another day—or to call my wife, for that matter." Even to his own ears his words sounded like an attempt to rationalize. He stood up to leave. "Look, I shouldn't have told you all this. I won't keep you up any longer. Get some sleep." He walked to the door.

Susan followed. "I'll say goodbye, then. I probably won't see you before your departure. Jack Burns wants to show me around the anthropology department tomorrow morning."

Zack smiled to himself as he left. It was obvious the Burns fellow was smitten by Susan. He couldn't think of a better circumstance for her right now.

* * * * *

ZACA

Zack woke the following morning to the simultaneous nag of alarm clock and the ring of his cell phone. He slammed his hand down on one and picked up the other. It was Luke Forrester, his boss, from Arizona.

"Hi, Zack. How's your trip going?"

"Just fine," Zack said, his voice a question.

"Don't worry Zack, this isn't an emergency. I just had a call from a Rick Malden, a National Forest Ranger out there. Says you helped him at a crime scene last night."

"Uh...yeah..."

"Wanted to know if he could keep you for a while."

"Well, it hardly seemed important enough to—"

"There've been some new developments since last night, according to Ranger Malden," Luke said. "He seemed to think he could use your, uh, particular skills."

Zack was befuddled, still groggy with sleep. "Well, I..."

"It's important enough to him to call me to clear the way."

"Well, I..."

"Fine. I won't expect you for a couple more days. Want me to call Libby?"

"Uh...no, no. I'll call her," Zack mumbled. He fell back on the cool sheets and let his brain catch up. He hated to be behind the eight ball before he was even out of bed. What could have happened that was important enough to call his boss? What did Rick Malden think Zack could do for him?

Well, he'd find out soon enough.

Zack called the airline and cancelled his flight, then he called Libby. To his surprise, Libby was fine with it; she had her hands full with little Bernie and her own projects.

Zack felt both excitement and anxiety as he hung up. He was excited for the chase. He had a mystery to solve; he loved that part. But what if his subliminal fears proved correct? Best put that part out of his mind for now.

He went to grab a shower. He thought he'd better have a cup of coffee before he called Barnard. He didn't have Malden's number, and he wanted to hear it first from Barnard, anyway.

Half an hour later Zack sat at a wrought iron table on a delightful patio just outside the dining room with a cup of coffee in front of him. He called Barnard.

"Sheriff's office, George Barnard speaking."

"Why am I here, George?"

"Well, that didn't take long."

"No, it didn't. My boss woke me up this morning."

"I hope you're okay with this," Barnard said. "It was Rick's idea. He had it all arranged by the time he told me. "

"I won't know if it's okay until I know what it is."

"First, let me tell you what we've learned since last night. The dead grower was Manuel Ortega, just as we thought. He was shot at close range with a Glock G21 loaded with .40 caliber bullets. The lab confirmed the blood in that blood pool is human, all from the same person. They found fingerprints on the Henry rifle. Some of them belonged to Manuel, some belonged to a person not in our data base."

"Nothing we didn't already suspect."

"True enough. They're running more tests. They'll search wider for the prints, and they'll check DNA and search hospital records for the blood. But all that will take a while."

"Okay. Got it. But you haven't answered my question. Why me?"

"I think it best if Rick Malden answered that. He said he'd drop by the hotel to see you first thing this morning. I'll give you time to get caught up, get back to you later."

Zack finished his coffee, felt his stomach growl. He had just ordered a muffin when he saw Malden at the patio doorway. Zack waved.

Malden saw him, came over. "Mind if I join you?"

Zack waved at the empty chair. "I've just ordered up a muffin but I could do with breakfast. You eaten yet?"

"Just coffee."

Zack signaled the waitress. "Barnard tells me you're the one made me miss my flight."

Malden looked sheepish. His official Forest Service shirt was tucked into worn jeans. Now in the morning sun Zack noticed long black hair curled at the ears, pale green eyes with white crow's feet etched into sun-darkened skin.

"Guilty as charged," Malden said. "But since you're here, I take it you're okay with it."

Zack gave a dry grin. "There's not a lot of choice when your boss calls to suggest it. As it happens, I've not got much else on my plate."

The waitress came to the table. After the men gave their breakfast orders, Zack said, "I am curious. This case has a puzzle or two, but nothing a good tracker can't resolve. Why me?"

Malden leaned back in his chair. "I'm a pretty good tracker myself, but judging from last night you're even better. Between us, I think we can get the job done. But there's another way you can help me, and that's the real reason I asked to borrow you. We need to work closely with the indigenous population."

Zack raised his eyebrows. "Indians?"

"Indians. Chumash tribe." Malden reached into his shirt pocket and pulled out a small map. "Let me show you."

He spread the map out on the table between them and slid his chair around. He plunked a long finger down. "Here we are in Santa Maria near the mouth of the Santa Maria River." He slid his finger south. "Here is Santa Ynez along the Santa Ynez River. Right there is the Chumash Indian Reservation and Casino." His finger moved again. "Over here is where we found the dead grower last night." His finger shifted and landed with authority. "Right here is Zaca Lake. This whole area is important to the Chumash, you might even say sacred."

Zack looked closely at the map. "Is this reservation land?"

"No, they don't own it. The Chumash knuckled under to the Spanish centuries ago and lost everything. This tiny reservation is all they have now."

The waitress arrived with their food. Malden folded the map up and slid his chair back. The men waited while the girl put down their plates, poured their coffee, and hurried away again.

"That's the only reservation they have," Malden said, picking up where he left off, "but that's not all the land they own. Their casino has made all the difference. They now have more power and influence in the Santa Ynez Valley than just about anybody, and that includes a whole lot of celebrities and nationally known politicians. So when the Chumash tell us an area is sacred to their tribe, even if it's on National Forest land, we listen."

Zack was puzzled. "You want me to help deal with the Chumash? Just because I work with other Indians?"

"Well, yes, in fact, that's a big part of it. It's not all of it, though." Malden took a deep breath and leaned in toward Zack. "It's not just that the ground is sacred to them, it's more than that. How shall I put it? They believe there are...spirits in there, the spirits of their forefathers. They think there's something else in there too, something...well, mythical." Malden sat back in his chair, watched Zack's face. "Your reputation precedes you. You are known to accommodate the beliefs and superstitions of the Navajo. Not many FBI agents are that open minded. That's why I want you." He smiled at Zack. "You okay with this?"

"Where do we start?" Zack said.

Malden chuckled. "I hoped that would be your answer. After we finish our breakfast, we'll meet some Chumash."

CHAPTER FOURTEEN

Jesus dreamed strange dreams. In these dreams he was unable to move, his body would not respond to his will. Beyond his vision were two men, low voices. They spoke English, one with a heavy Spanish accent. They played a game, a game in which they drew cards for Jesus' life. He didn't know how he knew this. Jesus strained to understand their conversation, but could not. He was very frightened.

When Jesus awakened, it was almost noon. He was wrapped in a sleeping bag, fully clothed but for shoes. It was unbearably hot, the bag wet with sweat. Jesus peeled it back, sat up, and stared at the interior of a wickiup. It was constructed of bent saplings bundled together with something like fishing line. There was an empty sleeping bag beside him, a jumble of paperback books at the head, a headlamp dangling from the low ceiling. Dirty socks emerged from a cloth bag. At the hut entrance he saw a tiny gas stove and fuel bottle on a wooden crate that served as a cupboard for food and supplies.

Blinding sunlight poured in the door but it was cool in the shelter. Jesus swung his legs around to put on his shoes. The pain from his leg screamed at him. He pulled up the loose leg of his pants; his knee was swollen twice its size. This is not good, he thought. I will be useless today.

A shadow fell over the entrance.

"So. You are awake."

It was Javier's voice, the man from last night, the man from his dream.

"I thought you might sleep the entire day." Javier's head appeared in the hut. His smile went away when he saw Jesus's knee. "Oh no, *amigo*, you will not work today."

"I can walk with a stick as a cane," Jesus said.

"No. It would be silly to make your injury worse. Better that you rest your leg today. We'll see about it tomorrow." Javier crawled into the shelter. "Let me help you with your shoes. I'll take you to a place where you can watch over the plants. You will be useful, but you won't need to move."

It was painful to put on his shoes, despite Javier's help. Yet somehow, with most of his weight on Javier, Jesus managed to crawl out of the tent. He stumbled up the slope to a place Javier selected. From there, seated, he could see the entirety of the marijuana crop. The plants were nearly two feet in height, about the same as the chaparral that intermingled with them and hid them from the air.

It was quite comfortable in the shade. Javier returned with something wrapped in leaves. "These are tortillas with pork I made for breakfast." He handed one to Jesus. "Here is a water bottle." Javier pointed down the slope. "Just below our wickiup there is a small spring. We

92

use that to irrigate the plants and to drink. When you can walk, I will show you how it is done."

Jesus was grateful for the food. The pork in the tortilla was cold but tasted wonderful. The water was refreshing, despite an acidic taste—the sun was hot, Jesus's throat was dry.

Javier lowered himself next to Jesus. "I will give you instructions while you eat." He waved his arm. "Before you is a moat, or as they say, a grow; a marijuana growing operation. It belongs to the Sonora Cartel. Marijuana growing is against the law in America. This crop is a threat to other cartels. They may try to take it from us or destroy it if they can. We must always work in silence, stay hidden as we move about, never give evidence of our presence by smoke or light reflections." Javier looked at Jesus' hands. "You must put tape over your wedding ring. If you have other jewelry, remove it." He put a sympathetic hand on Jesus' shoulder. "What I say is important. Your life may depend upon it."

Jesus nodded, his mouth full of tortilla.

"These plants are four months old," Javier said. "Soon they will reach the pre-flower stage. Until then they need lots of sun, water, and food. The soil nutrients that we use are in bags stacked behind the wickiup. There is a scoop and a bucket. We dig out soil around each plant, deposit a cup or so of food, then cover it over again. After that, we add water. Every two days we feed the plants. We water them every night. Down at the spring there is a hand pump connected to the irrigation pipes buried just beneath the soil. You pump it until there is dampness around the farthest plant. Simple."

Jesus nodded again.

"At the pre-flower stage, the plants will stop growing tall and begin to grow more branches. Nodes will appear where the branches meet, like tomato plants. As the plant fills out the male plant grows little grapelike clusters, the female develops white pistils, little hairs coming out of a pod. The plants will fill out even more and their flowers will grow. This will take one or two months. Then the male sacks burst"—Javier lifted his hands and spread them apart to demonstrate—"spread their pollen to the female flowers, which then produce seeds. In another two or three weeks the seeds mature within the female bud, maybe change color, the pod bursts, and the seeds drop to the ground." Javier indicated the plants before them. "That is the life cycle of the marijuana plant. You will not be here that long, however. Your shift will end and you will return to Señor Reyes's Ranch."

Jesus looked at the plants with wonder. "Does Señor Reyes know about this?"

Javier laughed. "*Madre de Dios*, no, no, no, no. He must never know. You must not tell a single person."

"What is my job when not watering or feeding the plants?"

"You guard them. All of our work will happen at night. During the day you sleep, watch, listen." Javier looked at Jesus. "Do you know how to use a gun?"

Jesus glanced at the holstered gun secured to Javier's waist. "I have never used one."

"It is simple. I will explain it to you. The gun is our last resort, to save ourselves. Silence is our safety. This crop cannot be seen, not even from the air. The rangers and the other cartels look for it. But they cannot find it unless you give it away."

Jesus remembered the trip up the mountain. "What about mountain lions?"

"The bears, lions, they will not bother you. They may pass by at night, but they will leave you alone."

They sat in silence, while Jesus absorbed it all. "What happened to Manuel?" he asked after a time.

Javier looked at him in surprise. "What do you know of Manuel?"

"I wear his clothes because he did not return."

Javier looked away, stared out over the trees across the canyon. He sighed. "Manuel was not careful. He gave himself away."

Jesus stared at Javier. "They killed him."

Javier nodded.

Fear caught hold of Jesus. The danger seemed real now; he was in the middle of a deadly war. He had accepted there would be danger from the sea, he knew the American police might catch him; he had steeled himself for a long absence from his family. But this was real physical danger. He had not bargained for this. "How long until I am relieved?"

"Not long. But don't worry; it is not so bad. Soon your caution will become habit and your worst enemy will be boredom." Javier laughed. "There are many books to read. Can you read?"

Jesus nodded.

"That is good. This is a beautiful place. Pretend you are a tourist in a lovely park." Javier smiled. "And think about your extra pay."

Jesus looked up quickly. "Extra pay?"

"Oh, yes. You will be paid handsomely for the danger you face."

That is well, then, Jesus thought.

CHAPTER FIFTEEN

Zack gave his teeth a quick brush, threw a daypack together, went down to the lobby to meet Rick.

Malden was stretched out in one of the chairs that lined the porch-like entrance of the Inn. He stood when Zack approached. "I've always liked this place. It's refined yet rustic at the same time." He grinned at Zack. "There's reputed to be ghosts here, you know."

Zack chuckled. "One set of spirits at a time. Where're we going?"

"Over to the Reservation. There's someone I'd like you to meet." Malden led the way to his official forest service pickup, a 2008 Chevrolet Silverado 1500. The logo on the door read Los Padres National Forest. Malden waved Zack into the passenger side. A long wet nose on a large chocolate-brown face prodded Zack from the rear of the extended cab when he climbed in.

"Down, Toker," Rick said, as he climbed into the driver's seat. "I hope you don't mind dogs. This is Toker, my best friend. He's a weed sniffer—that's his job, anyway. But mostly he's my companion." Rick stroked the big dog's head. "We've logged a lot of backwoods miles together, haven't we, boy?"

Zack let Toker sniff his hand. "He might smell Blue, my bloodhound. Best tracker dog you ever saw. My wife trains them." Zack stroked Toker behind the ear.

The truck pulled smoothly out into the traffic.

Zack looked down at the four-wheel drive shifter. "You go off the beaten path a lot, I imagine," he said.

"I do. I'm probably off pavement more than I'm on it. This old girl's got a 5.3-liter V8 with an automatic four-speed overdrive, so we do just fine on the highway as well. It's a comfortable truck." He looked at Zack, eyes somber. "Which is a good thing, 'cause I'm in it all day long."

When they reached the 101 they took the ramp south. Noise barriers and the backsides of buildings rolled by on one side, fields stretched out into the distance on the other. Eventually the highway bent east. They climbed into yellow grass hills with dark blotches of cattle. Vineyards cloaked south-facing slopes.

Zack was entranced. "Green valleys, steep mountains, rolling hills," he said. "You've got it all out here."

"There's more." Malden grinned. "Drive west a short ways and you'll come to ocean cliffs and sand dunes. I think some of the scenery we see today might surprise you." He pointed out prominent landmarks they passed— Solomon Peak, the beautiful hidden valley of Los Alamos, the vineyards of the Zaca River Valley, the transverse Santa Ynez Mountain range.

They turned off on route 246 and drove east past a flurry of fast food stores and strip malls. Then came an ostrich farm followed by a long tunnel of trees and horse pastures. They rounded a corner and abruptly faced a building with a thatched roof. Next to it was a windmill, complete with domed top and large blades, a Danish flag flying in front. Zack gazed in wonder. They might have entered a town in Denmark.

Malden watched Zack's face and chuckled. "Thought this might surprise you. We're in Solvang, home to a transplanted colony of Danes. They moved out here in the early 20th century and built the town. As the tourist industry grew, they added the building facades, just like in the old country. Make no mistake—it's a genuine Danish town. Most speak and write the language." Malden gestured toward a street sign. "Even the streets carry Danish names, like Attardag Road over there."

Zack watched the crowds flow along the sidewalks; throngs of tourists, families with cameras, sidewalk breakfast seating, colorful tour buses.

"It's a Danish Disneyland."

Traffic moved slowly through the town. Tourists mobbed the sidewalks and overflowed into the street. The buildings crowded together, one shop after another, bright splashes of color, all with the trademark tall chimneys and thatched roofs.

At the far end of town was another surprise—a Spanish mission, set on extensive grounds above the wide valley of the Santa Ynez River, a startling contrast to the bustling Danish village.

Malden glanced at Zack. He smiled at his expression. "Hope I haven't bored you this trip. We're almost there. The Chumash Reservation is just over this rise."

The Chumash Casino was imposing. Not in a skyscraper way, like the glistening towers Zack remembered in Palm Springs, but just tall enough to fit the landscape, and very extensive. They followed a drive next to it and entered a large parking garage.

"They must draw huge crowds," Zack said. Even at this hour, cars were scattered throughout the voluminous garage.

"That they do. Not just for gambling, although that draws people from all over the world, but also for the shows. They get name acts in here and charge half what you'd spend for the same ones in LA. They've got a nifty showroom. It seats a lot of people for shows, and then they can convert it over for Bingo."

They climbed the exit stairs and passed through a door to an upper level walkway. At the elevator, they dropped down two floors and followed a corridor tiled with brick with stone laid in a sunray pattern. Their heels clacked on the enameled floor surface. A sign announced Casino Offices. Malden pushed through the door.

A woman with short dark hair in a form-fitting business suit looked up from her desk and smiled. "Be right with you." She typed another moment or two. When she finished she came over to them. Her movements were fluid.

"How are you, Rick?" She smiled and extended her hand.

"I'm just fine, Rebecca. May I introduce Zack Tolliver? He's an FBI Agent who works with the Navajo People in Arizona. Zack, Rebecca Pace."

"Welcome, Zack. We've been expecting you." She turned to Rick. "It's a short ride down to Paula's place. Give me a moment, will you?" Rebecca disappeared into a back office.

"Expecting me?" Zack looked at Rick.

Malden made a sheepish expression. "I wanted to get things started in case you agreed to stay. Rebecca is in charge of public relations, for the Casino as well as the Tribe."

Zack looked around the office. He was drawn to the pictures on the walls. Some were contemporary photos of landscapes and wildlife; others were black and white portraits of people dressed in native clothing. All were quite good.

Rebecca returned, the business suit gone, a T-shirt, jeans, and boots in their place. "Shall we?" She led them out the door. They retraced their route back to the parking garage, took the elevator down to a subbasement level. When the door opened Zack saw a fleet of bright yellow Jeep Wranglers, tops removed, dried mud splattered on their tires and fenders.

Rebecca climbed into the driver's seat of the nearest one and waved the men in. Zack climbed into the back. The jeep started up with a roar that reverberated in the narrow concrete confines.

Once out of the garage, Malden shifted in his seat to talk to Zack. "We're on our way to meet Dr. Paula Sanchez. People here call her "Momma". She's a senior tribal member and a full professor at Cal State in Long Beach, in the American Indian Studies department."

"She's also on the board of the California Indian Storyteller's Association," Rebecca said. "She's a writer and a poet, and she's been like a mother to me since my own folks died. She lost her husband and fourteen year old daughter in an automobile accident years ago. I guess our relationship has been mutually beneficial."

The jeep roared down a tunnel-like road next to a deeply eroded, bone-dry creek bed shaded by oak trees. A break in the trees gave Zack a glimpse of the wide Santa Ynez River Valley flanked by tall mountains in a jagged line against the sky.

They spun around a corner, spewing dust. The jeep stopped. Rebecca jumped out and worked the lock combination on a steel gate, swung it open. "Paula is the only one in the entire neighborhood who has her place fenced," she said as she climbed back in. "She's a naturalist, among many other things, and she always has some strange creature running around her property." She grinned. "Don't worry, no lions or tigers."

Malden locked the gate behind the jeep. They
drove on. The road sloped through a grove of large oaks,
speckled lightly with morning sun. The underbrush was
gone, replaced by knee-high savannah grass. The effect
was serene. They wound down toward the river valley past
solitary trees. Zack saw mule deer grazing on nearby
slopes. Another turn and a yellow stucco house appeared
as if by magic. It blended into the grass, it's tile roof green
with lichens. A large open porch surrounded it.

They pulled up next to a tired looking Subaru,
covered in yellow dust. The jeep skidded to a stop in a dust
cloud of its own.

A screen door slapped open. A tall woman, her
raven hair streaked with grey tied back in braids, stepped
out. She stood erect, exuded authority. "I'm glad you called
when you did, Becky. I was on my way out to a meeting at
the University, but I'm always happy to find a reason to
cancel." Her chuckle was deep-throated, vibrant. "They
have too damned many of 'em." She waved them up to the
porch. "Sit down, sit down. I got lemonade, unless it's too
early for you, in which case I've got coffee." She looked at
Zack. "I guess you must be the FBI guy, since I know
these two. That's what, inference, or deductive reasoning?"
She gave a baritone chuckle.

Zack nodded. "A little of both, I'd say. Zack
Tolliver, ma'am."

"Well, Zack Tolliver, you can pour me a cup of
coffee, black, please. It's right there on the table." Momma
Sanchez wore jeans belted above a slightly bulging tummy,

boots, and a turquois and white shirt made from a hemp-like material.

They all found seats on wicker chairs. Zack poured coffee for Dr. Sanchez. Oaks draped in Spanish Moss offered shade for the house. The smell of sun-warmed grass was sweet.

"I was just watching a couple of Western Scrub-Jays, *Aphelocoma Californica*, out here," Paula said. "What a pair of clowns, so curious. Just before you arrived the male came right over here to the edge of the porch an' gave me the once over." She looked at Zack, her brown-black eyes twinkling. "You get those back home?"

"We've got jays in Arizona, but I don't think any are the California-whatsis," Zack said, and laughed. He handed her the coffee.

"We sure appreciate your time, Paula," Malden said. "Rebecca must have told you a grower was killed up in Rattlesnake Canyon. Zack here happened to be in town and we leaned on his boss to let us keep him for a while. He works as an FBI liaison with the Navajo in Arizona." Malden peered over at Zack. "We're glad to have a guy with his skills."

"Just what are your skills, Cowboy?"

"I think Rick is saying I'm a decent tracker."

"Zack accepts the spiritual side of the Navajo culture," Malden said. "In fact, he's here to assist an anthropology lecturer from UC Berkeley present a theory that supports the possible existence of an alternate human species."

Paula leveled a thoughtful gaze at Zack for a moment. She looked back at Malden. "We've had growers killed out there before. What's special about this one?"

"There's more goin' on out there than before. The death of the grower was an assassination, pure and simple——a rival cartel, no doubt. After the shooting, the killer walked off the way he came. We tracked him up until his footprints disappeared in a large pool of blood. Something bad happened to the assassin. There was so much blood whoever it belonged to couldn't have survived." Rick put his palms up. "But no body."

Zack watched Paula's face, saw a strange look come and go.

"Where do I come in?" she asked.

"I was hopin' you'd give Zack here a little background about the nature of the area we'll be in. You know, what do those hills mean to the Chumash? Why is the place so special to the tribe?"

Paula grunted. "Well..." She looked at her guests. "Would anyone like more to drink? This will take a while.

CHAPTER SIXTEEN

"Momma Sanchez has many titles," Rebecca said, her hand on the woman's arm. "The one dearest to me is her position on the Board of the California Indian Storytellers Association. No one knows as many Chumash legends and myths as Paula."

"That sounds like my cue to tell the legend of Zaca Wilderness," Paula said. "Okay, then. Listen closely, Cowboy, this one's for you."

"I'm ready," Zack said.

"A long time ago," she began, "before the white man ever set foot upon this land, a powerful sachem lived in a Chumash village in the foothills of the mountains. The village was in a lush green forest by a lake where a great river began its journey to the sea. The people were happy and prosperous. The sachem was well respected. He held a seat in the chiefs' council and advised the village elders. He was a wise man, but more than that, his eyes could pierce the veil of the Upper World and see what was to come. He used this gift to help steer the course of the village and so it was that the people were always prepared when drought dried up the land, or when the great serpent that held up the Middle World moved and made the earth tremble beneath their feet.

"The sachem had a beautiful daughter. She was known the length and breadth of the valley not just for her beauty but also for her kindness toward all creatures. It was said that the birds would land on her palm, that the deer would follow her when she walked in the forest. A more gentle soul did not walk the earth. She was beloved by her father beyond all things. But jealousy was in the hearts of many.

"One day the wise sachem prophesied that a great calamity would befall the village. For the first time his vision was unclear, he could not see the nature of the disaster and so was unable to help the village to defend against it. Soon a great fire came and the entire village burned. The people survived only by leaping into the lake where the flames could not reach them. All of their possessions were gone. The people were angry at the sachem. They forgot he had warned them of a calamity. They forgot that he too had lost all his possessions. Instead, they blamed him for their misfortune. The council decided the sachem should be punished. They declared he must give up his most beloved possession—his beautiful daughter. She was to leave home and enter the Upper World, lost to this world forever.

"Greatly angered and saddened by this injustice, the wise sachem prepared his beloved daughter for her journey to the place where the Middle World meets the Upper World. He watched her walk away from the village and into the forest for the last time. The sachem was mad with grief, inconsolable. He would neither eat nor drink. Soon he weighed less than the leaf blown about by the wind and it was apparent that he, too, would soon follow his daughter into the Upper World. Before he departed, the sachem had one last terrible prophecy to foretell. One day the paths his daughter trod so gently through the forest would become rough and uneven, the lush grasses and green trees would dry up and wither, the birds that came to her hand would grow large and ugly and mean-spirited, the animals that followed her with adoration would become dangerous and prey upon all who came that way. It came to pass as the wise sachem foretold. To this day no person passes that way without fear."

There was silence on the porch. Paula broke the spell with another baritone chuckle. "Well, that's the myth. Kind of beautiful in its way, don't you think?"

"To this day campers and hikers claim to see an Indian maiden walk among the trees," Rebecca said.

"I suppose anything that ever happens up in those canyons is laid at the door of that prophecy." Malden smiled.

"Has much happened?" Zack said.

"There've been a number of disappearances, all unofficial, of course."

"Mostly related to the drug trade, wouldn't you say?" Rebecca peered at Malden.

"Mostly, yes. That's why the disappearances are unofficial—the people who disappear are unofficial."

Zack cocked an eyebrow. "Is this legend our concern?"

Rebecca shook her head. "That whole area around Zaca Lake and Zaca Mountain is important to my people. Zaca Lake is thought to have a passageway our people used when they came here from the Channel Islands. The Old People used to make offerings there every year." Rebecca turned to Paula. "Isn't there a story about Zaca Lake?"

"There are many," Paula said, and laughed. "The Chumash name for Zaca Lake is Ko'o', or water. The word Zaca, on the other hand, means *in the bed* and was the name of a village located where Zaca Station is now.

"Zaca Lake was formed, according to the myth, by Thunder, one of two brothers from the Upper World, when he sat down and made a great hole in the earth. A man from the village saw him and said insulting things. The village people ran away in fear. When they returned the man was gone and so was Thunder. The huge hole was filled with water. So there it was—Ko'o'."

"The people in that village had trouble getting things right," Zack said.

"That they did, Cowboy. Another myth tells of a girl who drowned off the Channel Islands. Her Chumash lover used the lake as a pathway to follow her soul to the celestial realm of the souls. He brought her back through the gateway located at the bottom of the lake."

"As you can see," Rebecca said, "my people have a lot of tradition and ceremony associated with that region. When the drug cartels moved in and began growing marijuana, the issue became much more sensitive."

"Right. When growers went missing the cartels sent re-enforcements and the whole business escalated," Malden said.

Rebecca frowned. "It's gotten so bad, the Tribal Elders Council has threatened to take the issue before the Tribal Administration."

"To what end?"

"Leverage. The Chumash Tribe has its fingers in many projects dear to state and federal government. We supply a lot of financial support. The Tribe could threaten to rescind some of that, could force the government's hand to police the area. They could even establish an official Allotment for the Chumash there and keep everybody out."

"I for one think we should have done that a long time ago," Paula grumbled. "The forestry service is doing the best it can. They just don't have enough people."

Malden nodded at Zack. "You see how sensitive it all is. The murder of the grower is bad enough, but if word of the blood with no body to go with it got out—well, you can imagine how that legend will take on legs."

Rebecca looked earnestly at Zack. "This whole business could become a hot button issue for the tribe, the state, and the federal government."

Zack glanced at Malden. "So I'm supposed to be the guy who can keep this all in check?"

"Nah. You'll be the guy we point to when it all goes to hell," Malden said, and grinned.

"We'll find somebody from the Tribe to join you up there. If the Tribe is represented, there should be fewer incidents or complaints from our end," Paula said. "One last thing, Cowboy. This may be important, or it might be

110

meaningless. There are stories about—how shall I put this—a presence, something or someone who protects that forest, who hunts those who would desecrate it." Paula turned to Rebecca. "Becky, you know more about it."

"I don't know much," Rebecca said. "Hunting is regulated in the National Forest, right down to the types of weapons and projectiles for hunting mammals and game birds within particular seasons."

"Only with a valid California hunting license," Malden interjected.

"But it is permitted, and there's plenty of enticing game out there for hunters. But people don't hunt in the Zaca area anymore."

"That's right," Malden said. "The purchase of licenses has fallen off. We figure it's on account of the drug cartels. If you show up near one of their grows with a weapon, you could end up in a shootout."

"I'm sure that's part of it," Rebecca said. "But this other presence has something to do with it. Some claim to have seen it."

"What does it look like?" Zack said.

"A giant Indian."

CHAPTER SEVENTEEN

Malden drove north. The truck hummed past vast vineyards and elegant tasting rooms. To the east low clouds touched the tips of the San Rafael Mountains.

Malden glanced at Zack. "Now you have the folklore for this area." He gestured with his right hand toward the mountains. "What are your thoughts?"

"Very often myths and legends, no matter how absurd, have some kernel of truth. Part of our job here may be to sort out which kernel it is."

Malden nodded. "I didn't expect Paula to volunteer to ask a tribal member to join us. She must be taken with you." He grinned at Zack.

Zack glanced at him. "What's with the Cowboy bit?"

Malden shrugged. "I dunno, because of Arizona, maybe? She gives pet names to people she likes."

Zack changed the subject. "You spend every day out in that backcountry. You ever see the giant Indian, or the Indian maiden?"

"Naw, never have. To be fair, I cover a lot of other ground besides the Zaca area." Malden peeked at his side mirror. "I won't say I haven't felt as if something was around on occasion. The wilderness can get lonely." He smiled. "I've got a good companion in Toker, though."

"How will we get to the crime scene from here?"

"Well, a bird could fly right over Zaca Peak there to Rattlesnake Canyon in no time. But by road, we'll need to drive north up Foxen Canyon. It's long, but real scenic." He inclined his head toward the window. "Sit back and enjoy the ride."

Foxen Canyon was long. The valley grew wide as they progressed north. Vineyards alternated with cattle grazing, private ranches alternated with tasting rooms. A twin-spired chapel high on a promontory came into view.

"Sisquoc Chapel," Malden said. "It was erected by one of the pioneer families in the valley. We'll turn into the Sisquoc Winery just behind it."

They drove down the winery entrance road lined with olive trees, on beyond the tasting room to the fields. Malden engaged the four-wheel drive; they bumped across the river valley on a dirt access road. Once they entered the fold of the hills, the canyon narrowed. The road steepened, followed the meandering creek bed.

They drove past a primitive campground to an open area where two dry streambeds met.

Malden pointed left up a steep canyon. "That's Rattlesnake Canyon. We'll drive the road that climbs it. We can walk to the crime scene from up there."

The truck inched up the road in low range, around hairpin turns. The canyon fell away on Malden's side. At one extra wide turn Malden pulled off onto the shoulder, parked up against the cliff face.

"Here we are," he said. They climbed out. Malden flopped his seat forward and let Toker out. The dog ran around in circles, delighted to be free. The men meanwhile grabbed their packs from the truck bed. A faint trace of a trail dropped precipitously off the road shoulder.

Malden pointed across the canyon. "Up there is where we were last night. You see the cliff you rappelled down. Bring your eye down a bit. The marijuana crop is in there somewhere. They picked a good spot for it—you can't see it from the cliff above and you can't see it from over here. You pretty much have to stumble on it like those lost hikers did."

"How do we get there from here?"

"Follow me."

Toker led the way down. Malden followed. Zack skidded more than down-climbed the loose shale. The terrain leveled, a ridge led toward the arroyo. It wasn't a trail so much as bare rock. Coyote brush grabbed at Zack's pack. Beyond the ridge, the path wound toward the head of the canyon and dropped again. Zack watched Malden plunge down another near vertical drop, kicking up dust. Zack slid down behind him. They ended up on a rock ledge. It spanned the canyon, it would have been a waterfall, had there been any water.

"You good?"

"I'm fine." Zack wiped some sweat from his brow with the back of his hand. "How on earth did you find this trail?"

"I spend a lot of time out here in my line of work. Toker over there helps. He can smell which way the *sembradores* go."

"If you know all this, why are they still here?"

Malden held up two fingers.

Zack stared, puzzled.

"There's just the two of us," Malden said. "Between us we patrol the whole length and breadth of the Los Padres National Forest from the Santa Ynez Mountains north the San Luis Obispo County. We're not in one place very long."

Across the natural ramp, the trail became steep, stayed that way until it intersected a well-worn path across the slope.

"They call this *El Camino de Burro*," Malden said. "It's a connector trail. It takes you all along the length of this ridge. The *burros* travel along it to the most recent grow. The trail stays mostly in chaparral, it can't be seen from the air."

"Which way today?"

"We go that way a short distance." Malden pointed to the left. "From there we'll climb to the base of the cliff and work our way along."

It was another sweaty scramble to reach the cliff base where they found a worn, level path. Zack was grateful for the reprieve for his leg muscles. Soon he heard voices.

Malden stopped and put Toker on a lead. A few minutes later Zack recognized the place they climbed down the night before.

A tall lanky man in a trooper's hat climbed the slope toward them. Zack recognized Dom Antonio, from the roadblock.

He arrived breathing noticeably, stared at Zack, nodded to Malden. "Hello, Rick. George said you'd be coming." He aimed a thumb down the slope. "Darby from forensics is down there. He said send you down when you get here. He's got some questions for you." Dom wiped his brow. "I got to wait here for the ICE guys. They're comin' to destroy the marijuana."

"Thanks, Dom," Malden said. He turned down the slope.

As Zack turned to follow, Dom looked at him. "You enjoyin' your stay, boy?" he said. His mouth smiled but his eyes didn't.

"Seems like the fun's just begun," Zack said, surprised by the apparent animosity. He turned away to follow Malden and Toker down the steep path. Not love at first sight, he thought.

Everything at the crime scene looked different in the light of day. The marijuana grow looked much as he'd remembered, although many more plants were crushed underfoot. Zack could find nothing new where Manuel's body had been. Darby wasn't there, so after a thorough re-inspection of the scene, they descended the slope to the shelter. Again, their inspection revealed nothing new.

116

"I'm down here." Darby's voice floated up.

They went on down, found Darby at the mysterious blood pool, now black and viscous. He wore rubber gloves and knelt over an open toolbox. He placed a blood sample in a test tube.

"Any idea yet who belongs to this blood?" Malden said.

"Good morning to you, too." Darby glanced up at him. "The lab's doing a DNA search, but it will take a while." He lifted the test tube. "I've got a few more samples for other tests." He shook his head. "You may have heard I got prints off the rifle, but none are on file. Not so surprising, they're probably illegals. One set matches the corpse, again no surprise. I've sent both sets to Mexico with my fingers crossed. I can't tell you much from this blood, other than the fact that the guy who used to own it isn't in this world anymore." He stared up at Malden. "You got to find me a body."

Malden grunted. "We're sure gonna try."

CHAPTER EIGHTEEN

"I think that was our cue," Malden said. "Let's find a body."

Zack nodded absently, his eyes already on the ground. He walked over to the yellow tape, worked along it to the outside. After one complete circumnavigation he turned and retraced his steps. He stood and shook his head.

"Nothing?" Malden said.

"Not a trace."

"What now?"

"Let's try the approach path," Zack said. He stepped beyond the yellow tape, studied the ground. Every few feet he searched right and left of the path for anything out of place. The ground here was littered with live oak leaves, shaped like tiny cups, very brittle. Zack noticed some leaves looked crushed. He knelt, brushed the leaves away. There was a slight imprint in the earth. He studied it.

"Got something?" Malden stood behind him.

"Yeah. Take a look."

Malden knelt, inspected it.

"What do you think?" Zack said.

Malden stared at the mark. "It could be anything. It's just a slight depression."

Zack's eyes moved off to the side of the imprint. "Depressions don't just happen. Something makes them." He spoke with measured words, as if to himself. "I don't see any more, but I almost didn't see this one. Someone walked very softly here, barely crushed these brittle leaves."

"Why did he slip up here?"

Zack glanced at Malden. "He didn't. Think about it. The depth of the imprint depends upon the force he exerts, whether he walks, stands, jumps or whatever. The shape here is oval. It's a strong impression. It's the first we've found—"

"I get it!" Malden's eyes widened. "The guy was kneeling. That's the imprint of his knee."

"There you go. Now you're thinking like a tracker. I don't think he was kneeling, though. I think he was crouching." Zack traced the outline of the depression with his finger. "This is the ball of his foot. It's not a shoe; it's some sort of moccasin. If I'm right..." Zack pushed away leaves two feet to each side of the imprint, scanned the bared earth. He saw it now, a slight ridge. "Here's the other foot. The oval shape is distinct; all his weight is on the balls of his feet. It narrows toward the upslope side; he faced the blood, crouched here."

"I see it now," Malden said. "He crouched here, and waited?" Malden stared back up the path at the yellow tape. "Then...?"

"I don't know. We have to be patient and process the clues as we find them. This doesn't give us a lot, but we can take away a couple of things. He's a big guy, the width his forefoot and the distance between the impressions tells us that. He's at home in the woods; his woodcraft is among the best I've seen."

"He?"

Zack shrugged. "I've made that assumption from his size." He stood and stretched, pointed down the path. "He came from down there."

It took ten minutes for the men to work their way to El Camino Burro. They left no bush, twig, or leaf unturned. Once on the well-worn transverse path, they looked in one direction, then the other.

"How do we know which way he went?"

"Damn good question," Zack said. "We can't really be sure he was even here, since we've found no more sign." He studied El Camino Burro. "It's unlikely he would cross this path and go on down through that brush—it's very thick, it would be hard not to leave prints in that soft soil. We have to assume he went left or right. Left takes us back to the road, the campground, and more populated areas. I'm going with right." Zack looked down at Toker.

"Your dog has an opinion."

The dog tugged on his lead toward the right.

"Toker says turn right," Malden said.

They did. The hard packed earth of El Camino Burro left no prints. They relied entirely on Toker. The dog pulled Malden along at a steady trot while Zack watched for signs that anyone had left the trail. The well-traveled path led through tall chaparral and trees. Whenever a secondary trail turned off, the men gave the intersection a minute examination. Toker was impatient; he always wanted to go straight on. He whined impatiently each time the men stopped.

Malden's phone buzzed. He spoke in it for a moment, put it away. He grimaced. "Toker and I have to go. Jeremy Tusco, the other ranger, needs the dog. He's waiting up at the crime scene. You alright on your own for a while?"

Zack nodded. "Where shall we meet?"

"I'll come back here when I return. We can get to the truck along this same trail in the other direction."

After Rick and Toker left, Zack slowed his pace. Without Toker's nose and a second pair of eyes he needed to be more circumspect. He moved slow, found progress difficult.

"Hello."

Zack was startled. He felt foolish he hadn't noticed the person just off the pathway; a woman, a girl, really. She sat cross-legged, her back against a tree. A squirrel scampered away from her at Zack's approach. She wore buckskin leather pants, faded almost white, a beige tank top. Her shoulders and arms were brown from the sun. Chestnut hair, cut short at her ears, curled up, framed her face. Her arms lay in her lap, an acorn in her hand. Somber brown-black eyes regarded Zack.

"Hello yourself." Zack went from startled to confused. He didn't expect to see an attractive girl where he tracked a killer.

"I've waited a long time." Her voice was soft, almost a caress. She didn't smile, yet projected warmth.

"Waited for what?"

"You are the esteemed tracker from Navajo Land, yes?"

Zack was perplexed. "Uh, yes...I guess..."

She laughed now, a merry tinkling sound. "I am your guide."

"You?"

"Is there something wrong with that?"

"Uh, no. Of course not."

"You were focused on the ground as you came. What do you track?"

Zack felt a touch of annoyance at this interrogation. "Someone with moccasins...like yours."

Amusement flickered across her face. She glanced at her feet. "Not mine, I think. The moccasins you follow are much larger."

The girl was full of surprises. "You know who I'm tracking?"

She stood in one graceful motion. He noticed a bone handled knife at her waist. She stepped down to the trail. Long legged, she was as tall as he. "You are tracking a large man, very strong and agile. His stride is long. He moves as one with the forest, a predator."

"How do you know all this?"

"I follow the signs, as you do." Her eyes showed amusement.

"Then I must be on the right track."

122

"Did you doubt it, great tracker?"

"Look, who told you I—"

She put out her hand before he could finish. It was delicate, feminine. "I'm Tomasa. My friends call me Tommy."

Zack felt off balance again, yet couldn't help but grin back. "I'm Zack Tolliver."

"Well, Zack Tolliver, shall we do this?"

"Before we do, you need to know this man we follow is dangerous. He's killed a professional assassin and carried off the body somehow. You don't need to get involved in this."

Tommy's eyes glowed with amusement. "I will stay safely behind you."

Zack stared, confused again, uncertain. He shrugged. "Fine." He nodded toward the path. "Where does this trail lead?"

"It hugs the slope to where the ridge ends. There it intersects with the summit trail." Tommy stood aside for Zack to take the lead.

He did, but the man they followed left no sign of his passage. There were no disturbances, or other indications that he left the trail. Thirty minutes later the trail ended at the face of the ridge, as Tommy had said, and forced a choice. They could turn up the ridge trail and back along its crest, or drop down a steep path on loose shale to the valley floor.

Zack looked in both directions. From his vantage point the valley floor was a large brown clearing with green splotches where oak trees clustered. A stream bed the color of light coffee meandered through it. Steep slopes of black chaparral angled down on all sides. There was no way to know which way the man had gone.

Tommy pointed to the southeast. "The Sisquoc River Valley is over the next ridgeline. Beyond it is the backcountry east of Zaca Mountain. He might have gone that way."

Zack gazed out over the ranges. "What makes you think so?"

"It's desolate, uninhabited. He can disappear there." She peered at Zack. "What will you do?"

"Try to find him." He glanced at his watch. "Right now, I have to go back to meet up with the ranger, Rick Malden. I will try to get an early start tomorrow." Zack glanced at her. "Will you come?"

She nodded.

Zack watched her face. "You know this area quite well, I suspect, since the Chumash sent you to guide me. What do you know about this...person we follow?"

Tommy gazed out over the mountains. "I have roamed these hills for as long as I can remember. I love them. They are peaceful, restful. When the men from Mexico came to grow the *pagee*, the marijuana on these slopes, all that changed. They disrespected the land, polluted it. They disagreed among themselves, shot guns at one another." She waved an arm to encompass the mountains. "The peace that was here was disrupted." She studied Zack's face. "There is someone here, a protective presence, powerful beyond the evil of the drug traffickers. Their warlike ways stirred him to action. He hunts them now." Her steady gaze regarded Zack. "He is the one you track."

A dark foreboding seized Zack. "Have you seen this...presence?"

"I have seen signs of him. I have seen the sites of his kills.

"The blood?"

Tommy didn't answer. She looked away.

"You think the blood is from a trafficker, that this...protector killed him."

Gentle brown eyes regarded him. "You ask the question, yet you know the answer."

Zack stared off across the vastness. "I suppose I do."

Her words came with quiet authority, as if to a child. "It is your time to make a decision. Do you want to go on with this? You could go home, leave it alone. There is a balance to nature; this presence is part of it. You should think about that."

Zack stared off across the mountains, thoughtful, undecided.

"If you decide to return tomorrow, I will help you," Tommy said.

CHAPTER NINETEEN

Zack met Malden as planned, part way along El Camino Burro. He was *sans* Toker. Duty called: the dog's particular skills were needed in another part of the National Forest.

"That dog is more important to the forestry service than me," Rick said.

Malden had a lot of questions, and Zack had few answers. No, he did not know whom they tracked along El Camino Burro. No, he knew nothing about Tommy other than her name and her appearance. No, there was no rendezvous assigned to meet their Chumash guide the next day, she would find them. No, Zack did not know where she had gone, simply that she went another way.

Malden dropped Zack at the hotel, with plans to meet him for breakfast in the hotel dining room early the next morning.

In a day full of surprises, Zack had another one in store. As he entered the hotel lobby, his friend and mentor Eagle Feather looked up at him from an armchair. Zack failed to register him at first; when he did, he was overcome by astonishment.

Eagle Feather climbed up from his chair, amused by Zack's look.

"What are you doing here?" Zack demanded.

"Somebody's got to look after you, White Man."

Eagle Feather was Zack's first and best friend at the Navajo Indian Reservation in Arizona after he arrived as a young FBI agent fresh from the academy. He was assigned to the FBI liaison office in Tuba City, his job to work with the Navajo Nation Police, learn the ropes. Eagle Feather was his guide.

At first, the Navajo tracker didn't try to hide his contempt for the city-bred agent he guided. Zack proved he was different from other agents. He didn't put on airs, he asked questions, he listened to the answers. Eagle Feather took him under his wing, taught him the things he needed to know on the Reservation. Their friendship grew. They became a formidable team, Eagle Feather with his guide skills and his knowledge of Navajo ways, Zack with his stubborn persistence, FBI training and well-grounded logic. A marriage of opposites, the two friends learned to respect one another's differences, use one other as a sounding board.

The entry of a third party into this close relationship in the form of widowed bloodhound trainer Libby Whitestone did not disrupt their chemistry. She became someone special in Zack's life, yet always honored the deep friendship between the two men. Eagle Feather stood with Zack at his wedding, later agreed to be godfather to their firstborn.

Now he stood here, completely unexpected, a rare smile on his face from Zack's astonishment. "Libby said to tell you since she couldn't be here, it was up to me to keep

127

you out of trouble. Luke Forrester even promised a stipend to help you out."

All Zack could do was grin like an idiot. "How'd you get here so fast?"

"Forrester put me on a corporate jet headed from Flagstaff to Vandenberg Air Force Base on FBI business. They landed at Santa Maria Airport to drop me off."

"Well, aren't you something special."

Eagle Feather just smiled. "I noticed a bar down the hall there. Let's go grab a beer. You can tell me what's going on."

Eagle Feather drew the usual stares when they walked into the hotel bar. Never one to disappear into the woodwork, he wore a bright red paisley shirt with a black vest and black leather pants. He topped the outfit off with his signature black felt hat and solitary bedraggled eagle feather. He wore his silver-streaked black hair down his back in a thick braid, his rugged, sun-darkened face wore a habitual aspect of fierceness that belied the man's true nature.

The beers arrived. Eagle Feather took a long drink of his ale, wiped his mouth with his sleeve, turned to Zack. "What mess are you in this time, White Man?"

Zack laughed. "I've been asked to help local law enforcement with a case. It seems I somehow established a reputation as a good tracker who gets along with indigenous populations." He glanced sidelong at Eagle Feather. "Go figger!"

"Sounds like they screwed up on both counts."

ZACA

Zack shook his head. "They've got a real mess here. They've got cartels growing marijuana and killing each other off on National Forest land, land that's sacred to the Chumash Indians. They've got illegals and Panga boats and farm workers disappearing. They've got someone else out there killing off the cartel members. A Chumash guide tells me there's some sort of malignant presence in those mountains." He eyed Eagle Feather. "That's all."

"Sounds like old times." Eagle Feather set down his beer. "What's the plan?"

"Tomorrow I meet the forest ranger for breakfast. Then we find the Chumash guide and go back on the trail of the guy who killed the killer."

"You tracked him today?"

Zack nodded. "We had to give it up for the night. Tomorrow we'll stay on this guy's trail for the long haul. I came back to get my gear and some sleep."

Eagle Feather eyed Zack. "What's your jurisdiction here?"

"I guess the answer to your question is, my jurisdiction is muddy. I'm more of a guest, so technically I don't call the shots."

"Yeah, I thought so. You've got yourself into another mess."

Zack studied the lacing in his glass, glanced at Eagle Feather. "It may be worse than you think." He described the blood pool, the almost complete lack of sign left by the killer. "There's something unreal about it. I stared at all that blood, with no body, no clues, told myself, this can't be."

Eagle Feather put a hand on Zack's arm. "I know what you're thinking. Let's not go jumping to conclusions. Not every clever killer is a Skinwalker, or some other mythical creature."

"You're right," Zack said. His face dissolved into a warm smile. "I'm sure glad to see you."

CHAPTER TWENTY

When Jesus awoke early the next day, the swelling of his knee was down. He could dress and put on his sandals without much pain. His recovery had begun. In a way, this new assignment was a blessing; the constant bending in the fields did not allow his knee the time it needed to heal. Just one day of rest had done wonders.

Javier was in his sleeping bag, still asleep. Jesus crawled quietly out of the shelter, stood and stretched. The sun peeped over the eastern range to touch the upslope plants, the downslope still in shadow. Jesus found the spring, stripped off his shirt and slapped cold water over his torso. He filled a pail with water, brought it back to the wickiup. When Javier awakened it would be there for him to cook breakfast. Finally I can contribute, Jesus thought.

He walked up into the patch of sunlight, felt the sun's warmth on his shoulders. He inspected the young plants. All that Javier had taught him yesterday came to him. Birds chirped joyfully in the trees, the smell of new growth came to his nose.

There was a new sound, a low vibration at first that grew into a rapid thump and then a roar. The peace of the morning was shattered. He heard Javier yell, "Get down!" A helicopter materialized over the ridge and descended toward them, no more than a hundred feet above the trees.

Jesus dropped on the damp earth among the plants. He lay still. The craft hovered over them for several long seconds, then turned and roared south.

The moment it was gone, Javier hurtled from the wickiup. He spoke into a small radio he held in his hand.

Jesus found his feet, stumbled down the slope toward him. His knee flamed from the awkward landing when he dove to the ground. I've messed it up again, he thought, anguished.

"They found us," Javier said as Jesus approached. "We've got to move quickly. At least they didn't drop anyone, maybe they don't have enough men, but someone will come up the mountain soon. We have maybe an hour to clean up and get out."

"Where will we go?"

"We'll go deeper into the mountains, hide out until we get instructions. Quickly now, load up that box of supplies."

The two men worked feverishly. They packed up all they could carry and buried the rest.

"Load up as much water as you can," Javier said. "We don't know where our next water will come from."

When they were ready, Javier looked like a pack mule with his large pack, tools, and a gallon bottle of water dangling from his waist. Jesus was similarly loaded. He wondered how he could possibly hike any distance.

They brush-crashed down the slope beside a ravine, turned east on a worn path. After a kilometer or so,

Javier stopped. He put down his load and turned to Jesus. "Don't move. We have to do something about your knee."

Javier went into the brush, knife in hand. He reappeared shortly with two saplings, measured them against Jesus' leg, cut them to fit. He tore three strips of cloth from a T-shirt to hold them in place. "Try not to bend this leg," he said. "We must take the stress off your knee. We have a long way to go today. Our freedom and maybe even our lives depend on the distance we can travel."

Jesus managed to hobble along the path. He adjusted his stride to improve his pace incrementally. But when Javier turned off the path and thrashed directly up the slope, things changed. Jesus struggled to keep his knee straight, to keep the heavy load balanced. After a hundred meters Javier called a rest stop. Jesus moaned in pain.

"I know this is difficult," Javier said, breathing hard. "We must do the unexpected. There is a path here. It will be easier, but we have to go fast."

After they drank water, Javier led them along the faint trail deeper into the mountains. Several times Jesus heard the faint whomp-whomp of a helicopter somewhere behind them.

By noon, both were hot and exhausted. Sweat flowed freely down their faces and necks and stained their clothing. Jesus' knee throbbed. Javier called a halt above a narrow arroyo.

They removed their loads. Jesus sat on a boulder with his leg stretched before him. Javier passed him the water jug.

"Just a sip or two. We must preserve it."

"Where are we going?"

"I spoke to Jorge on the radio before we left," Javier said. "There is a cave to the east of us with supplies for emergencies like this. I have the GPS coordinates; we can locate it with my phone. First, we must put as much distance as possible between us and the grow."

"How far is the cave?"

"I don't know yet. However far it is, that is how far we must go." Javier's lips tightened. "There is another difficulty. Jorge has learned that men from a rival cartel search for us. They could be behind us right now."

"What will they do if they catch us?"

"They will kill us."

Jesus was stunned. "Why?"

"They want to drive us out. This cartel wants to take over our trade and become suppliers for this whole area. If they kill us, none of our people will dare work out here."

"What can we do?"

"Travel fast. A soldier from the Sonora Cartel will meet us at the cave. He can protect us." Javier grimaced. "Until then, we must look out for ourselves."

CHAPTER TWENTY-ONE

Jesus followed Javier down among rocks and scrub oaks
into a narrow gulch. Although the gradient was gentle, they
were often forced to leap over ledges or take large steps
over fallen logs. Each took a toll on Jesus' leg. The jury-
rigged cloth straps began to loosen. Jesus stopped several
times to tighten them, valuable time lost. Javier, as always,
was patient.

When they reached the valley floor they rested.
Javier produced cold pork wrapped in tortillas from his
pack. Beneath the sheltering umbrella of a large oak they
were protected from the sun and air surveillance. Jesus'
knee pain eased to an ache and throb. His fear subsided in
the framework of the bright bloom of the meadow around
them. Birds darted from trees, ground squirrels peeked
from their burrows. The sky was intensely blue, it was cool
in the shade.

Jesus thought how it might have been, in another
time, to live in such a valley with his family. In his fantasy
he saw Ana Dominga and Juanita play together in the tall
grass. Isabella fanned herself gently and smiled at the girls
from the porch of a tidy little cabin. He saw himself pause
to watch them fondly, laden with fresh deer meat, the
heavy meat digging into his shoulder, digging, digging...

Jesus woke with a start.

Javier's face was in his, his hand squeezed his shoulder. "Wake up, amigo, you can sleep when we reach the cave." He reached for Jesus' hand to help him stand.

The leg had stiffened. He felt a sudden cutting pain and gasped. Javier checked his splint, tightened it. The knee was swollen like a grapefruit. Javier grimaced with concern. He picked up Jesus' pack, helped him into it. "We must keep moving. We do not know how close our enemy may be."

They traveled east across the valley floor, kept to trees as much as possible. On the level ground, Jesus began to move better. He developed a rhythm, a step and a hop. His makeshift splint served him well.

The valley narrowed, sloped up into another arroyo. The terrain was tougher. The sides of the gully closed in, the way steepened, the sun burned even hotter.

The men sweated through their clothes. Jesus' shirt under his pack was a wet dishcloth against his back.

Javier paused, took out his phone to check their position.

Jesus sat at once, his leg one great throb.

"We're just two miles from the cave," Javier said. "When we reach the top of this arroyo, we will skirt the summit of the next mountain, cross a saddle, and then, *amigo*, the cave will be across a small valley." Javier tucked his phone away, reached down to help Jesus to his feet.

Jesus tried to straighten his leg with his hand. As he did, there was the sound a melon makes when it drops to the pavement. Javier let go of his arm, fell, his full weight on Jesus, crushed him against the rock where he sat. Jesus' leg doubled under him. He gasped at the sudden pain in his knee. He cursed, struggled to rise, tried to push Javier away. "Javier! What's the matter with you—get up, get up, you're hurting me."

Javier didn't reply, didn't move. Jesus felt moist warmth flow down his neck, over his chest, along his ribs. He squirmed, rolled downslope out from under the unresponsive Javier. Once free he turned on his side to straighten his leg, felt the shock of its pain, cried out. He touched the wet warmth on his chest, looked at his hand. It was covered in blood.

Alarmed, confused, Jesus turned to look at Javier. His head was on the ground, facing Jesus. His forehead and top of his skull were gone. A ragged red hole lined with brain matter and pulp was all that remained. Blood pooled on the ground.

Jesus panicked. He wriggled and clawed like a lizard away from Javier's body, into a clump of bushes, crouched there, gasped for breath. It was impossible to see beyond the steep side of the arroyo. He waited, searched with his eyes, tried to slow his breathing. The pounding of his heart was so loud he could hear nothing else.

He couldn't stay here; the killer would come looking for him. Where could he go? Where was the killer?

Javier had said they would climb to the top of this arroyo then go east to find the cave. The cave was his only chance. He had to reach it to live. There was no choice. He had to continue up this arroyo.

Jesus crawled, stayed low, used the cover of rocks and bushes. His right leg dragged behind him, the pain unbearable. His pack was a dead weight. He thought he should discard it, didn't do it; it was his protective shell. If the sniper shot again, maybe the pack would save him.

He crawled on, slithering snake-like up over rock ledges, clawing his fingers into the sandy earth to pull himself along. Any moment he expected to feel the punch of a bullet. The narrow arroyo was like a furnace. His thirst was overpowering, yet he dared not stop to drink water. Jesus measured his life in minutes, passing snail-like, one by one. He had one thought—he must survive for Isabella and the girls.

The climb up the arroyo was endless, but at some point he noticed it had narrowed, the slope had eased. He peered behind him; saw nothing. No dust, no sound. Up above him, the defile ended in a three-foot high wall of red soil. Beyond it, there were trees. *Santa Madre de Dios*, he thought. Let me reach them.

After another glance at the arroyo below, he pushed to his feet. His leg buckled, he almost screamed in agony but held his balance, clumped stiff-legged out of the arroyo into the trees and dropped to the ground. He tried to ignore the pain that coursed up and down his leg. He cocked his head and listened. All was quiet.

Jesus dropped his pack and found his water bottle. The plain liquid never tasted so sweet. His knee pain was almost unendurable, sweat poured from every square centimeter of skin, yet he was alive. Each mouthful of water restored him that much more.

There was no need for a plan, only one thing to do: try to find the cave. The trick was to survive that long. The assassin could be anywhere.

Jesus retied his leg, clawed to his feet, shouldered his pack, and stumped on.

CHAPTER TWENTY-TWO

The thick grove of oaks ended, the ground sloped away and knee high bunch grass began, the only cover occasional clumps of black sage and green-leafed coyote bush.

Jesus paused to listen, searched the landscape. He moved down through the grass, kept bushes between him and the distant ridgelines whenever he could. It took a long time to work down the open slope, with slips and falls. The agony that was his leg reached new levels of pain, but he dared not stop. Only when he came to a small stand of Chamise bushes did he pause to rest in its limited shade, his weight on his good leg. He wanted to sit, dared not. The faint trail led around the side of the hill. Javier had described such a route. It must be the right path. He pushed on.

Chamise and coyote bush were plentiful now. They made the going tough, tugged at his clothes, pricked his face and arms, yet he welcomed it for the cover it provided. His pace slowed still more, with frequent rests to catch his breath, take weight off his knee.

Around the face of the hill he came to broad areas of rockslide, difficult to cross, dangerous for the exposure. He crawled and slithered across these, his bad leg dragged behind him. Occasionally he gained a view; at one he saw a long saddle from his hill to the next, just as Javier had described. Jesus grew hopeful.

There was a loud crack against the rock next to his hand, an insect-like whine of a ricochet; particles of stone stung his hand and face like a mass of bees. He pancaked on the barren rock, his heart a drum against the hard surface. Before thoughts could form, he heard the thunk of a bullet against his pack, was jerked to one side. He thrust himself forward along the ground, his hands grapples. He furrowed into the dirt beyond the plate rock. Another bullet struck behind him. He scraped on until he was among bushes once again.

The sniper still pursued him, he thought in despair. He had followed, patient, waited for his opportunity, looked for him to grow careless. Jesus wondered why it had taken so long. How far behind was he? It didn't matter, he thought. The killer would come.

Jesus tried to stand in the shelter of the bush, wanted to see, but his stiff bound leg prevented it. Beyond panic, beyond caring, he wanted to give up. He couldn't. The image of his little girls was in his mind. He tried again to rise, heaved himself to his good knee, his useless leg stretched behind him like a broken rudder. With both palms on the ground, he brought his good leg under him, pushed upright, grabbed handfuls of prickly brush. His pack tried to pull him over; he teetered, held on, and half hopped, half bounced along the path.

The long saddle was just ahead. It offered no cover, a tin rabbit in a shooting gallery. There was no choice. Stay and he would die. Cross the saddle and he would die. He might as well try to cross.

Jesus hopped on, no hesitation at the exposed ridge, stumped ahead as fast as he could. His body was tensed for the bullet impact. He was a quarter of the way across, a third, almost half way. Was the assassin that far behind? Could he...?

A bullet kicked up dirt in front of him. A second exploded into the same place. Jesus stopped.

A voice came from behind. "Ah, *amigo*, what is your hurry? We have so much time. I have many bullets. Let's have some fun."

Another bullet struck, closer.

"Your friend is dead, *amigo*. He has no more head. He cannot live without a head, I think. Is that not true, *amigo*?"

This time he heard the bullet strike behind him.

The voice taunted him. "*Amigo*, you have hurt your leg. It makes you slow. I will remove it for you."

Jesus felt a punch to the back of his bad leg. It flew into the air of its own accord. He slammed down on his back, bounced to his side. His pack slid up over his head. Pain came from his leg in a fierce wave. Jesus cried out. The heavy pack pinned his head to the ground. From a far away place he heard the smack of a bullet. He waited to die.

A sound intruded into the twilight of his consciousness, cut through the waves of pain—a high-pitched scream. It was a cry of horror, of terror, the cry of a person frightened beyond endurance. It grew and grew. As he drifted into blackness Jesus wondered idly if he was hearing his own voice.

CHAPTER TWENTY-THREE

Zack arrived in the dining room for breakfast at six-thirty. Eagle Feather was already seated at a table, a cup of coffee in front of him. He looked up when Zack arrived. "I see your lazy habits haven't changed, White Man."

Zack grinned and lowered himself into a chair. "Seems to me my lazy habits usually follow a night with you and some alcohol."

Eagle Feather lifted both hands with an innocent expression.

Zack waved at the waitress, pointed to his empty coffee cup.

"What's the plan?" Eagle Feather said.

Zack looked at his watch. "Rick Malden should be here shortly. We'll drive to the upper Sisquoc River. Our guide will find us up there. We'll continue tracking where we left off yesterday."

"Sisquoc?"

"Rick tells me it's a river that rises in those mountains and flows into the Santa Maria River east of here. We can take a forest service road up to it, save ourselves some hiking." Zack watched the waitress pour his coffee.

"Sisquoc." Eagle Feather rolled it around on his tongue.

"Sisquoc means *stopping place* in the Chumash language." The voice came from behind Eagle Feather's chair. It was Malden. "Rancho Sisquoc was a land grant from Governor Pio Pico to Maria Antonia Dominguez Caballero in 1854. Now they grow grapes. You gonna introduce us, Zack?"

"Rick, meet my good friend Eagle Feather. He's been asked to come out here to watch over me."

"Somebody's got to do it," Eagle Feather said, held out his hand.

"Glad to meet you." Rick pulled out the empty chair between them, sat down. "Will you go with us today?"

"He will." Zack answered for him. "He's one of the better trackers you're ever gonna meet. I think we'll get the job done."

"Guess I can go home, then."

"Not so fast," Zack said. "We need a ride."

Malden chuckled. "We'd best get a good breakfast in us. I have a feeling it's going to be a long day today. Have you ordered?"

Zack called the waitress back, the men put in their orders. They chatted amiably during breakfast. It felt to Zack as if they'd always known each other. "What do you think about this mysterious presence people talk about in those mountains? The Chumash guide spoke of it yesterday."

Malden sighed and put down his fork. "Those are powerful images the Chumash people evoke. When you're

145

out in those woods alone they come back strong to your mind. I'd be lying if I didn't say I've felt something out there. But it's probably the growers watching me watch them."

"Nothing to it, then?"

Malden frowned. "It may sound silly, but I've noticed a particular smell on occasion, a strong sweaty-musk sort of smell. I know it's not my imagination, I've watched Toker react to something at the same time." He shrugged. "That's as close as I've gotten to any mysterious presence."

"Always trust your instincts. That's what I've tried to teach White Man here," Eagle Feather said.

"I'm slow, but I'm starting to get it." Zack grinned over his coffee cup.

After breakfast Zack and Eagle Feather went for their backpacks. Those went in the back of the truck, the three men on the big front seat. The truck sped down the straight ribbon of road that crossed the wide river valley.

"When William Brewer crossed this valley with the United States Geological Survey Team in 1860 he didn't like it much. As I recall, he complained that the ride was long and tedious with no water except one stinking sinkhole, as he put it." Malden waved at the vast panorama of green. "He'd be shocked to see it now."

They turned where they had the previous day at the twin-spired Sisquoc Chapel toward the Rancho Sisquoc Winery. At the Sisquoc River crossing they jounced down the bank and across the dry riverbed.

"Where's the river?" Eagle Feather said.

Malden glanced at him. "It's there. It's deep underground. Dig down ten or twelve feet and you'll find water. We'll follow the river a while."

Their road did stay with the river, crossed it several more times along its winding thirsty path. In a mile or so the road climbed away under sandy bluffs, narrowed, hugged the mountainside before it dropped back down to the riverbed. When the river forked, they followed the east branch, into the midst of the high mountains. The scenery was remarkable. The Arizona men were accustomed to spectacular vistas, yet were entranced.

At a point where the width of the riverbed dwindled to no more than a small stream, Malden brought the truck to a stop. "Let's stretch our legs," he said, and climbed out.

Zack took a few steps toward the river. "Hey, look at that. There's water in the creek."

"It's protected from the sun in these deep canyons, and we're nearer the source. But eighty percent of it's still underground." Malden pointed out a canyon just north of them. "Up that way is Rattlesnake Canyon, where Zack and I were yesterday. We're in La Brea Canyon now." He looked at Zack, pointed at a high ridge further left. "You were up there yesterday. You probably looked down at where we are now."

"Are we going to climb up there?"

"No need," Malden said. He pulled his pack out of the truck bed. "The man you tracked yesterday could only

147

have come down here. The trail is in that arroyo there. It crosses this little park." He looked at Zack. "Where was that Chumash guide gonna meet you?"

"Didn't say."

"Well, let's have some water and nose around to see what we can learn."

Zack didn't move for a while, enjoying the surrounding hills. He listened to the birdcalls, felt the waking warmth of the sun. Morning light crept into the canyon bit by bit, illuminated places hidden in shadow moments before. Raucous gold poppies and purple lupine staked their claims in patches on high slopes; fireweed grew in lower meadows. A blue scrub jay cocked his eye at Zack, came to land a few feet away for a closer look.

Eagle Feather put away his water bottle. He walked over to the arroyo, inspected the ground.

Zack joined him. "What do you see?"

Eagle Feather shrugged. "Not much. Nothing recent."

"He doesn't leave much."

"If he came this way at all." Eagle Feather sounded doubtful.

"You heard the man," Zack said. "He had to come this way."

Rick joined them, his pack already slung on his back. "He didn't necessarily come down the trail. He might've stayed high along the edge of the arroyo, bein' cautious."

"True enough." Eagle Feather glanced up at the arroyo bank. "He had to cross this creek bed somewhere, though. I couldn't of done it without leaving a trace."

"Let's follow the trail south. If he went this way, he'd have to cut back onto it somewhere," Zack said. He walked back to the truck for his pack.

Eagle Feather and Malden both nodded, followed him.

"The path is that way." Malden pointed toward a lone eucalyptus tree up the slope.

By unspoken agreement Eagle Feather took the lead, Zack followed and Malden brought up the rear.

"What about your guide?" Malden called up from behind Zack.

Zack turned his head. "Even if the guy we're following doesn't leave traces, we're gonna leave plenty ourselves. I'm pretty sure it won't be a problem for Tommy."

The trail angled south up the side of the ridge. Once they gained the ridge top, the track stayed high. The view west toward the Solomon Hills was impressive.

With no sign to follow, they moved at a quick pace. Eagle Feather studied the sides of the path for any indication their man returned to it. At the end of the ridge, the route divided.

Eagle Feather looked at Malden.

Malden pulled out a topo map, opened it. He held it out for Zack and Eagle Feather to see. "There are two obvious ridge lines here. This one takes you southeast, deep into the range. This one angles more southwest, stays close to the valley."

"What's your guess?" Zack said.

Malden folded the map. "Where did the Chumash guide think he'd go?"

"She mentioned Zaca Mountain."

"In that case, he'll most likely take the southwest ridge."

"Zaca Mountain?" Eagle Feather said.

"Zaca Lake and Zaca Mountain are special places to the Chumash," Zack said. "They guard the front range of the mountains."

"Why would this killer want to go to a Chumash sacred place?"

Zack shrugged. "I got no idea. Tommy seems to think this protective presence, as she called it, may have some sort of connection to the ancients."

"We'd better head out." Malden stuffed the map back in his pack.

They moved on. An hour later the sun blasted the ridge. The shade of trees they passed under came as a relief. They still had found no evidence to support their belief the killer had gone this way at all.

At a saddle between two ridges Malden called a stop. "How about a sandwich?"

Just off the trail where several trees offered shade, a flat rock made a table. It felt almost cold after the sun.

Zack removed his hat and wiped away sweat.

Malden opened his pack, pulled out sandwiches one by one. "I got turkey, ham, and, uh, let's see...turkey." His phone rang.

"Some wilderness," Eagle Feather said.

Malden looked at the phone. "I need to take this." He walked a few steps away.

Zack munched his sandwich. He could hear enough to know that Malden was doing the listening.

Malden put away the phone and came back. "I don't believe it. They found another grow, they need boots on the ground. I got to go back."

Zack looked at Malden, then at Eagle Feather. "Well, I guess we should carry on, at least a little while."

Malden considered. "Sure, why not. You don't need my authority. But I got to tell you, it seems we're following a will o' the whisp. Don't waste a lot more time."

"How will we get out?" Zack said.

"I'm not taking the truck. The only way to this new grow is hoofing it. I'll meet you at the truck tonight or early tomorrow."

The men shook hands and parted ways.

Zack and Eagle Feather finished their sandwiches in a leisurely fashion, enjoyed the shade and the view off to the east across the range of mountains.

Eagle Feather fixed an eye on Zack. "Partner, I know you got skills, and you say you had a trail, but there's nothin' here. I've not seen even a bent piece of grass."

151

Zack wiped crumbs from his lips. "I wonder if he took a different path after Tommy and I left his trail yesterday. I—"

"Well, hello there." Eagle Feather fixed his eyes on a point beyond Zack. "How long have you been there?"

Zack whipped his head around. There was Tommy. "Hey, Tommy. I thought you'd be along sooner or later."

"Tommy? But you're a girl," Eagle Feather said, despite himself.

Amused brown eyes regarded him.

Zack stood. "Eagle Feather, meet our Chumash guide, Tomasa..."

"Just Tommy." She nodded to Eagle Feather, looked at Zack. "Don't doubt yourself, Mr. Arizona Tracker. He came this way. I followed him to Zaca Lake."

Zack's eyes widened. "How early did you start out this morning?"

Her smile was gentle, as with a confused child. "I began after you left yesterday."

"But...how did you track in the dark? When did you sleep? What...?"

Eagle Feather considered her for a moment. "You followed his scent."

She observed him in return. "Yes."

"What scent," Zack demanded.

"The killer has his own particular scent," Eagle Feather said. "I caught it once or twice, but without other evidence, I dismissed it," He glanced at Tommy, returned to Zack. "Darkness can help rather than hinder you when you follow a scent trail. It forces your brain to prioritize that one sense."

"But you didn't sleep? Or eat?"

She raised her eyebrows. "I took care of myself. Thank your for your concern." She regarded Zack's friend. "Why Eagle Feather?"

"I was given that name by a group of hunters I guided a long time ago. It stuck."

"What is your tribe?" she said.

Eagle Feather gave a mischievous grin. "Jewish, mostly...and some Navajo."

"Eagle Feather is my partner back at the Reservation," Zack said. "His father was Jewish and his mom Navajo. That's why he's...different."

"You think we should give it up; he's gone already," Eagle Feather said, ready to change the subject.

Tommy nodded.

"He disappeared at this Zaca Lake?" Zack said.

She nodded again. "He must have been there some time yesterday. He probably used the lake to hide his scent, he could be anywhere now."

"We might as well turn back, in that case," Zack said. He felt a bit let down.

They gathered up their things, slung on the packs, and turned back along the ridge trail. Tommy led off at a good pace, the men followed several yards behind.

"She always that antisocial?" Eagle Feather said in a grumbled whisper.

"I think she's shy, she doesn't know you yet." Zack gave a fatuous grin. "If she did, she'd be even farther ahead."

"Keep it up, White Man, keep it up."

Zack looked up. Ahead, Tommy was stopped, listening. They heard it now, a rifle shot. Two more sounded in rapid succession.

"Those were up ahead, toward the truck."

Eagle Feather nodded. His face showed concern.

"Malden." Zack began to jog. Eagle Feather ran with him. Tommy let them pass. The ridge evaporated under their rapid steps. They came to where it fell away into the river valley.

Eagle Feather grabbed Zack's arm. "You packin'?"

"Just a handgun."

"That was rifle fire. Don't let's rush into anything."

CHAPTER TWENTY-FOUR

Zack and Eagle Feather scuffled and slid down the steep trail. Five minutes later they entered the shady tree-filled arroyo that opened to the riverbed where they'd left Malden's truck. Zack heard no further shots, knew he might have missed one in the noise of their travel. One came now—loud, staccato, echoed off the canyon walls. The men stopped, listened. It was not repeated, they moved ahead.

Eagle Feather touched Zack's arm. "Wait. Where's Tommy?"

Zack looked behind. She was gone. "I don't blame her. I'm sure a gun fight was not part of her agreement."

They pressed on. Moments later the arroyo opened to the narrow river valley. The truck sat on the far side of the riverbed, about a hundred yards away on open sandy ground. Nearer them, by fifty yards, was a driftwood log, no more than two feet high. Malden was scrunched behind it. Another shot sounded, a chip of wood flew off the top of the log. They heard the thunk when the bullet hit the wood.

The men crouched behind cover.

"He's pinned down," Eagle Feather said.

"That one came too close. Someone has him zeroed in." Zack cupped his hands and yelled. "Malden. You okay?"

Malden turned, looked. Another shot smacked into the log. Malden curled smaller, adjusted his body to face them. He pointed to his right leg.

"He's hit," Eagle Feather said. "He can't make a run for it. Looks like it's up to us."

Zack studied the grassy slope on the far side of the canyon. A ribbon of trail led up into some trees. The rifle fire seemed to come from up there. He took off his pack, took out his bottle and had a long pull of water. Then he was up, running low out into the open, yelling at Malden as he ran. "Stay there, Malden. Don't move."

Eagle Feather yelled after him. "Are you crazy...?"

A puff of dirt flew up near Zack's foot. Staying low as he ran, Zack changed direction. He heard the whir of a bullet pass close, another rifle report. He turned and ran back toward Eagle Feather. Dust spit up near his feet. When he was close enough he launched himself behind the cover of some brush, scrambled behind a tree. Bullets came like hard rain into the brush he had just left.

"What the fuck are you doing?" Eagle Feather's customary calm had dissolved.

Zack glanced at him from behind the tree, grinned. "I had to take pressure off Malden. Now the shooter knows he has to deal with more than one person." Zack breathed hard, looked across at the far trees. "Can you tell if there's more than one up there?"

"So far just one rifle." Eagle Feather peered from behind his cover. "My guess is just the one shooter. If there'd been more, they all would have unloaded on you."

Zack, still breathing hard, nodded.

"If there had been more than one, they'd have got you." Eagle Feather muttered under his breath. "Crazy White Man."

It was quiet now, a bit unnerving for Zack after his mad scramble. His heart thumped. While he caught his breath he considered the situation. The shooter was deliberate and accurate. He'd hit the log twice, and he'd hit Malden. He missed Zack only because Zack changed direction at the right moment; he was sure a bullet would have hit him had he not. He dug in his pack for his handgun, attached the holster to his belt. He found his phone and called Barnard, the only local number he had in memory.

Barnard was shocked. "You're what? Where? Malden is hit? Christ! What did you guys stir up out there? Yes, of course, right away. Jesus!" He rang off to organize a rescue.

There had been no more shots since Zack's run. He called out. "Rick! Can you hear me?"

He saw Malden stir. A hand waved.

"Listen, Rick. Don't move. Help is on the way." Rick nodded. Zack spoke to Eagle Feather. "I'm gonna work around behind him."

Eagle Feather shook his head. "It'll take you all day. You'll have to go way up the valley to get across the river, and you'll have to stay behind cover the whole way. If he's in those trees, he's got a great view up and down this river."

"He might be gone by now," Zack pointed out. "He knows there's at least one more of us."

"Are you gonna do another crazy run to find out?"

Zack grinned and studied the slopes across the river. He needed a better fix on the shooter. He had a general idea of the direction of the bullets. There were limited options for concealment at the range the rifleman needed for accuracy, maybe a thousand yards or so. He doubted the sniper had a scope and stand; that would be a lot to haul around these mountains. Say a maximum of 1200 yards. That logic placed the rifleman in those trees where the trail disappeared, as he had first thought.

Zack leaned around his tree. "You're right, man. There's not enough cover to do a run around. Let's show him there's two of us, make him believe we're gonna work around behind him. That might force him to withdraw."

"How we gonna do that?"

Zack picked up a baseball size rock, studied the slope on his side of the arroyo. There were stands of Mazanitis. It was the way Zack would go if he tried to work behind the shooter. He picked a spot, stood up behind his tree for more power, threw the rock at the slope. He watched the trees across the river. There was a glint of light. Dust spurted right where Zack's rock had landed. The rifle report came moments later.

ZACA

Eagle Feather's rock landed in some brush on the slope on his side of the arroyo, making it sway slightly. There was no shot.

Zack smiled to himself. The sniper would now be thinking some serious thoughts. He'd know now there were at least two of them, think they were circling behind him from two different directions. His eye traveled back to Malden behind the log. Rick's head was angled back toward them. He seemed all right so far. He'd be getting thirsty, though. Zack hoped the leg wound wasn't too bad.

There was no further sign of the rifleman. Their wait lasted another 45 minutes until they heard the sound of an approaching helicopter. It came right up the river, hovered over Malden, and landed on the riverbed between Rick and the rifleman's position. Zack used the dust and flying sand as a screen to run to Malden.

Rick tried to stand.

Zack got there and supported him. "Where are you hit?"

Malden pointed to his right thigh. A large dark stain soaked his pants. "It's the muscle of my thigh. Hurts like hell, but I can move the leg."

Another forest ranger sprinted up. "Rick, are you okay?" he said.

"I'll live to protect the forest another day." Malden gestured to Zack. "Jeremy, meet Zack. Over there is Eagle Feather. This here is Jeremy Tusco, my other half." Rick's face twisted with pain. "I didn't expect you guys would meet under these conditions."

159

Jeremy was a large beefy man with deer-brown eyes and a black beard. "Hey," he said, and grabbed hold of Malden. "Rick, there's a first aid kit in the bird. We can help you with the pain when we get you there." He wrapped a big arm around him and half carried him toward the helicopter.

Zack and Eagle Feather watched.

"You coming?" Malden yelled back over his shoulder.

"Nope." Zack had to yell over the noise of the blades. "This guy pissed me off."

They watched Jeremy help Malden up into the helicopter. A moment later, Tusco came back to Zack, a rifle in his hand. "I'll send some help along," he said. "Don't do anything crazy until they get here. Meanwhile, you might need this." He handed him the rifle and a box of shells. "I'm sure you know what to do with it."

"We'll figure it out."

Jeremy ran back and the copter rose in a cloud of sand grit, angled back down the river.

"If you'd be so kind as to go get the packs, I'll make sure nobody disturbs your walk." Zack lay down behind the log, sighted the rifle, and sent a bullet into the thicket where he'd seen the metallic glint. Nothing happened. There was no further indication of anyone in the trees.

Eagle Feather returned with the packs. Zack took his and shouldered it, handed the rifle to Eagle Feather. They walked over to the trail that wound up the slope, climbed toward the trees. Eagle Feather kept the rifle trained there, although both knew the rifleman was long gone. He'd have given up the minute he heard the chopper.

Zack came into the shade of the trees first. He set his pack down and studied the ground. Eagle Feather joined him. Shell casings lay scattered near a dead log, the man hadn't bothered to pick them up. Without bending over, Zack saw they were .308 Winchester cartridges; great range, good power, inexpensive.

"You're not likely to find prints on those," Eagle Feather said.

Zack knew he was right. "We'll leave 'em for the lab boys."

Eagle Feather studied the rifleman's hide choice. "This guy was a professional." He pointed out where the grass was matted the length of a man's body. The rifleman had stretched out, firing leisurely from a prone position.

Zack sighted over the dead log to the riverbed. "Like shooting ducks in a barrel. He didn't need a scope. With an accurate rifle and a good stock, he could pick Malden off before he knew he was there."

"Why didn't he?" Eagle Feather eyed Zack. "We figured he's a professional. Why just the leg?'"

Zack thought about it. "I think he knew we were here. I don't think he came to kill anyone, just scare us off."

The men studied the ground for additional evidence. Finding none, they shouldered their packs. Law enforcement would come up here to investigate. It was important they find it just as it was.

Eagle Feather looked for tracks. He found them, coming and going. Zack looked; Vibram soled shoes about size eight and a half or nine, headed back up the trail with long strides. They followed.

CHAPTER TWENTY-FIVE

The sniper was easy to follow. He didn't try to hide his tracks. Zack figured he didn't expect them to follow him, he'd think they boarded the helicopter with Malden. Still, the men were careful, watchful.

After a steep ascent from the river, the trail leveled off, ran beside a narrow gulch and entered a grove of Mazanitis bushes. Here thick red branches protruded into the trail, limiting their view; a perfect place for an ambush.

Zack led, gun in hand. The ground was soft underfoot; they made no sound. The trail eased to the right, moved out of the thick brush. They faced a small meadow covered in knee-high bunch grass rippling in the breezes, touched by the sun's golden glow. A solitary oak tree commanded the space. Zack's eye caught movement beneath the tree, in the grass. When he moved forward an ominous hiss stopped him, a loud flap of wings startled him. A vulture rose from the grass, struggled for lift, flew off. A moment later two more of the large birds erupted from the grass, careened off into the sky. Zack had a bad feeling.

The two men approached the tree, ready for anything. They found the grass well trampled beneath, coated in a reflective substance; blood, Zack realized. Recently spilled, thick, it coated the grass and filled the crevices of the hard-packed earth. A strong musty smell permeated the air around them.

His handgun ready, Zack moved to the edge of the clearing, walked a wide circumference around the meadow. Eagle Feather went to the tree and studied the ground.

Zack came back to him. "He's gone now, I think." His voice came loud in the stillness.

"Not long gone, though. The blood still drips." Eagle Feather pointed to a rifle abandoned in the grass.

Zack walked over to it, knelt and inspected it without touching it. "This wasn't just some amateur trophy hunter. This is a long-range outfit, a Savage HB 110FV Rifle, looks like a Lothar Walther barrel, plastic stock, maybe a Bell and Carlson, the barrels equipped with a Miculek AR-15 muzzle brake. This outfit is a perfect fit for those .308 Winchester cartridges we found back there." Zack stood and looked at Eagle Feather. "This man was professionally equipped to hunt at long range, but not elk or bear, I'm thinking."

"Question is, where's the body?"

Zack looked at the blood spill. "This looks just like the other one, not forced in any direction as from an impact or directional wound." Zack looked up at the limb just above them, then down at the blood. "Some droplets shot further, the rest just sort of flowed."

"There's a piece of cloth tied around that branch." Eagle Feather reached up with the barrel of the rifle, pushed at it. "It's hard to see, kind of blends into the bark."

"So what is it, some sort of token?" Zack looked closer at it.

"You ever hunt deer?"

Zack looked at Eagle Feather, puzzled by the question.

"That cloth's been cut just under the limb. Something was hung from there."

Realization began to dawn. Zack felt a little sick in the pit of his stomach. "He hung the guy up there..."

Eagle Feather nodded, his face grim. "Yep. He hung him up there by some part of his clothing, maybe his shirt sleeve, and gutted him out, just like you'd dress a deer in the woods."

"Jesus!" Zack stared at the limb, picturing the man hanging beneath. He looked at the ground. "Then where are the guts?"

Eagle Feather crouched. He poked his forefinger into the blood. When he raised it, something chunky rested there. "Those vultures do a real good job of cleaning up. Here's a bit of tissue, might be from something stretchy, like intestinal wall."

The sick spot in Zack's stomach grew. "The vultures ate it all."

"It wouldn't take 'em long. Be like Vienna sausage to those boys."

"Jesus, Eagle Feather." Zack threw him a look, askance. "But where's the body? Those birds couldn't have eaten the whole thing."

Eagle Feather shook his head, looked around. "That's a fact." He stood. "What now?"

Zack considered the question. There were no more answers here. "We keep going." He pulled out his phone. "I'll tell Barnard what we found, give him the coordinates." He glanced at Eagle Feather. "Maybe we can't follow this...whatever, but we can backtrack the assassin, learn where he came from."

Eagle Feather hitched the rifle up on his shoulder. "Let's go."

CHAPTER TWENTY-SIX

Eagle Feather led off. He inspected the trail surface,
grunted in satisfaction. He'd found prints. The killer
moved rapidly coming toward the river. He jogged along,
like he was worried about getting somewhere on time.

"Any sign of whoever killed him?"

"No, nothing."

They traveled in silence, intent on the ground. The
trail steepened as it wound up the side of the mountain.
Another half-mile took them out of the chaparral into
open terrain with a view of neighboring mountains, and
glimpses down into valleys. They slid and scrambled over
shale and tread across large expanses of smooth ledge. The
trail was visible far ahead; it wound along the slope like a
thin line drawn in pencil.

"We're vulnerable to snipers up here," Eagle
Feather said during a brief rest stop.

"Yeah, I thought of that. I don't see many
options."

"Just sayin'."

The men crossed the open slopes without incident.
The path dropped into a forest of pinyon pine where the
smell of pine needles and cool air in the dells refreshed
them. The trail continued to lose elevation until it reached

the bottom of an arroyo. Here the damp dirt path captured every impression. Their progress was swift.

The arroyo intersected with another one. They stopped. A small stream entered the narrow canyon from the right, pooled up into a small pond. Mud at its edge recorded deer prints and raccoon. Eagle Feather scouted around the pool while Zack explored the dry arroyo entering to the left.

Zack heard Eagle Feather call, returned to the pool. His friend pointed to the far edge of the water. "Look behind that big rock. See that bit of black? It's small diameter tubing, someone is irrigating from this pool."

They walked upstream until the irrigation tube resurfaced. It led them up the arroyo. The ravine was rock-choked with no obvious path. They hopped from rock to rock. The way steepened, here the boulders seemed pre-arranged almost like steps. Beyond the steep section the ravine leveled, vegetation grew thick. Here they found another path, moist, impressionable.

Eagle Feather went to one knee. "The sniper was up here. Those are his tracks. Here's another print, a guy with big heavy feet." He glanced up at Zack. "This might be the operation they called Malden to handle."

Zack took out his handgun, checked the load. Eagle Feather unlashed the rifle, held it in one hand. They came to a grove of oak where the arroyo widened to form a small valley. The men squatted, surveyed the scene.

"We must be close," Zack said. "We could stumble into it any moment."

"Or get shot. You want to lead for a while?"

Zack grinned. "You hear your ancestors calling?"

Eagle Feather's lips twitched. He let Zack pass.

Gun in hand, Zack stayed low, crept up the path. A few yards ahead the underbrush gave way to grass. He saw the camp. The black tubing terminated at an electric pump connected to a car battery. Beyond it were two wickiups, roofs covered with tarps, a fire pit between them with a frame of saplings overhead to diffuse the smoke. Supply crates were stacked near the huts. Empty pesticide containers lay in a heap. Several propane tanks were stacked in a pile next to a tree. Plastic water bottles and empty Corona bottles were scattered everywhere.

Zack and Eagle Feather stole toward the shelters. There was no sound. Zack went to the first one, Eagle Feather to the other. Zack peered in. No one was home.

Eagle Feather looked in the second one, shook his head. No one was home there, either.

They walked on up the slope. Ten yards further on they came to the marijuana crop. The entire operation was deserted.

Back at the camp, Zack sat on a log and watched Eagle Feather study the signs. "It's amazing that they found this from the air."

"Maybe they didn't, maybe this is a different one." Eagle Feather came back and sat next to Zack. "I've found sign for a total of four men. Two, including the one we've been following, were here briefly. They were the last to arrive and the last to leave. Since their tracks overlay the prints of the other two, they must have been following them. Everyone left by that trail over there, the second pair still following the first."

"They were in a hurry." Zack pointed to the supply crates. "They left all their essentials behind."

Eagle Feather nodded. "We can assume the first two were the growers, the second two came to kill them."

Zack stood, walked to the trail, scouted the ground. "The growers must have been warned about the assassins somehow."

"The killers arrive, see they're gone, go after them."

Zack's brow furrowed. "Just one thing. Why did the sniper come after us? How did they know where to find us?"

"Here's another question," Eagle Feather said. "Where's that second assassin right now? Did he follow the growers, or is he out there waiting to ambush us?"

"They might have radios, somebody directing them."

"Maybe." Eagle Feather stood. "So what now, boss?"

"The way I see it, there's one way to go from here. We know what happened to the first sniper. Now its time to find the other one."

Eagle Feather grimaced and picked up his pack. "How'd I know you'd say that?"

CHAPTER TWENTY-SEVEN

Jesus opened his eyes to bright light and the hazy outline of man above him. The image cleared, he saw the face of a stranger, the shooter, the killer of Javier. He thought he would die now.

The man reached an arm under his shoulder, lifted him to a sitting position. He held a bottle of water to his lips, had him drink.

Jesus almost choked in his fear.

The man spoke Spanish. "Don't worry, you are safe. I work for the Sonora Cartel. I am a friend of Jorge. I have been sent to protect you."

Relief swept over Jesus. He trembled, his eyes watered from emotion.

"Your pant leg is covered with blood. Have you been shot?" The stranger eased him back down.

Pain swelled from the movement of his leg and Jesus cried out.

The stranger had a large knife in his hands. "I am going to cut away your pant leg. I need to see how serious your wound is."

Jesus felt a strong tug on his pants, almost screamed at the pain. Then the tugging stopped. He heard an intake of breath.

"The bullet passed along the outside of your upper calf," the man said. "It left a large cut but the bleeding has nearly stopped. It is not serious. It is your knee that is bad. What happened? It is swollen and purple. You can't walk like this."

"I hit it several days ago. It has not had a chance to heal." Jesus was still groggy and confused.

"You were lucky with the bullet." The man continued to examine the leg. His eyebrows were black and thick, Jesus noticed, like bristles in a hairbrush.

"The bullet hit your stick splint, broke it. That changed its path just enough to save your leg."

Jesus was relieved. He remembered how the bullet knocked him right off his feet. He was sure his leg must be broken.

The stranger stood. He was a large man, barrel chested, big hands. "There is no time for your knee to heal now, either. We must find a way to bind the joint for you to travel. We need to get you to a safe place."

The man rifled through a pack—his own pack, Jesus realized—found a shirt, tore it into strips. Then he took the broken splint and cut it shorter with his knife. After gently rolling Jesus on his side, he placed the piece of wood behind the injured knee, tied it above and below the swollen area with the cloth strips. He reached under Jesus' shoulders and lifted him on his feet as easily as a feather pillow.

Waves of pain came from the knee. The pant leg was blood soaked, the torn material flapped, but he could walk. The new splint was less awkward yet effective.

Jesus looked back toward the hillside. "Where is the man who shot me?"

The stranger shrugged. "There was no one here but you." He picked up Jesus' pack. "He could come back at any time. We must move." He turned and walked across the ridgeline.

Jesus stumbled after him. His memory of the bullet impact was vivid. He felt fearful, exposed. His heart rate slowed only after they entered the cover of the brush on the far side.

They paused for water.

"What shall I call you?" Jesus said.

"I am Pablo."

"My name is..."

"Your name is Jesus Hermenegildo Romano," Pablo said. "I know all about you. It is my job." He passed his water bottle to Jesus. "Where is Rafael?"

A tear came to Jesus' eye. "He is dead. The sniper killed him."

Pablo made no comment.

"Where will we go now?"

"Not far. There is a cave close by. We will go there until the danger has passed. After that, we'll get you out of these mountains."

"But my job...?"

"Your job is done. You are in no shape to continue as a *sembrador*. When you recover, others will decide what you can do." Pablo stood. "Enough chatter. None of that will matter if we are killed. We must keep moving."

Jesus followed Pablo along the flank of the mountain on a gradual descent into a narrow valley. The canyon wall was steep; there were many switchbacks. They came to a small stream of water on the valley floor.

"That is our water source. The cave is over there." Pablo gestured across the valley. "But first, we must hide our tracks." They turned off the path upslope of the stream and walked along a patch of exposed rock parallel to it. Several yards on, they descended.

Across the creek there was a meadow, alive with wildflowers. Great oaks surrounded it, their arms stretched far beyond their thick trunks, as if awakened from a long nap. At the far side of the valley a Mazanitis grove, red branches intertwined like a loose-knit sweater, blanketed the steepening terrain. Pablo led across the meadow to the grove. Beyond the thick shrubs the steep valley wall was layered with loose rock.

Jesus stared at it in despair. "I can't go up there."

"You don't have to." Pablo slipped in among the Mazanitis bushes and disappeared. Jesus followed. He came to a tunnel through the twined branches. On the far side was the entrance to a large cave. He stared in wonder.

"We will be safe in here," Pablo said.

Jesus went in. A dank, musty smell greeted him. It wasn't completely dark, there was light enough to see, aided by cracks where daylight found a way in. The roof was comfortably high, the room large and spacious.

"This is where I sleep, over here." Pablo gestured toward some personal articles next to a sleeping bag. A rifle with a scope lay on the bag. A small gasoline stove, a pot, packages of Raman noodles sat nearby. "You can sleep over here." Pablo put Jesus' pack down next to a second sleeping bag near the far wall.

Jesus went to it, sat, his leg stretched out before him. The relief was immediate. He glanced around the cave, started when he saw a bleached skull with a long narrow jawbone.

Pablo grinned at his expression. "A deer. The previous occupant had a large appetite." He passed a water bottle to Jesus. "Drink, eat something, sleep. We could be here a long time."

Jesus took a long sip, handed back the bottle. Without another word, he lay down, turned his face to the wall, and went to sleep.

CHAPTER TWENTY-EIGHT

Zack took the lead to give Eagle Feather a mental rest. The trail was easy to follow; the men they pursued took no care to cover their tracks. Back on the original path, the prints led east; two sets of sandals and a sneaker overlaid.

Zack spoke over his shoulder. "The second assassin has followed the growers."

"Another sniper, likely. He'll be patient, wait to get his shot. The two growers might not know they're being followed."

Zack read something else in the dirt. "One man is injured. He's favoring his right leg." The dirt surface was smooth, the story clear; the injured man was struggling. At one point Zack found thread among a jumble of prints. He showed Eagle Feather.

"That's from ripping material. They might have torn some cloth strips to bind the leg somehow."

Zack moved on. The injured man's strides were longer now. It seemed the new support helped. Next moment, the path surface before him was empty, the footprints gone.

Zack doubled back, scanned the sides of the trail, found what he expected. "They left the trail, turned up the hill here."

Eagle Feather peered at the signs, nodded. "They expect followers." He grunted. "They didn't fool the assassin, though."

Zack tracked the men up the hillside. After a steep climb they came to a place where the grass was crushed, where the two growers had rested. "It must have been agony for the man with the bad leg."

Eagle Feather pointed to a sneaker print. "The assassin is still with them."

Zack's eye searched ahead. "They began a traverse over here, on a deer trail." He followed. The sun sent shafts of light through the scrub oaks to dance on the scuffed dirt and set the grasses glowing. The day was fading. When the sun sank behind the mountain ridge behind them, pursuit for the day would end. Zack picked up the pace.

An hour later their quarry led them on a steep descent down a hillside. They stepped out of the brush into a wide meadow, the bottom of a bowl shaped by the surrounding mountains. Their trail led to a huge oak tree, the centerpiece of the grassy tableland. Thick limbs reached out, almost touched the ground, rose again with a burst of branches. The growers had rested here. The shade at mid-day would have been welcome.

Eagle Feather studied the sun. "We ought to camp here. It'll be too dark to continue in an hour."

"Let's leave our gear and go on for a while. We can return when it gets too dark."

"Typical White Man; has to have it both ways."
Eagle Feather grinned, shrugged; dropped his pack.

They kept only their weapons and a water bottle,
followed their quarry on across the meadow. The tracks of
the two growers were obvious. Where the meadow ended,
their tracks led on a gradual ascent up an arroyo. The
assassin's sneaker prints went another way.

Zack looked up at the mountain slopes. "The only
way out of here is up. Why did the killer go another way?"

Eagle Feather studied the slopes. "I see two
obvious ridges. The killer knew he was close, knew they
had to climb, that they'd be slow. He decided to go up the
other ridge. He figures he can pick them off from over
there without exposing himself."

Zack stared at the two ridges. He could almost see
the scenario play out. "So what now? Follow the victims,
or follow the killer?"

Eagle Feather's face was grim. "Ten to one we'll
find a couple of bodies up there. Best go see if anyone is
still alive."

Zack nodded. "Your turn. Lead on." The better
tracker, Eagle Feather would be faster. Time was critical
now with the sun nearing the western ridges.

The slope steepened, narrowed into a tight ravine,
a bone-dry slash up the mountain. Rocky outcrops and
occasional stands of coyote bush impeded their progress.
It was clear the injured man had struggled. Long grooves
in the sandy dirt showed where he had dragged his injured
leg up and over ledges. He must have been in serious pain.

ZACA

The sun cast long shadows. Details of tracks became difficult to read. They'd have to stop, or risk missing an important sign. They had come a third of the way up the arroyo, turned back with reluctance.

Under the great oak they emptied their packs and made camp. It was dusk, a fine soft evening. Zack collected wood, Eagle Feather built a small fire. They made a meal of beef jerky and Clif bars while they waited for the water to heat.

Zack glanced up at the disappearing ridges. "I can't imagine how those men feel tonight, cold, miserable, and hunted."

"They might not be feeling anything."

"Always the cheery one. On the bright side, I never heard any shots."

"I don't think we would, necessarily." Eagle Feather checked the water pot, put it back to heat some more. He peeked at Zack. "I'd be willing to call that a good sign, though."

Some stars pinpricked the dark blanket of sky. More and more appeared until it seemed they would join into a single glow. The men made tea, sat back, watched the display until the rising moon stole the stars and washed the world in its own beams. The near full orb, huge over the mountain ridge, climbed high and bathed the mountains in soft light. In the meadow, brush, fallen limbs, trees and stumps took on different meaning as strange new shapes.

Zack placed his handgun next to his blanket. He lay back, tilted his worn Stetson over his eyes, prepared for sleep.

"Don't shoot yourself in the foot with that thing." Eagle Feather's voice came far away and drowsy from beneath his blanket. But for the hoot of an owl, all was still.

Zack drifted off to sleep.

* * * * *

A hand over his mouth, warm breath on his face, Eagle Feather's barely audible whisper in his ear.

"Don't move and don't make a sound."

Zack could see without moving, the jacket he used for a pillow elevated his head. The meadow was bathed in bright moonlight, the bushes and stumps grotesque creatures. The more Zack stared the less he saw. Each shadow moved as his eye left it, stopped when it returned.

There was a sound behind their tree, Eagle Feather pivoted that way. Zack sat up, his hand found his gun. Movement across the meadow caught his eye, a bush that wasn't a bush. Zack brought the handgun from under his blanket. Something separated itself from the bush, grew large, a shape, the figure of a tall man. It's long black shadow described a giant with two feathers, arms crossed. Zack looked for Eagle Feather; he was gone. He looked back at the figure, an indistinct form, blacker than the surrounding blackness. The shadow moved, raised an arm toward him.

Zack raised his gun, aimed.

His arm was pushed away. "Don't shoot, Zack."

It was Tomasa's voice. Zack turned his head, surprised. When he looked back, the shadow was gone.

Eagle Feather had returned with his headlamp. He cast its beam around the meadow. It illuminated the shadows, changed them back to the familiar snags and dead limbs. No giant.

"What the hell..." Zack lowered his gun, stared at Tomasa.

"I didn't want you to shoot him," she said.

"He pointed something at me."

"He protects these woods. If you fired, he would consider you his enemy."

Eagle Feather's headlamp shown on her face. "How do you know its rules?"

"He would not have harmed us," she insisted.

"It didn't feel that way to me." Zack said.

Tomasa shook her head. "He presented himself as a warning. He's letting you know he will protect this land."

Zack stared at her. "How—"

Eagle Feather grabbed his arm.

They listened.

Zack heard it now, a cracking of the underbrush beyond the meadow. They heard a snap of branches, the sound of running, a loud thrashing—silence. A scream pierced the night with a suddenness that set Zack's hair on end, a woman's scream, piercing and shrill. It was cut off. The sound reverberated off the mountains for long moments.

"Jesus Christ." Zack's eyes searched the dark.

"That may have been a deer," Eagle Feather said.

"Deer don't scream."

"Yes, they do. Rarely, but they do. Something caught it, killed it."

"Something like what?"

"A mountain lion, probably." Eagle Feather stirred the fire, threw on more wood.

"I'd believe you about the mountain lion if I hadn't just seen what I saw," Zack said.

There was no more sleep that night. Dawn was close. Zack helped Eagle Feather build up the fire so that every nearby haunted shadow revealed its true self. Zack set water on to boil for coffee.

Eagle Feather stared at Tommy. "How is it you happen to get here just in the nick of time?"

"Just good luck." Her soft smile was disarming. The fire's stuttering light danced shadows on her face. "I found your trail on the river bank. I followed you. When it grew too dark to see, I came directly here. I know this place; I thought you might camp here."

"You came on in the dark?"

"I know these mountains quite well."

Zack watched her. She had fine, gentle features; an attractive female, yet dressed as a man. "What about that giant Indian shadow creature? How well do you know him?"

She smiled, as with one too simple to understand. "He protects this land and my people."

"You already told me that."

Eagle Feather looked from one to the other. "In the dark, with the moon behind him, an ordinary person can appear large and ominous. Especially at a distance."

"You think that was just a man, nothing more?"

Eagle Feather shrugged. "We'll know better when it's light."

They stared into the fire, keeping their thoughts to themselves. Zack believed Tommy knew more than she let on. He waited, but she said no more.

CHAPTER TWENTY-NINE

The first ray of dawn's red sun reached across the meadow, found Zack where he'd dozed off despite himself, warmed his cheek. He opened his eyes. The fire embers glowed red and white. Tomasa leaned back against the tree, her eyes closed, face serene. Eagle Feather was gone.

Zack pushed aside his jacket, stretched, walked to the trees to empty his bladder. When he returned, Eagle Feather was by the fire, stirring it back to life.

"Where you been?"

"I went to locate the assassin's trail."

Zack knelt beside him. "Any luck?"

"It's there. He headed up another ridge, as we thought." Eagle Feather poured water from his bottle into the coffee pot.

Zack stared into the fire. "I fear the two trails will merge sooner or later."

Eagle Feather nodded. He gestured across the meadow. "There's very little sign where we saw that giant, just some pressed grass."

Zack saw that Tomasa's eyes were open.

The water boiled. Eagle Feather poured coffee for them. The sun was full on the meadow now, the day warmed quickly.

Zack brought several Clif Bars out of his pack and offered them around. "Not exactly eggs and bacon but it'll keep us going." He took his coffee and strolled across the meadow to where he thought the giant had been.

Tomasa and Eagle Feather watched.

"Is this where he was?" Zack called.

"Right where you are," Eagle Feather said.

Zack studied the ground. As Eagle Feather had said, there was nothing but some pressed grass in two places, now springing back. "Yeah, not much here." He grimaced. "So why did I expect to find anything?"

"You just don't want to believe, White Man."

* * * * *

By the time they packed and saw to the fire, the sun was high and hot.

Zack looked at Tomasa. "You coming?"

"I might be able to help."

Zack made a gallant bow and ushered her ahead of him. They crossed the meadow, headed up to the arroyo.

Eagle Feather showed where the assassin's prints diverged from the others. "He went off that way. Probably up that ridge over there, where the afternoon sun would be behind him for his shot."

They retraced their steps up the arroyo. Tracking wasn't difficult. The steeper the terrain, the more obvious the drag marks from the unfortunate man's leg. The prints of the two growers moved steadily upward.

185

Eagle Feather gave a grunt, held up. A body lay across the gulch above them. The man might have been resting there but for his awkward position. One side of his face was gone.

They studied the ground as they approached, read the story. Eagle Feather peered at the ridge west of them. "Like we guessed, he had the sun behind him. Easy shot."

Zack looked at the man's legs. "This is the healthy one. There's no sign of a leg injury."

"The sniper was smart. He left the slow one to kill at his leisure."

Eagle Feather stepped around the body, eyes to the ground. "He twisted as he fell." He put his hand in some depressed earth. "I think he came down on top of Injured Man, who was right here." Eagle Feather stood straight, looked across at the ridge, eyes measuring. "The way I see it, the healthy guy was standing upright, head and shoulders visible above the arroyo. The sniper shoots him in the head, he falls"—Eagle Feather stepped to the side, angled his shoulders in pantomime—"right on top of Injured Man, maybe pins him to the ground."

"Good God," Zack said. "He must have been terrified."

Eagle Feather moved up the slope, intent on the story spelled out in the arroyo. "Injured Guy wasn't hit, no blood up here. He crawls along on his stomach, like a snake. He's desperate, knows he's in deadly danger. Look at those flat handprints where he pushes himself up to look around." Eagle Feather dropped on his stomach near

186

the prints, raised his head. "He can't see anything. The arroyo walls are too high. He doesn't know where the killer is, can only keep worming his way up."

Zack and Tomasa followed, intent on the life-like scenario Eagle Feather demonstrated.

"He crawls, rests—see the deeper impression? Then crawls on again. He goes on, and on." Admiration crept into Eagle Feather's voice.

They were at the lip of the ravine. They climbed out of the arroyo, saw a swale where the man crawled to the trees.

"He crawled that entire way," Zack said.

"He had a strong will to survive. Question is, what will we find in those trees?"

They followed the trace, reluctant. Yet when they entered the tree grove, no body awaited them. They saw where the man had rested before moving on.

"He's okay so far. He managed to walk." Zack pulled out his phone. "I have to tell Barnard about the body."

Barnard did not sound pleased at the news. "What the hell are you stirring up out there? I can't get any work done."

"Believe me, I'd rather be sitting where you are right now."

Barnard sighed audibly. "I'll call the troopers and get back to you. Don't leave the body unattended. You got a good signal?"

"Right here I do."

"Okay, stay there. I'll get right back." He hung up.

Zack found Tomasa and Eagle Feather across the knoll at the far edge of the trees. Ahead an open slope descended to taller growth. The injured man made no effort to hide his tracks; his thoughts were on speed alone.

"I can keep going with you as long as I have a signal," Zack said. "Barnard's gonna call back."

They followed the man's tracks down the hillside. He made no attempt to hide them; speed was the key.

Zack's phone rang. "You two go ahead. I'll go back and wait."

He answered.

"Barnard here. The troopers will send a crew in by helicopter. Have you got coordinates where they can land?"

Zack gave directions to the meadow. "What's their ETA?"

"One hour."

Zack spent the hour sitting with the body. Black flies swarmed and buzzed. He sorted recent events in his mind. Interesting that Tomasa seemed to know, and believe, the legend of the giant Indian protector. She'd been certain enough to risk pushing Zack's pistol aside. She appeared to know more than she was saying.

His ruminations were interrupted by the thump-thump of a helicopter. He heard it long before the tiny speck appeared over the distant range. He watched it land in the meadow below. His phone rang.

"Zack? This is Darby, from forensics. Where are you?"

Zack directed him up the arroyo, saw the little figures cross the meadow, three...no, four of them.

He called Darby. "Bruce, you're headed just right. Come straight up the arroyo. It's narrow up here; you can't miss the body. We're going on ahead to try to find the other man. If you need me, call."

Zack retraced his steps over the summit and down the open slope into the chaparral. Tomasa and Eagle Feather were not in sight. He followed the faint trail on a traverse of the mountain across several areas of rockslide. On the far side of the mountain he found Tomasa standing near a long exposed ridge.

"Eagle Feather went back to see if he could cut the trail of the assassin up there somewhere." She waved up the mountainside. "This poor man dragged himself all the way here. In places, he was flat on his stomach, pulling himself along. We think he was fired upon."

"He went out there?" Zack said, nodding toward the long narrow saddle.

"There's no where else to go."

Zack scratched his head. "Maybe he got a reprieve. I don't see a body out there."

They heard a shout behind them.

Eagle Feather stood high up the slope in some brush. "Bang," he said, pointing his finger down at them. "The sniper was right here. I've got shell casings."

Zack and Tommy watched him work down the slope toward them, slow and careful, eyes on the ground. They saw him stop near a solitary tree.

"You'll want to see this," Eagle Feather said.

They climbed up to look. In the pit of his stomach, Zack knew what they would find. He wasn't wrong. A large area of blood lay thick on the ground, the nearby vegetation splattered with it. This sniper had met the same fate as his comrade.

CHAPTER THIRTY

It was dark. Jesus was lost, struggled to orient himself to time and place. He moved, felt stabbing pain in his knee. It all came back. He was in a cave, injured, helpless, hunted.

Light came from beyond the cave mouth. It was day; his watch said nine o'clock. He had slept long. Pablo was gone, his rifle missing. He would be out there, on guard. For the first time in a long while, Jesus felt safe.

He didn't try to rise; more important to rest. Jesus recalled that first morning at the camp, when Javier insisted he rest for the day. Javier had been right, of course. That day of inactivity had done wonders for his knee. At the thought of Javier, tears came to his eyes.

There was food near the head of his sleeping bag: a snack box of cheerios, several sticks of beef jerky, some chocolate bars, water. None of it looked appetizing to Jesus yet he must eat. He unwrapped a chocolate bar and nibbled at it, felt a surge of energy, made himself finish it, sipped some water.

Jesus looked around the cave interior. He felt restless, wanted to move, to get away. He longed for the safety of the Reyes ranch, to be done with the Sonora Cartel, to go home. Somehow, he must find patience. It was more important to stay safe for his family.

A shot sounded, far off. It was impossible to tell how far. Another shot came, then another. They were sharp reports, powerful, like a rifle.

Jesus pulled himself from his sleeping bag, crawled to the cave mouth. It was brighter here. He waited, listened. There was the occasional birdcall, some small animals rustling, nothing else. Minutes went by. He waited.

Many shots came, four, five, all in a bunch. They still echoed in his ear when a scream sounded, powerful, high-pitched, terror-driven. Then nothing.

Jesus cringed with fright. Despite the distortion of distance, he knew in his heart the scream was Pablo. Something unspeakable had happened.

There would be no more protection for Jesus; he was next. He crawled deep into the rear of the cave. Like the fawn that blends with sun-dappled leaves when the wolf hunts, his safety must come from the cave's dark interior. He lay perfectly still. His back against the far cave wall, Jesus stared at the patch of light. Hours crept by. Soaked in sweat, eyes wide, breathing shallow—he waited.

The afternoon wore on; the sun moved across the mountains, the light at the cave mouth grew dim. Still Jesus waited. Whoever, whatever caused Pablo to utter that scream could be just beyond the cave mouth. The shadows deepened. Dusk approached. Darkness might be his only chance. He'd need full dark to leave the cave...to go where? He had no idea where he was, no idea where to go.

Jesus waited, undecided.

CHAPTER THIRTY-ONE

They could find no prints or sign beyond the area of blood, to no one's surprise. As before, the body was gone, the only tracks those of the victim where he walked to his death.

Zack had to walk back around the mountain to get a cell signal. He called Darby, told him about the new blood they'd found. He gave Darby the coordinates, promised someone would wait there to assist him.

When he returned, Eagle Feather was out on the saddle, tracking. Tommy watched nearby. As Zack went to them, he followed the running, hopping prints of the injured man, clearly etched in the dirt.

Eagle Feather showed him a second pair of footprints, large Vibram soles. "It's Grand Central Station out here."

"I wonder which team this new guy plays for."

"Maybe for the good guys," Eagle Feather said, and pointed. "This deeper imprint suggests Vibram Sole took on extra weight. Right there you can see Injured Man's heel dig in deep. Vibram Sole apparently helped Injured Man to his feet." Eagle Feather leaned back on his haunch, looked up at Zack. "Now we got to wonder if Vibram sole had anything to do with the blood, and those missing bodies."

They followed the prints on across the saddle: the Vibram sole and partially weighted, partially dragged sandals.

"They stopped here, under cover," Eagle Feather said. "One sat, the other stood or crouched nearby. Maybe they had water or re-bandaged the leg."

"Maybe both. Look here." Zack pulled broken pieces of sapling from the brush.

Eagle Feather continued to scout.

"You go ahead," Zack said. "I have to wait for Darby to lead him to the blood area."

"Can't he find his own way?"

"Probably." Zack grinned. "I've got to show cooperation with these guys, or my boss will get complaints."

"Politics." Eagle Feather snorted. He looked at the sun. "Okay, say another half hour, if he's coming right out. I'll be back by then."

Tommy went with Eagle Feather.

Zack walked back across the saddle. It was long past noon, his stomach told him. He found another energy bar and chewed on it until Darby arrived.

An investigator from the California State Police came with Darby.

"Zack, meet Clem. He's helping with the investigation. Forestry will send their own team out from Washington as soon as they can mobilize."

Zack shook hands. The uniformed trooper was short and wiry, maybe Irish, from the smile lines and general look of him.

"You've got a mess here, it seems," he said to Zack with a shake of his head.

Darby glanced at Zack. "Everybody's in a stir. When Malden got shot, it started a wildfire."

Zack led them up to the blood-coated area.

Darby stared down at it. "I saw the blood spill near the Sisquoc River yesterday. This looks the same. These are nasty. I'm almost ready to believe someone robbed a blood bank and dumped this stuff around just to blow our minds."

"Would that it was so harmless," Zack said. "For each of these we've got good evidence that a man has gone missing. We just can't find their bodies."

Darby bottled blood samples. "It takes a while to get a full DNA profile and to check CODIS. I already know there's no match for the first blood. At least not in this country."

"How about Mexico or South America?"

"We're trying to get cooperation from those authorities right now," Darby said. He capped off a tube. "Still, they'll need to be on file. They have DNA markers for active criminals down there, but not as many as I'd like."

Clem walked around the blood pool. "Somebody walked here before me. Was it you?" He looked at Zack.

"My partner looked for signs. He didn't find anything."

"What do you make of it?"

"I don't know what to make of it," Zack said.

"Who's that?" Clem stared at the saddle.

Zack looked. "That's my partner, Eagle Feather."

"Indian?"

"Navajo." Zack walked down the slope to meet Eagle Feather. "Where's Tommy?"

"She went on ahead. She's very concerned about the injured guy, wants to see where he ended up."

They climbed up to join Darby and Clem. Zack made introductions.

"There's nothing more for us to do here," Darby said. "It's past four. By the time we get back and remove the body, it'll be late." He looked at Zack and Eagle Feather. "You fellas want a ride back?"

"We've got more to do here. There's an injured Mex grower out there." Zack waved toward the mountain ridges.

"You've got to stop when it gets dark anyway," Darby pointed out. "We could use your help with the body. There's another team flying back first thing in the morning. You could hitch a ride with them."

Zack looked at Eagle Feather, who nodded.

"What about Tommy?" Zack said.

"She told me not to worry about her, said she'll find us if need be."

ZACA

* * * * *

That evening Susan returned. Zack got a note she'd left at the reception desk of the hotel. He called and invited her to dinner.

Susan and Eagle Feather had not seen one another for more than six months. The reunion called for a special wine. Zack sent the waiter to find one.

"Every time the three of us come together, there's a mystery to solve," Eagle Feather commented as he studied his menu.

"So." Susan glanced at Zack. "It's still a mystery, is it?"

"It is." Zack set down his menu. "We know a rival cartel sends people to kill the growers in those mountains. The mystery is who kills those cartel mercenaries, and what happens to their bodies?"

"Dump the blood, steal the body, leave no trace." Susan said.

"That's about right."

"Something from the air? You know, one of those personal jetpacks? Or a personal helicopter?" Susan's eyes twinkled.

Eagle Feather smiled. "Count on the scientist to think of something like that. Unfortunately, it doesn't fit. A jet stream or rotating blades would leave a disturbance on the ground. There wasn't any. At a couple of sites, overhead foliage would prevent direct access from the air."

"Hmmm." Susan grew thoughtful.

197

"Any explanation you can come up with is welcome at this point," Zack said. He grinned at Susan. "Unless you're going to propose a creature with wings."

"Could happen." Susan smiled back.

The waiter arrived with a wine selection. "I think you will appreciate this Red. It's a Zaca Mesa 2006 Mesa Reserve Syrah—earthy, rich, with a sweet berry taste going away."

"Sounds perfect." Zack tasted, nodded and the waiter poured. The friends toasted their reunion. Soon after, the conversation turned back to the mystery.

"Allow me to establish a baseline for you," Susan said. She pulled a pencil and a small pad from her purse along with a pair of rimless glasses, which she slipped on. The professorial effect was immediate. "You have three questions to answer: why, how, and who. First, why does the perpetrator kill these people? What possible motive could there be? Second, how on earth does the perpetrator manage it? Third, who or what is this perpetrator?"

Susan drew a straight line across the pad. At three equal intervals she intersected the line with the questions *Why, How,* and *Who..* She looked at them over her glasses. "These questions are necessarily related. We'll list as many answers as possible under each question. These answers should be based on evidence or strong surmise." She jabbed her pencil toward them. "It is important that you not restrict your responses in any way, no preconceived notions, no limitations. Okay?"

198

The men nodded. They'd been through this exercise before.

"Okay, go."

Zack jumped right in. "Toward motive, someone or something doesn't want cartel assassins in those mountains."

"That's good Zack, but too general. Do you think it's just cartel killers the perpetrator desires to eliminate?"

"Maybe not."

"Okay, simplify."

"The perpetrator doesn't want anyone killing others in those mountains."

"Can you make it even simpler?"

Zack scratched his head. "Uh, the perpetrator doesn't like killers."

"Do you believe what you just said to be true?"

Zack shrugged, then nodded.

"Good. Let's put that under *Why*." She wrote it in. "Next?"

"That's interesting," Eagle Feather said. "One might be tempted to say the perp doesn't want any drugs there, but if that were true, he'd kill growers as well. He hasn't."

"It's killing he wants stopped," Zack said. "Any killing."

"Very good. You get the idea. What's next?"

Eagle Feather tried this time. "Under *How*: the perp drains the blood."

"Duh." Zack said.

"No, Zack, Eagle Feather is exactly right. You must put down what you know, no matter how simplistic it may seem." She entered it.

"Okay, then," Zack said. "Under *Who:* someone who has lived there a long time."

"You have evidence?"

"A witness who has known of his presence all her life."

Susan wrote it down. "Anything else?"

"He's a big guy," Zack said. "According to the prints of his soles he left at the first kill, he's substantially larger than either of us."

She wrote that also. When she'd finished, she looked at what they had so far. "Let's revisit 'Why'," she said. "Can you think of a second reason or motive?"

Zack shook his head. "We have no evidence of any other reason. Unless it's just random."

Susan nodded, wrote *random*. "You sound doubtful about that one. Why?"

"I don't know, maybe it's because the killings were so specifically directed toward the drug mercenaries."

"Why haven't you suggested the possibility that the perp works for the rival cartel?" Susan said.

"It's the timing." Eagle Feather looked at Zack, who nodded. "The perp had plenty of opportunity to kill these guys before. He didn't. He killed them right after they killed someone else."

"Okay, it's time to take this to the next level," Susan said. "We will re-apply the same question to our most likely answer. So, we ask *why* again—*why* doesn't the perpetrator want any killing in those mountains?"

Zack answered this time. "The perpetrator feels that killing disturbs the peace or sanctity of the place."

Eagle Feather nodded his agreement.

"Put it more simply," Susan chided. She looked up as the waiter arrived with their entrees. They waited for him to finish passing the plates.

After the waiter left, Zack groaned. "This is too much like classwork. More simply, the perpetrator protects the area."

Susan wrote it down. "How does he drain the blood?" She looked at each of them.

"The blood flows, it doesn't spatter or fly around," Eagle Feather said. He played with his spoon as he thought. "He somehow immobilizes his victim. Then he hangs him up from a limb. He must cut the abdomen, maybe from below the naval on up into the heart." He glanced at Zack. "Like gutting a deer."

"That's right," Zack said. "He must remove organs and allow free flow."

"He's hunting them down and dressing them like a deer." Susan wrote it down.

The waiter appeared. "Is everything all right?" He looked pointedly at their plates. No one had touched the food.

'Uh...yes, looks great," Zack said. He realized he'd never seen it arrive.

As the men began to eat, Susan went ahead with the exercise. "Let's consider the last question, *who?* Our answer was someone who has lived in those mountains a long time. Let's dig deeper. How long do we think?"

Zack waved his fork with a chunk of steak on it. "I know where you're going now. To develop such a proprietary feeling for the place, the perp must have lived there a long time. Tomasa told us she wandered those woods her whole life, and has always known of the presence of this...creature. So he's been there at least as long as Tomasa. She's what, 17? 18?" He looked at Eagle Feather.

"I'd guess 16."

"Am I correct in assuming you have no evidence that says this person preceded Tomasa?"

Both men nodded.

"But nothing to say he didn't?"

More nods.

"Pass the salt," Zack said.

Susan studied her pad for a moment. "Here's what I see in all this. Your perp is an Indian, or closely related to the Indians, who feels a responsibility to protect these mountains. He's traditional, loyal, protective. He has a sense of entitlement, or of authority, and operates under his own specific guidelines. Physically, he is uncommonly large, very agile, extremely strong. He may well have capabilities beyond our expectations. We surmise his weapon must be a knife, or similar cutting tool. He is very stealthy, practiced in woodcraft." She looked up over her glasses at the two men. "There are remaining questions. How does he sustain himself? Do the Chumash shelter him? And here's an interesting question—is there only one of him?"

Zack and Eagle Feather stared at her.

"Shit," Zack said.

"Do you have any questions about this analysis?"

"Why an Indian?" Zack said.

Susan looked at her notes. "His woodcraft, hunts people like deer, your Indian friend senses his presence, he operates in an area the Chumash hold sacred—lots of little things that add up."

Eagle Feather studied Susan's face. "You haven't proposed a different species of human."

Susan smiled back at him. "That doesn't mean it hasn't crossed my mind. It might well come to that. To propose it now, however, would be to get ahead of ourselves. This exercise was to pool the evidence, evaluate it, and draw conclusions from it. As Zack says, when the only possibility left is the impossible, then we must include it."

Zack eyed Susan with respect. "You have a real talent for synthesizing data, although I don't see how it will change our plans."

Eagle Feather held up his fork. "Maybe it will. For one thing, we need to observe Tomasa a little more closely, follow her cues. By the way, do you know why a hunter drains away the blood from the deer as quickly as possible?"

Zack shook his head.

"It's to eliminate the gamey taste—the longer it's left, the gamier the meat."

Susan stared at him. "Are you suggesting..."

"That this hunter eats the meat? We haven't found the bodies, they've gone somewhere, right?"

Zack dropped his fork with a clatter. "Okay, my dinner is done."

CHAPTER THIRTY-TWO

Jesus waited until the cave mouth was but a faint outline against the darkness beyond and pulled himself upright against the earthen wall. He knew he must go soon, or not go at all. Pain shot through his knee, but thankfully it subsided when he eased weight onto it. The splint distributed his weight, made it possible to stand. He took a step. He looked up. He was too late. The cave entrance was no longer empty. A shadow obscured the faint glow of the entrance. Someone was there. Jesus held his breath, hoped the intruder couldn't see him against the blackness of the cave's interior.

"What is your name?"

The voice that came to him was gentle, soft...feminine. Jesus was startled.

"You are safe with me," the voice said. "What is your name?"

Jesus spoke in a hoarse whisper. "I...I am Jesus."

"Jesus, don't be afraid. I will protect you."

Jesus was afraid.

"Jesus?"

"Who...who are you?"

"My name is Tomasa."

"Are you from Mexico?"

"I am Chumash. Spanish is also my language."

A riot of confused thoughts crowded Jesus' brain. None of this made sense. "But what...how did you come here?" And then in a rush, "It isn't safe."

"It is safe now." The words were gentle, comforting. Jesus did not reply.

"May I come in?"

"I was...I was about to leave."

"Where will you go?" The voice was nearer now.

Jesus trembled, flattened against the wall of the cave. He had heard the terrified cries of Pablo. The tough mercenary had screamed like a baby. Jesus recalled folk tales from his childhood, stories of shape shifters, evil creatures who could assume any shape, any voice. He knew only that a woman simply should not be here, not now, not in these circumstances, not in this place.

She seemed to know his thoughts. "Jesus, the danger has passed. The people who would harm you are gone. I followed you here. I have come to help you."

Jesus heard a scratch sound and a match flared. In the sudden light he saw a girl, tall, slender, boy-like. Her eyes were soft, compassionate. Then the match died.

"How do I know you are who you say?"

"Who else could I be?" She paused. Then she said, "You must trust."

She was right, Jesus knew. He had no other choice.

Jesus felt her touch on his shoulder and shuddered. The momentary glimpse of this woman's face in the light of the match had comforted him in that moment, but now this person stood next to him, touched him. He was afraid.

"You are safe with me, Jesus," she repeated, her voice soft, patient.

"What...what do you want?"

"What do you want?"

"I want to go home." All of Jesus' pent up fear was in his response.

"That is what I want as well. I want to help you go home."

"But how...?"

She did not answer. Instead, she grasped his hand, led him toward the cave door. He came with her. Her touch brought a tingle to his arm, like a small charge of electricity. In a moment they were outside the cave.

It was lighter here. Jesus saw the outline of trees; far above there were stars. A touch of moonlight shimmered on the path. Jesus knew he should be afraid, yet he wasn't. When the girl Tomasa held his hand, his fear left. He hung on tight. He saw her in the dim light, more movement than substance, like fish that would rise to his bait in the murky bay waters back home. He clung to her hand and followed her. He noticed something else. He could walk without pain, still awkward but without the customary painful jolts.

The night air felt cool against his sweaty face. They came to the stream, and to his surprise Tomasa led him into the water. It lapped cold against the bare skin in his huaraches. They turned upstream, stayed in the middle of the current. At each obstacle, stone or deadwood, Tomasa warned him with a quick squeeze of her hand. Invariably, he moved up and over it with ease. They traveled as in a dream.

Jesus followed Tomasa up the rivulet for a long time. It was almost pleasant, the breath of night air on his face, the cold water on his feet, the heat of his body from the exercise enough to keep him warm. He sensed the canyon walls narrow, the slopes grow steeper. The stream itself funneled, steepened, bubbled over high step-like rock ledges. The higher they climbed, the brighter shone the moon. It glistened and sparkled on the froth of the rushing water. It frosted the meadows, leant a mystical glow to the valley beneath. Neither spoke.

Jesus kept a firm grip on Tomasa's hand. As long as he held on to her, he felt he could surmount any obstacle. Trust her, she had said. This was what she meant.

* * * * *

The light of dawn had begun to outline the blackness of the mountain summits when Tomasa led Jesus across a field and among rows of grape vines.

She dropped his hand. "You wait here. The workers will come soon. Tell them where you need to go." She patted his arm gently. "Your troubles are over now."

Jesus stared across the vineyard toward distant buildings. He was bone weary yet he needed answers to a thousand questions. He turned to ask Tomasa—she was gone, only mist between the vines where she had been.

Jesus slumped to the ground, his buttocks on the soft earth; a thick vine supported him like a chair back. His mind raced, went back to the night, the trudge up and down the mountain slopes, hour after hour. It all should have been torture, somehow it wasn't. Each time Jesus thought he could go no farther and stopped to rest, he was overcome by restlessness, had to go on.

Tomasa said little on their journey. She appeared indefatigable, her breath never labored, she moved with such grace she seemed to dance up the mountainsides. Never once had she released Jesus's hand.

He looked at it now, palm up, the thick fingers, the calloused skin. Energy had come to him from her soft hand. The power of her will, like an electric current, had surged into him. Now she was gone, her energy with her. Jesus collapsed like a puppet dropped by the puppeteer.

Jesus woke with a start at a touch on his shoulder. The rising sun cast the face above him in shadow.

"*Que pasa, Amigo*? Who are you? Why are you here?" The voice was rough.

Jesus squinted up.

Other figures stood nearby, curious.

"*Me perdi*," he said. "The truck left without me. I became lost." Jesus struggled to rise. His knee was agony; he fell back.

A strong hand gripped his.

Jesus stood, his weight on his good leg. "I walked and walked, it was dark. I tripped and fell. I injured my knee." Jesus rubbed his bad knee to show them.

The voice sounded less harsh. "Where do you come from?"

"I work for Señor Rufus Reyes in Santa Lupita. The driver left without me."

"Come. Lean on my shoulder. We will go to my supervisor. He will help you." The man was big and very strong. He half carried Jesus down the rows.

CHAPTER THIRTY-THREE

Zack left Eagle Feather and Susan to catch up on their news. He went to find Malden.

Rick Malden lived in Orcutt, a town by name but a community so melded into the sprawl of Santa Maria that Zack didn't know when he had left the one and entered the other. His wide front porch faced east to catch the warm morning sun; now it was dark, the only light a moth-clustered porch lamp.

Malden opened the door at the first knock. A long black nose poked around him to sniff Zack. Malden held the dog's collar. "Come in, Zack. I was glad to get your call."

Zack stroked Toker's head as he stepped into the front hall.

"Let's go to the sitting room," Malden said, steered him down a step to a room with overstuffed chairs and a large TV. He pointed to one of the chairs. "Coffee, soda, beer?" When Zack declined, Malden sat opposite him.

Toker took up residence next to Zack's chair.

"I'm glad to see you moving so well on that leg." Zack scratched behind Toker's ears.

"Oh, it really was nothing. Hurt like hell, but it's what they call in the movies a flesh wound." His eyes narrowed. "Barnard tells me the guy that shot me didn't fare so well."

Zack shook his head and grimaced. "There was nothing left of him but a pool of blood." He went on to describe the day's events.

When he had finished, Rick sat back in his chair. He let out a long whistle. "We've got a serial killer loose in the forest."

"That's about the size of it. Fortunately, he seems zeroed in on the drug traffickers. We think he may have been around a lot longer than this, that nobody knew it. The recent spate of killings might be due to increased drug activity in this guy's domain."

"You're going back out there tomorrow?"

"Yes. The injured grower is still out there, so far as we know. We'll get on his trail again, see where it takes us." Zack leaned forward. "Which brings me to another question. You must have wondered how the sniper knew exactly where to find you to ambush you."

Malden rubbed his thigh, nodded. "That question did occur to me. At first, I figured it was pure coincidence, the rifleman saw my truck from a distance, thought I was a rival." He shook his head slowly. "After some thought, I no longer buy that."

"Why not?"

Malden regarded Zack. "I think the real target was you."

"Me?"

"Consider this." Malden's face grew animated. "I've been in and out of all those locations almost every day. I've probably stumbled right by grow sites more than once. No one ever shot at me. I'm old news. These guys had me factored in." He pointed at Zack. "You are the news, a strange fed nosing around. I think they wanted to send you a message."

"I'll confess, I hadn't thought of that."

"But for the fact I got the call to help process the new grow, we'd all have come out together. The rifleman——"

"That's it," Zack exclaimed. "No one knew Eagle Feather would be with us, let alone Tomasa. The assassin would expect me to come back with you." Zack eyed Malden. "That is, after you got the call."

Malden sat still, absorbed it all. He stared back at Zack. "The telephone call was the key. That's how they timed it."

"Right. So who called you?"

"Jeremy Tusco, my partner."

Zack watched Malden's face, waited.

"No, no. If that's what you're thinking, not a chance. I've known Jeremy a long time. Besides, he only passes along the orders from the command level."

"Which is..."

"Which can be a number of people. When a ranger locates a large crop operation, he reports it to the department. A day is selected, the other rangers up and down California are notified, and we all gather at the

213

appropriate station the night before to make plans. Frequently, there are not enough rangers, so state troopers are called in to augment the force."

"You didn't know in advance about this raid."

"Right. Sometimes the operation is small, only one or two rangers required. Sometimes we have to move quickly, before the growers can start destroying stuff, or a ranger is endangered, that kind of thing. In those instances, a state police sergeant or some other administrator might call the shots. Sometimes it's even someone lower down the chain of command in the forestry service." Malden shrugged. "It's hard to know sometimes."

"But you can find out..."

"Oh, yes, I can most certainly find out, and I will."

* * * * *

At 6 AM the following morning Zack and Eagle Feather were at a hanger at the Santa Maria airfield as a crew rolled out the CHP helicopter. The marine layer, as the locals called the morning fog, enveloped men and machine in a ghostly aura. Soon after, Darby turned up, then other men straggled in, yawning, coffees held in a death grip.

"It's gonna be a bit crowded," Darby said. He put his large kit down on the tarmac. "We have two teams going in, forensics and investigative. We'll be one person over listed capacity, but it won't be the first time. This is a brand new MD500E; we use it for the quieter four-bladed tail rotor. It will handle all of us easily."

"Well look here, it's the rent-a-fed."

Zack turned, saw the towering figure of Dom Antonio. He had a small pack on his back and a rifle case in his hand. The man grinned at him.

Zack shook his hand. "For a rental, you folks are getting a bargain." He gestured toward the case. "Why the fancy equipment?"

Dom's grin turned evil. "You never know when you might get a shot at a bad guy. Who's your friend?"

Zack made the introductions.

Dom looked from one to the other. "No rifle?"

Zack shook his head. "We're not after a killer. We're trying to rescue a wounded, frightened man."

Dom shook his head in disagreement. "We've already got a man down from rifle fire. I don't plan to be pinned down without a way to talk back." He patted his case.

The helicopter rotors turned slowly, sped up, and the men climbed in. Darby took a seat on the floor, his case in his lap. They took off and in five minutes had popped out of the fog into a crystal clear day. The flight was brief. A half hour later they climbed out into the now familiar meadow. The sun already felt hot.

Zack and Eagle Feather set out across the meadow and up the arroyo, left the four troopers to organize themselves. Despite steep slopes, the way was familiar, their progress swift.

Once across the saddle, they rested. Eagle Feather led from there. A faint path around the mountainside took them on a gradual descent toward a deep valley nestled among hills. Eagle Feather was along this track the day before and moved now with confidence.

With each foot of descent vegetation grew more thick and green. It was a place the sun reached indirectly, a secret Eden. The light felt different, diffused by thick foliage; gentled in its passage through the green canopy, it arrived on the forest floor friendly and bright. The cool of night was imprisoned within the valley and hung in the air, as refreshing as a waterfall mist.

There was something magical about the place. Zack felt refreshed, his senses sharpened. The sharp demand of the scrub jay, the sad question of a mourning dove came like music in an iPod to his ears. He stopped to listen, entranced. Unseen creatures rustled somewhere on the forest floor, he caught the scent of moldering wood and wild ginger. Somewhere below them a stream bubbled and chuckled its way down the valley.

Zack caught Eagle Feather eyeing him.

"The ancients live here," the Navajo said.

The trace path they followed widened, other animal paths joined. The trees were tall here, stretched toward the sunlight. The frothy water of the brook cascaded over boulders and pooled behind mossy logs. The valley was long, deep, narrow. Trees of many varieties stood in groves, vines draped rocky cliffs, lichen and moss draped rotting logs like green caps; boulders, rounded by forces of nature clustered here and there like great forgotten marbles.

They came to the stream. The path, a moist film, presented a maze of animal prints etched clear in the damp earth, but the footprints they followed were not there.

Eagle Feather crossed the rivulet, knelt to study the ground on the far side. "If they came this way, they left no sign." He looked back across the rippling water. "They must have turned off sooner."

Zack nodded, went back up the path. A few yards along, he saw where a line of exposed rock traversed the slope. He walked along it, found a telltale swale in a patch of grass. From there it was not difficult to follow their tracks across the creek through the meadow to a large stand of brush where they found a well-concealed gap through the tangled branches. They passed through. Beyond was a clearing, beyond it a sheer rock cliff, in it the dark maw of a cave.

Eagle Feather went toward it, cautious. He signaled Zack to wait, crept in. A moment later he reappeared. "Nobody's home."

Zack went in. Light near the cave entrance was enough to judge size and depth. He noticed painted handprints and other pictographs on the walls. Deeper in the cave was evidence of modern man in the form of discarded food wrappers and tin cans. Sleeping bags and clothing strewn against the far walls indicated this cave was used frequently—and recently.

Eagle Feather scanned the dirt near the cave entrance. When Zack re-emerged he pointed to the ground. Footprints of both Injured Man and Big Man proved they both were here. "Someone else was here, too."

Zack followed Eagle Feather's finger, saw a smaller impression, a moccasin print. "Tomasa?"

Eagle Feather nodded. He stood and stared back at the cave. "Everything points to a hasty departure."

"They were discovered?"

"Maybe. Yet I can find no other prints."

They searched the ground together. The small clearing yielded nothing, so they worked their way through the brush tangle to the outside meadow. Trapped moisture from the stream left the grass spongy. There were traces of passage but no distinct footprints. Not until they increased their perimeter to include the slopes beyond the meadow did they find useful tracks. Eagle Feather found them first.

"I have prints for Big Man here. They lead up the valley."

"Alone?"

"So far. His strides are long, not shortened as they were with Injured Man."

"You go ahead. I'll search in the other direction," Zack said. He set to work, crossed and re-crossed the meadow, then the forest floor beyond. There was no sign of Injured Man or Tomasa. He was ready to give it up when he heard an urgent call from Eagle Feather.

Zack found Eagle Feather at a point where the canyon steepened and narrowed into an arroyo. He was near one of the last tall trees, an oak with thick outstretched branches. His eyes were on the ground. Zack came closer; saw a dark substance on the forest floor. It matted the leaves and covered the debris. He didn't need to be told what it was.

"He was running before he arrived here. Something frightened him." Eagle Feather pointed to a leafy area outside the blood smear.

Zack looked, saw a shell casing.

"Whatever it was, he shot at it."

Zack searched among the leaves and found three more shells. "These are from a handgun. He must have emptied it." He stooped, picked up another.

Eagle Feather opened his palm. In it was a different shell. "This is a .358 Winchester cartridge."

"A rifle."

"Yeah," Eagle Feather said. He pointed down the slope. "He first shot at something from down there. Then he dropped the rifle, ran this far, turned and fired multiple shots with his handgun."

"The guns didn't save him."

Buzzing flies covered the large pool of coagulated blood. Red-black matter coated leaves and dirt over a three-foot square area, as if a giant water balloon filled with the liquid had burst above it.

Zack felt sick. Had something similar happened to the Mexican? What about Tomasa?

Eagle Feather pointed. "Here's a branch where he could hang the carcass. There's evidence of abrasion on it."

Realization dawned for Zack. "Big Man shot at him, and so he died. Just like the others, just like I would've if Tomasa hadn't stopped me."

"I don't think we're gonna find a body here, either."

Zack felt something close to panic. "We've got to find out what happened to Injured Man and Tomasa." He jogged back toward the cave.

CHAPTER THIRTY-FOUR

A search of the ground near the cave again revealed nothing. They searched the stream banks for 100 yards in each direction; examined every leaf, scrutinized the tiniest overturned stone.

Zack shrugged, admitted defeat. "It's as if they evaporated."

Eagle Feather eyed the rippling current. "They must have used the water to hide their tracks. I would do that. It gets rough, though. They'd have to step high up over logs and stand on tipsy rocks with slick surfaces." He shook his head. "I don't see how Injured Man could do that."

"If we suppose they did manage it, how can we know whether they went upstream or downstream?"

"Right. If we pick wrong, we lose all that extra time. Even then, there may be no evidence to support the idea." Eagle Feather shook his head. "You tell me how this man who can barely walk on a flat surface could walk in that creek."

Zack thought about it. "I guess we're done here." He walked to the tree where he'd left his pack.

Eagle Feather followed. "What now?"

"Let's have lunch, then head back." Zack sat and leaned against the tree.

Eagle Feather brought his pack over.

Silence ensued while the two tired, hungry men refreshed themselves. Now that they were still, the forest came to full life with birdsongs and the rustle and whisper of wind in the treetops. The rushing waters bubbled a cheerful accompaniment.

Warmed by the sun, Zack grew drowsy. Yet something nagged him, some piece of the puzzle he couldn't place. "You wonder how these cartel assassins got their information."

Eagle Feather's eyes were closed. He kept them that way.

"They seemed to know just where to find those hidden marijuana grows," Zack said.

Eagle Feather said nothing.

"You wouldn't send professional hit men across the border from Mexico, and into a forest just to wander around hoping to find something."

One of Eagle Feather's eyes popped open. "Where're you going with this?"

"I don't know. I don't believe in coincidence, and there's a bit too much of that going on."

The eye closed again.

"Think about it." Zack scratched his back against the tree. "These two assassins knew exactly where to find those two growers. They went directly there, there was no hesitation. They split up, and one knew just where to go to find Malden...when he'd be there. Malden agrees that someone must have tipped off those killers to know when we'd be at the river. They split up at the camp; one followed the growers, the other went directly to the river to shoot Malden—again, no hesitation. They had to have received information."

"You think they're on radios, an inside man cues them."

"That's got to be it, right?" Zack waved an arm around. "This is a huge place. You could spend weeks trying to locate a well-hidden marijuana crop like that. But they went right to it. What does that tell you?"

"It tells me I'm not gonna get my nap." Eagle Feather opened both eyes. "Okay, suppose you're right. Who could this inside guy be? It'd have to be someone in the loop, someone who knows everything going on. He'd need access to law enforcement, and to forestry service planning. He'd need access to cartel information, too. Who could possibly do all that? Seems a stretch to me."

"Yeah, I suppose."

"Unless..." Now Eagle Feather couldn't let go. "Suppose someone on the law enforcement side is on the payroll of a cartel, and this particular guy can access surveillance photos from helicopter flyovers? If he worked for the rival cartel, he could give them exact coordinates for the crops. And if he was aware of copter flights, he might know the rangers' movements. He might have all the pieces."

Zack stared at Eagle Feather with raised eyebrows. "This is why I keep you around."

"Who called Malden to send him off to the new grow, I wonder?"

"I asked him that. His partner called him, but he thinks someone higher up set it up. He plans to find out." Zack chuckled. "When you think about it, everyone in that helicopter this morning fits the criteria you just outlined."

Eagle Feather stared at Zack. He wasn't laughing. "That's right, you know. If it is one of them, he's thinking we're going to figure it out, sooner or later, and—"

"And that's something he can't allow," Zack finished, his eyes scanning distant trees. At that very moment there was the bright flash of reflected light. "Down." Zack launched himself away from the tree. He heard a bullet enter the tree where he had just been. The report of a rifle came a fraction of a second later.

CHAPTER THIRTY-FIVE

After Zack's headlong dive he ended in a small hollow behind a rotting log, not much protection. He squirmed his body around, inched his head up. A crack in the log gave a narrow view of the opposite slope, but he saw nothing. "Eagle Feather?"

"Over here, behind the rock."

Zack could barely hear him over the chattering stream. "Have you got a weapon?"

"Yeah, a knife, but I can't quite reach him with it."

"I have a handgun."

"We're gonna have to ask him to come a lot closer, White Man."

"If this is one of our buddies from the helicopter, he knows we don't have a rifle."

Zack waited for that thought to strike home.

It did.

"Shit."

"He can wait us out, shoot us the minute we move."

"Yeah, yeah, I get the picture."

Zack heard Eagle Feather grunt, as if he had changed position. "He'll ease down the slope toward us, just out of pistol range, wait for us to show ourselves."

"Any ideas?"

"Depends on whether there's just one shooter."

"I think just one."

"How sure are you, White Man?"

"Not that sure." Zack reached under his thigh, moved the stick that ground into him. He waited. The silent forest waited with him.

Eagle Feather's voice drifted to him. "I know where there's a rifle."

Zack was puzzled...remembered—the rifle abandoned by Big Man. "You got a plan?" Zack's pistol was in his hand. He scanned the slope.

"Here's plan A: you go get it."

"Good plan." Zack grinned despite himself. "You lay down a covering fire with your knife."

There was no reply, no responding chuckle. Eagle Feather was gone.

Zack looked out at the slope. There was nothing to see. There had been no indication of the gunman's presence since the one shot. A ray of sun sifted through the leafy branches onto his leg, heated it. He wanted to move it, but there was no place to put it.

The sniper would work his way behind them. He'd find a place where he could see them; just pick them off. Zack would first know he was there when he felt the incoming bullet. There was no way to protect both sides. Not a good situation. He hoped Eagle Feather got clear away, could create a diversion.

Perspiration formed on his back, trickled along his spine. His legs threatened to cramp. The beam of sun cooked his leg. He was thirsty. If Eagle Feather could to do something, he hoped it would be soon.

His thoughts were interrupted by a shot. It sounded like the same rifle, more distant, off where Eagle Feather had gone. If the rifleman was there, he couldn't be here. Was there another shooter? Like Eagle Feather said, how sure was he? No choice. Zack eyed the next bit of cover, breathed in, jumped up, ran. He dove behind a tree. No shot. Had he surprised the shooter, or was no one there? He peered up the slope...nothing.

Zack took several deep breaths, ran again, dropped behind a bush. Still nothing. He was sure now. There was only one rifleman. The bad news, he may have just shot Eagle Feather.

Zack slipped out of cover, his confidence growing, moved in the direction of the second shot. He followed the stream up canyon, the way they'd gone this morning. When he reached the kill site, he took cover. His eyes searched the forest floor. He was sure he was in the right place. Big Man's rifle was gone. Zack hoped that meant Eagle Feather had it.

Now what? Where was Eagle Feather? The second shot had come from up here somewhere, impossible to pinpoint the spot. He would keep going, hope to run into Eagle Feather, not the sniper.

Zack sprinted from cover to cover up the slope. He rested until his breath quieted, ran, dove for cover, did it all over again. He'd come far up the valley wall now; fewer trees, the undergrowth thick but short. He launched himself into a thick stand of Mazanitis, landed prone. He stared at a man's leg, followed it up—Eagle Feather. The Navajo was seated, his back against a thick trunk, his legs stretched out. The rifle lay across his lap.

Zack came to his knees.

"You sounded like a tank coming up the slope, White Man. Maybe you should announce your arrival with a megaphone next time."

"Christ, Eagle Feather. You scared the hell out of me. I thought the sniper shot you."

"He didn't shoot me. He didn't even shoot at me."

"What did he shoot?"

"I have no idea."

Zack slumped down opposite Eagle Feather, glanced at the rifle. "Now you've got that, I feel a bit better."

Eagle Feather grimaced. "We need to find him before he finds us."

"Where'd that shot come from?"

The Navajo pointed up the slope. "Up there somewhere. I've been waiting for him to come down. I don't think he's coming."

"Maybe we should go there, see what's holding him up," Zack said.

"My thoughts exactly." Eagle Feather led out. The red-limbed brush thinned. They took cover in clumps of sage, felt more exposed. Zack left distance between them; why give the shooter two targets at the same time? They neared the top of the slope, moved into tall grass, much less cover. Dry, brittle debris underfoot made stealth difficult.

Eagle Feather disappeared into a clump of sage. Zack waited, followed. When he got there Eagle Feather was in a crouch, his gaze on something beyond the sage bushes, his palm toward Zack. He turned, put a finger to his lips, motioned him down.

Zack dropped on his stomach, wormed his way forward. He raised his head until he could see beyond the shrubs. He saw a grassy meadow, a large oak tree with ravens clustered in its upper branches. He heard their raucous cries. At the foot of the tree was a huge man, his back to them. The muscles of his bare shoulders and arms undulated; his head was down, intent on his work. Two feathers projected from a headband, a thick black braid hung halfway down his massive bare back, the spine deeply hollowed where lower back met waist, a dark leather breechclout partially covered brown muscular buttocks above thick thighs, long legs, the feet hidden by tall grass. The Indian was focused on something obscured by the giant's bulk, something suspended from a thick oak branch a dozen feet above the ground.

The head and shoulders of the colossus bent lower, as if his work took him there. To Zack's horror, the head of a man with close-cropped hair came into view. The head jerked side-to-side as the Indian worked. When the giant moved to a crouch, his work became clear. The man's chest and upper abdomen were revealed, slashed open. The Indian busily removed the man's organs. The victim's face seemed familiar, yet indeterminable at the distance.

The giant stood, stepped back, seemed to consider his work. He put back his head as if to sniff the air, swung around. His fierce gaze traveled along the perimeter of the meadow.

The suspended body of the man came full to Zack's view. His arms dangled at his sides, his shirt hung in strips, his abdomen gaped open, intestines hung like a grotesque rope. His pants drooped over his shoe tops like a collapsed tent, drenched in blood.

Zack's glimpse was momentary. The Indian's slow scrutiny came toward him; he flattened. As he did he uttered an involuntary gasp, for in that moment he recognized the victim.

The two men waited, neither man breathed. When at last Zack dared lift his head, in by inch, he saw the giant was back at his gruesome task. His big hand reached deep inside the body cavity, grasped organs, and pulled them out. He worked efficiently, used a large knife to slash the trailing tissue and sinew. Zack could see the victim's face now, frozen in death in a blend of surprise and horror. There could be no doubt—it was Dom.

The Indian was methodical, a hunter field dressing a deer. The body cavity emptied and scraped, he started to dismember it, severed the body parts cleanly at the joints with quick slashes of his great knife, sectioned Dom's body from bottom to top. A neat stack of body parts grew, until at last nothing remained suspended from the tree but

Dom's head. The giant removed it, placed on top of the pile, removed the leather belt and cloth strips that had suspended the trooper from the branch, used them to tie the body parts into a tight bundle.

For his next chore he picked up the intestines and organs and draped them over branches. Before he had finished a black cloud of birds descended, fought and clawed over each morsel. The giant ignored them, lifted the bundle of body parts, swung it over his back. He surveyed the ground. Apparently satisfied, he turned away. One powerful leaping step propelled him forty feet across the meadow. In moments he was gone.

The squabbling black flock finished and flew off, a few at a time, until only one or two remained searching the limbs and ground beneath the tree for missed morsels. After the very last bird had flown, nothing remained on the flattened, blood-slicked grass.

The two men waited a long time in silence. Zack struggled to keep his gorge down. He glanced at Eagle Feather. His friend was white. "That was..."

"Yeah, I saw. That was Dom." Eagle Feather shook his head, awed.

"It came for Dom because he tried to kill us."

"Maybe, maybe not. The shot we heard; I guess Dom must have seen it."

Zack stood, stared where the monster had disappeared. "Did it know we were here, do you think?"

"Ordinarily, I'd say no. We weren't that close, the wind was toward us, our approach was quiet. But this thing? Did you see it sniff the breeze?" Eagle Feather shuddered. "Who knows?"

The men walked toward the tree. Before they'd gone far, Zack saw a scoped rifle. It lay in the grass near the edge of the meadow, likely dropped there after Dom's futile attempt to kill the monster.

Eagle Feather put a hand on Zack's arm. "Right now we've got a choice. We can go over there, leave prints, become involved in Dom's killing, or move out of here right now.

Zack paused, thought it over. "You're right. Leave the rifle where it is. Let police investigators discover this scene." He turned a grim face to Eagle Feather. "We know now that Dom tried to kill us. We don't want anyone to think we killed him. It may be wise to keep our presence here a secret, at least for now."

"What about the Indian monster?"

"I think we need another chat with Paula," Zack said.

The friends walked back down the canyon to the stream crossing. They found their packs, picked them up, and headed up the trail.

CHAPTER THIRTY-SIX

Jesus ogled the room with wonder. He'd never been inside Don Rufus' ranch house. The tile floor glistened like the shimmering waters of the bay near his home, the red-toned Mazanitis furniture spread about like driftwood on a beach, the great windows opened to a matchless vista. He marveled and waited.

Jorge came for him that morning in his rattletrap pickup. He asked no questions, he seemed already to know the answers. He brought news of his own. Rafael Rodriquez had been fired. The foreman tried to tell Don Rufus that Jesus attacked him for no reason and should be arrested. Candida came forward to accuse Rafael of rape. After that, the floodgates opened. One by one, the women came forward, complained about Rafael and his sexual harassment. Rodriguez was arrested, would be brought up on multiple charges of rape. Jorge was made supervisor in his place. Jesus was vindicated. Jesus listened in amazement. So much happened in so short a time.

These events were on Jesus' mind when Don Rufus entered the room, Jorge behind him. The rancher pointed to a chair, spoke in Spanish. "Sit."

Jesus sat.

Don Rufus leveled his gaze on him.

Jesus hung his head.

Señor Reyes was gruff yet kindly. He spoke in English now. "We'll get a doc to take a look at that knee. Jorge has fresh clothes for you, an' I'm sure you'd like a shower." He looked at Jorge, who translated.

Jesus nodded.

"What I'm gonna say, don't get me wrong," Reyes said. "I'm glad you did what you did, believe me. If you hadn't roughed up that bastard, who knows how many women he would 'a hurt."

Jesus waited.

Reyes spread his hands wide, a man with a dilemma. "But son, I can't let you stay here. You attacked my supervisor, even if he did deserve it." He ticked off on stubby fingers. "You were up in those hills hidin' from the law when you was supposed to be right here workin'. If you'd come to me, I'd 'a listened to ya."

Jesus hung his head again.

Reyes sat in a large leather armchair. He eyed Jesus and sighed. "I got to let you go, son. But you did me a favor by standin' up for your amigos and stoppin' that bully. I always repay a favor." Reyes gestured to Jorge to listen as he spoke. "You're gonna go to the hospital until they say you can travel. I'm gonna cut you a check for a year's work an' I'm gonna buy you a ticket home. Then we'll be square." Reyes waited as Jorge translated.

Jesus felt a surge of joy. He would be going home. He would see his family. He would come home with money. "Muchas gracias," he said in a hoarse whisper.

Don Rufus smiled. He rose to his feet. Jesus also stood. Reyes reached out and took Jesus' hand. "Good luck, Amigo" He walked away.

It wasn't until he was out in the driveway that Jesus remembered his obligation to the cartel. His bliss evaporated. Panicked, he turned to Jorge. "I can't go home," he said. "My agreement—"

"Wait. We can't talk here. Get in the truck."

Jesus climbed into the passenger side.

Jorge started the motor, turned to Jesus. "I have good news for you. The cartel says you may go home."

Jesus waited. There must be more.

"They know what you have gone through. They have seen your loyalty. They will pay you the money they promised."

Jesus was in shock. How could he have so much good luck after so much bad? It was hard to comprehend.

Jorge engaged the clutch. "There is one thing, though."

Jesus's heart stopped.

Jorge peered at him. "Listen carefully. Your contract has been extended—for life. If ever the organization needs you, they will contact you. They will expect you to respond at once. You understand? Can you accept this?"

That was all? Jesus could not believe his good luck. He nodded many times. "*Si, si, si.*" He felt enormous relief. His rigid body relaxed. Then, as he let down, his injury, exhaustion, and dehydration took over; he was overcome. Jesus clung to the truck door. The pain in his knee raged.

Jorge looked at him. "I think the change of clothes and shower must wait, Jesus. We will go to the hospital right away.

CHAPTER THIRTY-SEVEN

Darby was packing his kit when Zack and Eagle Feather found him. He looked tired, his shirt damp on his back, yet his mood was good.

"I found tissue in with the blood." A sample bag was in his hand. "This should yield more information." He opened the cooler chest and dropped the specimen in a compartment with dry ice, leaned back and stretched. "Did you figure out where the wounded grower went?"

Zack shook his head. "He completely escaped us. We located a cave where he hid, but from there..." He shrugged.

Eagle Feather looked sidewise at Darby. "We found the guy in the Vibram-soled shoes, though, or at least what's left of him." He pointed to the pool of blood at their feet. "He looked pretty much like that."

Darby stared at Eagle Feather, then groaned. "Not another one." He looked at his watch, called up the slope to his assistant. "Clem, they've found another blood pool."

"The copter's leaving in an hour," Clem called back. He sounded anxious.

Darby sighed. "We'll have to come back tomorrow, I guess." He glanced at Zack. "Will you come back out again?"

"I can't say. It's likely, though. If not, I've got the GPS coordinates for that new blood in my phone. I'll send them to you."

Eagle Feather handed Darby the rifle he carried. "This might interest you. We found it near the big man's blood."

Darby inspected the weapon, holding it by the tip of the barrel.

"There may still be some of his prints on it along with mine," Eagle Feather said. "I'd have left it, but someone was shooting at us at the time and I needed it."

"Someone shot at you?" Darby stared from one to the other.

"Tried to kill us," Zack said. "If I hadn't seen the sun glint off his rifle, I wouldn't be here."

Darby inspected the rifle in his hands. "Did you get him?"

"No, we didn't," Eagle Feather said. "We went toward the sound of his rifle, but he didn't hang around. Left no trace, like he got carried off or something."

Darby shook his head. "There's entirely too much of that going on. We need to break this case—and soon." He picked up his kit and the cooler. "Let's get back to the bird. The investigating team will want to debrief you."

Late afternoon in the mountains was hot and dry; the dusty earth seemed to float into their lungs like smoke. Zack helped Darby with the cooler. Eagle Feather carried the rifle again, since his prints were already on it, as Darby pointed out.

As they straggled across the meadow toward the
helicopter, one of the investigators near it hailed them.
"Have any of you guys seen Dom?"

They all shook their heads.

Eagle Feather said, "We didn't hang around with
him."

Zack threw him a warning glance.

They loaded the equipment into the McDonnell
Douglas craft. Everything was ready for departure, yet still
no sign of Dom. They stood there, talked and waited.

"Does anyone know where Dom went?" Darby
said.

"He left the crime scene up in the arroyo after an
hour or so," one of the investigating team said. "He just
picked up and left with that fancy rifle. He didn't pass
you?"

Darby shook his head. "Never saw him. I was at
the other blood slick all day."

The man eyed Zack. "Where were you?"

"We tracked the wounded man from the second
crime scene. His tracks went west to a deep valley. As we
told Darby here, we found another blood pool down
there."

All conversation stopped; heads swung toward
him.

"It wasn't..."

"Oh, no," Zack said. "It wasn't Dom. It was the
guy with the large Vibram sole footprints."

"But someone shot at Zack and Eagle Feather," Darby said.

All eyes went back to Zack. He retold his story. "Someone was shooting to kill out there,' he said. "If Dom was out wandering on his own, I'd be concerned for him."

Shadows were already deep in the meadow. The pilot looked at his watch. "I have to get you gentlemen back," he said.

Darby took charge. "Climb in, everyone. I'll call the sergeant and let him decide what to do next."

There wasn't much talk on the trip back; it was too noisy to converse anyway. Zack used the half hour ride to think about recent events. They were right about Dom, he was sure of that now. The trooper must have been the inside man for one of the cartels. It made sense, how he volunteered to help Malden all the time. What better way to access information about ranger activities and marijuana crop locations? Dom must have figured Zack and Eagle Feather were on to him—or maybe he thought they would learn something if they caught up to the grower. Either way, it all began to make sense.

His mind went to the other problem, the mystery he didn't want to think about. Who or what was that giant Indian? Could the legend actually be true? Or was someone enacting the legend for his own purposes? No ordinary person, though. He'd need to be abnormally large and possess strength and agility beyond the greatest athlete anyone has ever known.

Zack shook his head, stumped, unhappy with his conclusions. He remembered his own words to the law enforcement students: once you've eliminated all other possibilities, whatever remains, however improbable, must be the truth. So deal with it, Zack told himself.

By the time the copter set down on the airport tarmac, Zack was no closer to answers. He jumped down from the craft...and came face to face with Rick Malden.

Rick stood on the tarmac supported by a crutch. He had a wide grin stretched across his face. "I had to see with my own eyes that you two characters are alive," Rick said. He had to yell over the noise of the blades.

The three men walked into the terminal together.

"How about a bite?" Malden said. "There's a nice little Mexican restaurant here."

Pepper Garcia's was near the baggage claim, at the south end of the building. They found it nearly empty— Happy Hour was a half hour away, the downstairs bar was empty. Malden steered them to a corner table in the restaurant. A waiter appeared at once with menus.

"You should try the shrimp fajita," Malden said. "But don't worry, everything here is good."

The waiter went to get their Margaritas, the men settled in to talk.

Zack gave an account of the long string of events of the day.

The Ranger's eyes grew wide as the story progressed. Malden did not interrupt even once; he sat perfectly still and listened.

241

After Zack described their narrow escape from the sniper in the hidden valley, he paused, glanced at Eagle Feather.

Malden waited. After a moment, he said, "Well? Did you catch the sniper?"

"No, we never caught him," Zack said.

"When we got back we found Dom missing," Eagle Feather said. "He didn't make the flight back."

"Dom's missing? Do you think this sniper got him?"

Before anyone could answer, the waiter was back. They gave their orders; she took them and bustled off.

Malden put the question again. "Do you think Dom's in danger?"

Zack fiddled with his knife. "You're pretty close to Dom?"

Malden stared at him. "We've known each other a long time."

Zack sighed. "You may find this difficult. We think it was Dom who shot at us."

Malden went pale. He scrutinized their faces, one after the other. "How can you possibly think that?"

Eagle Feather counted on fingers. "First, he had a long range hunting rifle with him, real fancy, probably scoped. I wondered about it when I saw that fancy case. Did he plan to hunt deer while the others investigated a crime scene?"

Zack leaned toward Malden, studied his face. "So far as Dom knew, all the cartel killers were dead, nothing but blood smears in the hills. The only folks left alive out there were an injured grower and some guy who helped him to escape. Dom knew that."

Eagle Feather held up a second finger. "We heard just two shots all day. One was aimed at us. The second we heard across the ridge from us. It was faint, but it was the same rifle."

Malden's face was a picture of doubt. "You don't know that was his rifle you heard. It could have been another cartel killer who shot at you first, then at Dom."

"Look, Rick," Zack said, "we won't say this to anyone else until the search team has a chance to locate Dom. We can't prove anything directly, not now, anyway. I wanted you to know what we believe, in advance."

Eagle Feather lifted up a third finger. "I found his footprints, right where the sniper stood to ambush us. I'm not guessing, I know."

Rick looked unhappy, but he agreed to keep this news to himself, at least until they saw the results of the search. The meal ended on a less jovial note than it began.

Malden dropped them off at the hotel with the promise to contact them the following morning. He wouldn't stay for a nightcap; he had a lot to think about.

The desk clerk signaled to Zack as they entered the lobby. "You have three messages, sir."

Zack glanced at Eagle Feather, his eyebrows raised. "I'm the man tonight."

The clerk handed him three folded slips of paper.

Zack read the first. *Please call Chief Barnard at your earliest convenience.* He opened the next. *Come by my room when you get back. Susan.* The final one read: *Please call. Rufus Reyes.*

Zack called Barnard as they walked down the corridor.

The sheriff sounded terse. "I thought you were going to keep me updated?"

"Uh, sure, Sheriff, I'll tell you what I can." Zack retold the events of the afternoon, omitted his knowledge of Dom and the giant Indian.

Barnard sounded mollified. "You got no idea who sniped at you, huh? Probably another of them cartel killers. They're crawling all over those hills now. You say Dom's missing? Well, I wouldn't worry too much. He can take care of himself. "

Zack rang off after promising to call Barnard more often.

They had come to Zack's room, he waved Eagle Feather inside, followed. He touched Rufus Reyes' number on his phone.

Rufus picked up after several rings.

"Rufus? Zack Tolliver."

"Zack, thanks for calling. I wanted ya to know one of my workers came down from the hills today. He's been lost and chased and all sorts of crap. They found him over at Rancho Sisquoc, dehydrated and wounded. I sent him to the hospital."

Zack struggled to keep the excitement out of his voice. "Where was he wounded, Rufus?"

"He has a badly swollen knee from crackin' it on somethin', and a big gash in his leg he says came from a rock. Looked like a bullet wound to me, though."

Zack didn't know what to ask first. "Who else knows about him?"

"Well, just my supervisor Jorge, I guess. He went and got him, then took him to the hospital for me. Why, does it matter?"

Zack was firm. "Yeah, Rufus, it really does. If we want to keep him alive, we've got to keep this to ourselves. Please tell your man Jorge not to say anything. What hospital is it? What's his name?"

"Whoa, there, podner, slow down. His name is Jesus sumthin', Romano, I think. We sent him to Marion. And yeah, I'll talk to Jorge. What's this all about?"

"I don't know as much as I should just yet. I'll just say there's been several murders, and I think there could be an inside man assisting the cartels, which is why we need to keep this to ourselves. Are you okay with that?"

"Uh, yeah, Zack, at least for now. I can't make any promises long term."

"I know that, Rufus. Just for now. I'll get back to you soon, I promise."

As soon as Zack rang off from Rufus, he called Barnard back. "George, listen, we need to put a guard on a hospital room. Can you arrange that?"

"What's happened, Zack?"

"I can't go into it all just now," Zack said. "He's a Mexican worker. He just returned from the hills and he may know something to help us. I'm going over there right now with Eagle Feather to see if we can talk to him." Zack paused. "This is important, George. People have been trying to kill this guy all over the mountains."

"Sure, Zack. I'll get hold of the Chief at Santa Maria PD. We'll get someone there right away."

"Thanks, George." Zack rang off. Without pause he punched another number.

Susan answered.

"Hello, Susan. We're back in the hotel, but something just came up. I'll be back in an hour or so. Can we see you then?"

"That would be nice," Susan said. "I'll be waiting."

CHAPTER THIRTY- EIGHT

At first the room spun, nothing would stay in focus. He waited; lay still until the double outlines merged into one. The room seemed too bright.

"How are you feeling?"

It was a woman's voice, in Spanish. For a dozy moment he thought he was home in Mexico. Somehow, he knew he was not. Jesus let his senses reassert themselves, fearful of what they might tell him. He was relieved to feel no pain. His eyes moved. He could see his toes beneath a white sheet. His right arm was at his side, a tube protruded from a bandage around his wrist. A thicker bandage with support rods encased his entire left leg.

"You had ligament tears, bruised bone, and a bad infection," the voice said.

Jesus slowly turned his head. The woman wore a white nurse uniform. She had a pale face with blue-green eyes surrounded by light brown hair. Jesus was surprised. Her Spanish was flawless. He had expected her to look Hispanic.

"Would you like some water?"

He was very thirsty, he realized. He nodded his head. The movement caused his head to ache.

"A simple yes might be best," the woman said in gentle reproof. "You're on drugs for the pain. You were seriously dehydrated." She poured water from a small pitcher into a paper cup, lifted his head with a hand beneath the pillow so that he could sip the water without spilling it.

The water was life giving. His energy returned. "Will my leg be alright?"

"I'll let the doctor explain. He'll be along after his rounds." She smoothed out the sheet. "A man from the FBI is here. He wants to speak to you. The doctor said you could talk for a short time after you woke up." She went to the door. "I'll ask him in."

Jesus felt a chill. The FBI? Wasn't that like the secret police?

The man entered the room. He looked perfectly normal, dressed in casual clothes, a pleasant face. He held out an open wallet with a card and a shiny badge. Another man was behind him. That man wore a black felt hat with a feather and had a dark complexion. Jesus felt a bit more comfortable.

The FBI man spoke in English, his voice calm and soothing. The darker man translated. "Good afternoon. I hope you are feeling better."

"*Si*."

The FBI man dragged a chair close to the bed, sat down. "You know, we're old friends."

Jesus stared.

"Yes," the man said. "We walked a long way together in the forest, you and I."

"I did not see you," Jesus blurted.

The man laughed. "No, I didn't see you, either, but I saw your footprints. I followed them a long way."

Jesus felt the blood drain from his face. He didn't respond.

"How is your knee?"

Jesus had forgotten his knee. His left hand went to it.

"Yes, it must have been most painful on that long walk," the FBI man said.

Jesus was confused. "How did you know?"

The FBI man smiled. "There is no mystery to it. I could see you favored your leg from your tracks." He leaned forward. "Someone shot you in that same leg. You were lucky; something turned away the bullet. Did you wear a brace?"

Jesus nodded. It all came back to him in a rush. He was afraid now, wary. "I did not hurt anyone."

The FBI man smiled. "Oh, don't worry, I know that. You are an innocent victim."

Jesus stared.

The man stuck out his hand. "I am Zack Tolliver. This is my friend Eagle Feather." The man named Eagle Feather translated, then nodded.

Jesus liked the feel of the man Zack's grip. It was firm.

"I am Jesus."

"I'm glad to meet you, Jesus," Señor Zack said. He crossed his legs, sat back. "Jesus, I'm curious. I followed you and your poor friend for two days; all the way from

the marijuana crop to the cave. I know what happened.
But I still have a few questions. Will you help me out?"

Jesus was depressed. This man knew everything.
He nodded.

"Who was the man helped you after you were
shot?"

"His name was Pablo."

"Did he work for the *narcotraficantes*?"

"*Si.*"

"The same *financiero* family that pays you?"

"*Si.*" Only after he spoke did Jesus realized he had
just made a full confession. His heart sank.

Señor Zack looked at him with a sympathetic
expression. "I am not here to put you in jail. I am here to
find the people who killed your friend."

Jesus nodded, felt hope rise again.

"What happened to the big man?"

Jesus's mind flew back to the gunshots, the scream
he heard outside the cave. "I do not know. I was in the
cave. I heard many shots. I heard Pablo scream."

The FBI man glanced over his shoulder at the
Indian, looked back at Jesus. "How did you escape the
cave?"

Jesus hesitated. It seemed a sacrilege to talk about
the angel. He did anyway. "The Holy Mother sent an angel
to me. The angel found me in the cave and took my hand
and led me away from there. It was a miracle. We flew over
the tops of the mountains. When I awoke, I was in a

vineyard. The workers found me." Jesus felt his eyes water. "Jorge came for me in the truck and I was safe."

"Jorge? Oh, yes, the supervisor at Mr. Reyes' Rancho."

"*Si.* Jorge is my friend."

"Did you tell your story to Jorge when he came for you?"

"*Si.*"

"Who else did you tell?"

"No one."

"Not even Mr. Reyes?"

Jesus shook his head. "No"

Señor Zack leaned toward him. "Someone wants to kill you. Do you know why?"

Jesus' mind was once again filled with horrible images from his near escapes. His eyes brimmed. "I have done nothing to anyone. Javier said the other cartel wishes us dead. That is all."

Señor Zack patted his shoulder. "You'll stay right here in the hospital until you are completely recovered. A policeman will guard your door at all times." He pointed to the Indian. "My friend and I will catch the person who tried to kill you. We will come back tomorrow to speak to you again."

Jesus looked at him.

"You help us out and we'll see what can be done to get you home."

Jesus again felt hopelessness surge toward joy. This time he held his emotions in check. He no longer trusted the feelings.

CHAPTER THIRTY-NINE

Susan's blue eyes were alive with curiosity when she welcomed her friends into her hotel room. She had engaged a large room, well appointed, with ample desk room for her work. Zack plopped down in the large sofa with a sigh. Susan joined him. Eagle Feather pulled a damask upholstered chair close.

"Have you learned more about our mysterious killer?" Susan said. She looked intently from one man to the other.

"And how are you? It's nice to see you too," Zack said.

"We saw him." Eagle Feather decided to put her out of her misery.

"You saw him," she breathed.

"You were right on," Zack said. "He is an Indian, a really big Indian."

"We caught him in the act." The two men were like boys eager to be the one to tell the tale. "He strung the man up, just as we surmised, emptied out the body cavity, butchered him, fed his entrails to the birds, and carted him off."

Susan breathed deeply, her eyes glistened.

"Unfortunately, the man happened to be a state trooper," Zack said.

"A policeman," Susan said. She gasped. "You saw all this?"

"We were a captive audience," Eagle Feather said.

"Oh, I wish I'd seen this thing," Susan said.

"Thing?" The men surveyed her.

"You saw it. Do you really think it was an Indian with a thyroid problem?"

Eagle Feather lifted his eyebrows. "You think it's a shape-shifting creature."

"Well? Think of the size, the strength, the appearance and then disappearance of this Indian. Neither of you could track it successfully." Susan looked from one man to the other.

Zack stared. "We're back to the alternate species."

"Exactly. We know they're out there. We don't always know what form they take." Susan was excited.

Eagle Feather looked at Zack. "We tend to consider such creatures as we would animals, expect them to all look alike and act alike. Shouldn't they be more like humans with their own minds, own personalities? This Indian, if it actually is one of those creatures, might just be a solitary individual who loves the mountains, loves to hunt, and doesn't want people poaching on his ground."

"We could surmise that these creatures all share the ability to shift shape. It would explain how they've survived all these years undetected," Zack said.

Susan continued the thought, her excitement palpable. "Just like humans, there would be good ones and evil ones." Her mind whirred on. "There can't be too many of them, or we'd know more about them. But there must be families of them, hidden away."

"With shape-shifting capability, they could hide in plain sight." Zack pointed out. "You could be one, Susan."

"I think White Man is one," Eagle Feather said. "He's pretty shifty."

Zack grinned, held up a hand. "We're getting a little carried away. Our immediate problem, believe it or not, isn't this Indian, it's the humans who initiated this drug war." He peered at Susan. "We're pretty sure this trooper the Indian killed, Dom, was connected with the cartels in some way. He tried to kill us today to prevent us from learning something."

Susan grabbed Zack's arm. "He tried to kill you?"

"We were lucky. The danger isn't over, though. There is someone in a high position who helps one of the cartels. He doesn't want us nosing around either."

"How do you know this?"

"The cartel assassins we've followed have information they could only acquire from a ranger or law enforcement administrator. They knew spot-on where to find the marijuana grows—and us, for that matter."

"We've not told anyone what happened to Dom," Eagle Feather said. "That's our ace in the hole. All they know is he is missing. Only Rick Malden, the ranger, knows we believe Dom tried to kill us."

Zack nodded. "The other link is the Mexican worker in the hospital. He knows more than he thinks he knows. They've tried to kill him too." He glanced at Susan. "We've got him under guard."

"What will you do now?"

"We'll wait," Zack said.

CHAPTER FORTY

Jesus had a headache. The nurse showed him where to squeeze the tube in his arm if he needed more pain medicine. He did it now. He lay back and waited for it to take effect.

The guard was outside his door. He'd poked his head in to introduce himself after the FBI agent left. The man spoke passible Spanish, which made Jesus feel better.

Jesus tried to sort it all out in his mind. What he didn't get was why, or who. Why did the FBI man think he needed protection? Who would want to kill him? He wasn't in the mountains anymore, no threat to anyone.

Señor Zack said he'd be back to talk to him. Maybe he could answer those questions. Meanwhile he'd wait, try to be patient.

Jesus felt surprisingly good, despite his leg. Sure, his head ached and the knee still sent needles of pain when he moved it. He felt well enough to climb aboard a plane, though. That's all he wanted to do.

He listened to the sounds of the hospital, the swish of soft-soled nurses coming and going, the quiet hum of voices, the click of bottles in the carts, the rattle of dishes. Everything was hushed, subdued.

He looked around the room for the first time. It was spare. His eye roved to a plastic curtain across the room. Another patient. He hadn't noticed. He looked the other way, saw a tall metal table set out from the wall, his personal items on it, beyond it the open bathroom door, a sink. His bed faced a TV screen hung high up in the corner. There was a clock over the door. It was 5 PM.

The nurse appeared in the doorway, smiled, came to his side. "How are you feeling?"

"Better." Jesus said.

"You should stay still for a while yet." The nurse busied herself with his fluid bag. "I came to tell you my shift has ended. The night nurse will be in shortly to take your dinner order." She smoothed his sheets. "Has the doctor been in?"

Jesus thought, realized he hadn't. "No."

"I'm sure he'll be here soon." She beamed a warm smile. "I'll see you tomorrow." She swished out the door.

Confined, his pain medication kicking in, Jesus became logy. His lids crept down. He dozed.

When he awoke, the clock over the door said 6 PM. His stomach churned. The night nurse hadn't taken his order; maybe her shift hadn't started. He was hungry now.

He reached for the button to summon the nurse; something made him pause. Outside, the corridor was silent. The nurse's chatter, people walking, bottles clinking; all gone. He became still, listened for any indication of human presence out there—heard nothing. He tensed, sat

258

up. His head felt like an empty room with dull pain bouncing off its walls. He looked at the clock. 6:05 PM.

There'd been no noise since he awakened. Not a sound in this large, busy hospital for a full five minutes. He did not think that was normal, not even for the night shift. A lurking fear clutched his mind.

He called to the guard in a loud whisper. "Señor?"

No answer.

"Señor, are you there?"

Still nothing.

Something was wrong.

Jesus didn't wait. He pulled the bandage off his wrist, removed the intravenous needle. A bright red dot blossomed on the sheet. He climbed from the bed, careful, wary of pain, moving as if a glass balanced on his head. He crept to the door, his hospital booties noiseless, inched his face around until he could see into the corridor.

The chair against the wall was empty. The corridor stretched far away in either direction, a glistening tunnel of white light. Nothing moved. Part way along, the nurses' station jutted out; even there he saw no movement, heard no rustle of paper, clicking of keys—no sounds.

Jesus ducked back into his room. He tried to tell himself not to worry, to go back to bed, but he couldn't. All his internal alarms sounded. Something was very, very wrong.

They were coming for him, to finish the job. That was it. There wasn't much time. He dared not try to escape along the corridor for fear he'd run into the arms of the assassins. Nor was there a way out from the window, even if he could get it open.

He had to think of something else.

He turned to his bed, pulled the sheets taught, folded them over crisply, fluffed the pillow. The bed must look unoccupied. He removed the water pitcher, cup, paper towel, everything the nurse put on the tray table for him, hid them in the bathroom. He rolled the empty table back against the wall, pushed the intravenous feed stand deep into the corner. Then he lowered the bed, flattened it out.

He glanced at his roommate's curtain. There'd been no sound from the patient. He peered around the divider, saw a balding head; the patient's back to him, on his side, apparently asleep. Jesus removed the medical chart from the foot of the bed, replaced it with his own. He hid the other patient's medical chart in the bathroom. His eyes flew around the room, he thought hard. It would have to do. Jesus grabbed his bedpan, crawled under his bed, placed the pan between himself and the door, lay still. He waited.

Jesus had no sense of time, no idea how long he lay there. Someone was in the room now. There had been no sound. Jesus saw running shoes, orange and black, frayed cuffs of jeans. The feet paused just inside the door, slightly apart, facing Jesus. His heart thumped.

There was a soft metallic click, a slight sound of metal brushing metal. The feet moved to the next bed, disappeared. Silence hung. Then it came: *pffft* and another *pffft*, followed each time by a low thunk.

The shoes returned, came directly to the foot of his bed, faced it, stayed there. Jesus thought the thump of his heart against the floor would give him away.

He heard another sound of metal brushing metal, another click. Jesus closed his eyes, waited.

The feet turned, walked briskly out of the room.

Still Jesus waited. Was it a trick? Would the killer return, catch him unaware? Four or five minutes passed, hour-like. Nothing. Jesus could wait no longer. He had to get out of this place.

He crawled out from under the bed, looked for his clothes, had another thought. He went to his roommate's closet—found jeans, a collared shirt large enough to squeeze into, leather boots. He should look different; whoever tried to kill him might still be around. He pulled on the strange clothing, tried not to look at his roommate's bed, did anyway. Red encroached on white beneath the man, spreading. Jesus walked away. He crept from the room, found a stairwell, went down it two stairs at a time. His head throbbed at every step.

The bottom door opened to a maintenance area. A straw hat hung on a hook. He put it on his head, pushed out the side door. He blinked in the sudden glare.

There was one person Jesus thought he could trust. He walked south, toward Santa Lupita.

CHAPTER FORTY-ONE

They didn't have to wait long. Susan had just begun another speculative discussion about the giant Indian when Zack's phone vibrated. It was Barnard. Zack listened to his news. He put his phone down, stared at Eagle Feather, stunned. "Damn."

"What now?" Eagle Feather said.

"That was Barnard. Someone just killed Jesus. Shot him to death right there in the hospital."

Eagle Feather breathed in. "Where was the guard?"

Zack was angry. "Barnard said they hadn't got around to posting one yet."

"So. The last possible witness against an inside man is gone," Susan said.

"I should have stayed. I should have stayed right there until the guard was set."

Eagle Feather shook his head at Zack. "White Man, you take yourself too seriously. There was no way to know they wanted Jesus that badly."

Susan nodded, shrugged. "They took a huge risk."

Zack couldn't excuse himself. He'd been a step behind this entire investigation. Meanwhile, bodies piled up all around him. Now there was nothing to be done. As Susan pointed out, the last witness was gone, their last clue erased.

Zack's phone rang again. He looked down at it, reluctant, picked it up. It was Barnard again. "Yeah?" He listened to the sheriff. His eyes widened. He put down the phone, shook his head in wonder. "You're not gonna believe this. Barnard now says the dead guy isn't Jesus after all. He says Jesus shot the man in the next bed and ran."

The three sat in silent amazement.

"What...why would he do that?" Susan said.

Zack shrugged.

"Where would he get a gun?"

Eagle Feather regarded Susan. "Not from the guard. There wasn't one." He turned to Zack. "What does Barnard think?"

Zack stood, agitated. "He seems to think Jesus is more involved with the cartels than he let on. He thinks they smuggled a gun in to him somehow. Jesus shot the bedmate because he was a witness." He eyed Eagle Feather. "What do you think? You saw Jesus."

"I think he was scared. He really didn't understand why someone wanted to kill him. I don't buy it."

Susan looked from one to the other. "What do you think happened?"

"I don't think Jesus shot the man, but someone did. That means an assassin came to the room. Why?" Zack ticked a finger. "We know someone wanted to kill Jesus. We don't know anything about the guy in the other bed. Did someone want to kill him too? That's a bit too much of a coincidence." Zack shook his head. "No, someone killed the wrong man. Jesus escaped somehow."

Eagle Feather nodded in agreement. "What could Jesus possibly know that makes him so dangerous to these people?"

"I don't know." Zack headed for the door. "There's only one guy who can tell us. Jesus himself."

"Where're you goin'?"

"I'm gonna find him."

Eagle Feather stood. "Here we go," he said under his breath. He looked at Susan. "Coming?"

The sun was low in the sky. The heat of the day lingered. Zack kept the car windows open; put the AC on low.

Eagle Feather raised an eyebrow at Zack. "You got a plan?"

"Of sorts." Zack brought up a city map display on the dash screen. "If Jesus left the hospital grounds, and I think he did, he'd have nowhere to go except back to Rufus' ranch. It's the only place he knows that's safe. So assume Jesus headed south. The most direct way from the hospital is Main Street." Zack pointed to it on the map. "We're on Broadway, about four blocks away from the hospital. How long do you figure it would take him to walk those four blocks on his bad leg?"

Eagle Feather rolled his eyes. "Talk about long shots. Okay, I'll play. Let's call it ten minutes. Add another five or so for him to escape his floor and leave the hospital grounds. If we assume Barnard called us right away, Jesus should have hit this intersection about twenty minutes ago."

"So turn left?"

Eagle Feather chuckled. "Yeah, turn left."

The light at the intersection took forever to change. At the green arrow, Zack made a wide left turn. He stayed in the right lane and drove slow. The three scanned the sidewalks. The buildings were larger south of Broadway, more industrial. The sidewalks were wider, more open.

Eagle Feather whistled under his breath. "I don't believe it. Look. See that guy with the hat pulled low in the tight jeans? Isn't that him?"

Zack looked. The man walked with a distinct limp. "I'll pull up beyond him and park. We'll wait for him. I don't want to startle him into running."

They pulled up opposite a Hyundai dealership and parked. All around them were large windowless buildings with huge parking lots. There was nowhere to hide.

When Jesus came abreast of him, Eagle Feather stepped out. He said in Spanish, "Jesus. Remember me? I'm Eagle Feather. I was with the FBI agent in the hospital. I'm here to help you."

Jesus looked up, startled, turned as if to run.

"*Espera¡* Wait. We are here to help you."

Jesus paused.

Susan stepped out of the car. Her presence seemed to quiet him.

"There is nowhere for you to go. The killers will find you," Eagle Feather said. "If you come with us, we can save your life."

265

Jesus looked suspicious. "You said I would be safe in the hospital."

"We thought so. We didn't know we shouldn't trust people."

Jesus didn't move.

Susan laid a hand on his arm.

"No one will know you are with us," Eagle Feather said. "Agent Tolliver will protect you."

"How did you...?"

"Jesus, we can't stand here in the open. We will be seen. When you are in the car, we can explain along the way." Susan held the rear door.

Jesus' shoulders drooped, a defeated man. He climbed into the rear seat. Susan went to the other side, climbed in next to him.

Zack pulled out into the traffic. He looked in the rear view mirror at Jesus, smiled. "*¡Hola!*"

Eagle Feather introduced Susan. He turned to Zack. "Where will we take him?"

"Back to the hotel, I suppose. We can add a couple of items to his disguise, bring him in the back way." He paused. "We can't tell anyone else about this. We'll be harboring a fugitive until we get this straightened out."

CHAPTER FORTY-TWO

They decided Jesus should stay in Susan's room. If the inside man they sought suspected Zack of harboring Jesus, he was least likely to search her room. Susan would take Zack's room; Zack would sleep in Eagle Feather's extra bed.

Jesus was demoralized, on the edge of panic. Zack would have preferred to let him sleep, interview him in the morning, but time didn't allow this. It was critical they learn all they could from Jesus that evening. The four of them gathered in Susan's suite.

Zack wanted to include Rick Malden.

"Malden could be involved," Eagle Feather said.

Zack nodded slowly. "I know. I feel it's a chance we have to take. My instinct says he's clean."

"It's a risk." Eagle Feather glanced at Susan.

"Zack's instincts have kept me alive," she said.

"Okay, call him."

They made Jesus as comfortable as possible in an armchair, with a hassock to rest his foot. He was hungry. Susan offered him a Subway sandwich she had in the small fridge. Jesus demolished it in short order. When the last crumb of the sandwich was gone along with half a bottle of water, the interview began.

Zack knew very little Spanish, Susan knew some. Eagle Feather would have to translate.

"Will you tell us what happened in the hospital?" Zack said.

Still panicked, almost unable to talk about it, Jesus relived those moments. As the story unfolded, the listeners were filled with admiration.

"You did well," Zack told Jesus. "Not many people would have thought so clearly."

Jesus said nothing. He didn't feel the hero.

"Who wants you dead?"

Jesus responded to Zack with a mixture of fear and puzzlement. "I don't know."

"It is important we know everything. It is the only way we can help you and bring the killers to justice."

There was a knock at the door.

Jesus swung his feet down as if to run.

Susan held up her hand. "Don't be afraid, Jesus. The man at the door is our friend. He can help us."

Eagle Feather peeked past the security chain, saw it was Malden, let him in. He introduced him to Susan and Jesus.

Malden wheeled the desk chair over. He inquired about Jesus' family in Spanish. It was just the right touch.

Jesus' face lit up when he spoke of his wife and two little girls. "I could show you a picture, if I had my own clothes." His face fell when he realized the picture was lost.

"Let me tell you what's happened since we last saw you," Zack said to Malden.

The ranger listened without interruption. When Zack came to the part about Jesus' escape from the hospital, Malden gave the Mexican a respectful look.

"Pretty quick thinking there."

Zack studied Jesus. He spoke to him through Eagle Feather. "We need to know everything that happened to you, from the first moment you decided to come to America, until you went to the hospital. We need every detail."

Jesus began. It was the start of a long night. Zack wrote down names as they poured out: Sonora Cartel, Jorge, Candida, Raul. They interrupted Jesus frequently with questions.

As the night wore on, Susan's head nodded several times. Finally she dozed.

The men kept the small coffee maker steaming.

It was two in the morning when Jesus finished. The men sat in silence, absorbing it all.

"Let's adjourn to the other room and let Jesus and Susan get some sleep," Zack said. He gave Jesus strict instructions not to open his door under any circumstances. If someone knocked, he was to call Zack on his cell.

Zack let Susan into his room. She flopped down on the bed and went right to sleep.

Zack locked her in. They went to Eagle Feather's room and cooked up yet another mini pot of coffee.

"I heard nothing to implicate anyone but this Jorge guy," Malden said, and went to pour a coffee.

Eagle Feather watched him. "I heard nothing to suggest why anyone would want to kill Jesus."

"We're missing something here," Zack said. "Jesus must have seen, heard, or learned something important, maybe something about the inside man."

Malden glanced at them over his shoulder. "You two think Dom tried to kill you. Could he have been connected to the inside man?"

"Good thought." Eagle Feather went to join Malden at the coffee. "If we assume that connection, we can look at Dom's associates as a place to begin."

Zack rocked back in his chair, clasped his hands behind his head. "That opens a lot of possibilities." He peered at Malden and grinned. "Rick Malden, for one."

Malden sat on the edge of the bed with his coffee. He grinned back. "Should I confess now?"

The others chuckled.

"It's true I spend a lot of time with Dom," Malden said. "He's always Johnny-on-the-spot when I need assistance. I'm grateful to him. That's why I find it hard to believe he would try to shoot you."

Zack eyed Malden. "The inverse of that is he uses you to gain information."

"Yeah, he could do that, all right."

"Who else does Dom hang around with?" Eagle Feather said.

Rick put his empty coffee cup on the bedside table, leaned back against a stack of pillows. "For a real fierce looking guy, he's friendly with a lot of people—my partner Jeremy Tusco, for one, and Barnard, of course. Then there's Darby and the other troopers." He sighed. "I dunno. It just seems like he's always around."

"I guess we know why, now," Eagle Feather said.

"What about Rufus Reyes?" Zack cocked an eyebrow at Malden.

"Rufus?" Malden shook his head. "I don't know that I ever saw them together, to tell you the truth. What made you think of him?"

"Jorge works for him."

Eagle Feather rotated the desk chair to look at Malden. "We know Jorge works for the Sonora Cartel. It seems obvious he helped recruit and manage people for them. Should we believe this Rufus is entirely unaware of that?"

"I just can't see it," Malden said.

"There's two things against that conclusion, in my book," Zack said. "First, Rufus is the guy who brought me into this. If he's guilty, that's a lot of hubris. Second, this man has no hubris."

"I agree with Zack. Rufus is just plain good-hearted. A guy like Jorge can flourish at his farm because Reyes will always believe the best of everybody." Malden shook his head. "No, not him. Speaking of him, Jesus says Jorge is the ranch manager now. I guess we better clue Rufus in."

271

Zack put up a hand. "No, not yet. We need to keep all our cards close to our chest until we know more."

Malden got up, rolled the chair back under the desk. "I'm goin' home. My brain stopped workin' an hour ago."

Zack stood, shook his hand. "We've got a lot to think about. Let's get back together tomorrow morning, talk some more. Dining room? Eight o'clock?"

CHAPTER FORTY-THREE

Zack dreamed about a large swarm of bees, woke to find his phone vibrating on the bedside table. He looked at it. It told him 7 AM. He groaned. It also said California State Police.

He answered it. "Zack Tolliver."

"Hello, Agent Tolliver, sorry to wake you. My name is Jeff Montana. I'm sergeant in charge of the North Santa Barbara County State Police district. I'd like to ask you some questions. Can you meet us in the lobby?" The voice was strong and officious.

"When?"

"Right now."

"I'll be right down," Zack said. He washed up, splashed cold water in his eyes, dressed. He tugged at Eagle Feather. "The state troopers want to talk to me. They'll want to talk to you sooner or later. You might as well get dressed and meet us down in the lobby."

Eagle Feather looked at his watch. "Three hours sleep. Great."

Zack stepped out of the elevator, walked to the lobby.

Darby stood near the front desk. He waved. "Hi, Zack. Jeff is in the dining room. Come join us for some coffee."

Zack followed Darby to the table.

Sergeant Jeff Montana was a stocky man, crisp blue eyes in a block-like face. He rose, grabbed Zack's hand. "I'm sorry to disturb you so early, Agent Tolliver. As you know, we have a trooper gone missing. We've still had no word from him. I'm quite concerned." He sat down, motioned Zack to an empty seat.

The rich aroma of fresh-brewed coffee was in the air, smelled mighty good to Zack.

Montana leaned toward him. "I've got a search team going out with Darby here and his forensic team. Bruce can steer them part of the way." Montana pushed an empty cup toward Zack, signaled the waiter. "Coffee, Zack?"

Zack nodded.

The man arrived with the coffee pot, poured.

"Have a couple of sips," Montana said with a knowing grin. "I can talk while you drink."

Zack sipped the strong brew.

"Darby tells me you and your friend—Eagle Feather, is it—heard rifle shots. Could be it was Dom, could be he was at the ass end of them. Either way, I'd like to establish where they were fired. What do you think?"

"We heard two shots," Zack said. "The first one was directly at us. Have you got a topo?"

"Happens I do." Montana reached for a briefcase and took out an iPad. He flipped it onto its stand, touched the screen, angled it for Zack. "That X right there is where the helicopter landed. Here is where the body was, and

274

right over there is where the blood is. Can you show me where you were when you heard those shots fired?"

Before Zack could respond a hand reached past his shoulder, a finger landed on the map.

"We were right here when we were shot at," Eagle Feather's voice said.

"Meet my friend Eagle Feather, Sergeant."

The two men shook hands. Eagle Feather sat down in the empty chair next to Zack.

"Please go on, Mr. Eagle Feather."

Eagle Feather grabbed Zack's coffee cup, took a sip before he spoke. "Zack and I had just found another blood pool, right about here." His finger pointed. "After we took fire, I went back there to get a rifle that had been left by the victim. That's when I heard the second shot. It came from over this way." Eagle Feather moved his finger up the slope.

"From where I was, it sounded over here," Zack said. "I thought someone shot at Eagle Feather."

Montana marked each position with a virtual flag. "So best guess from each of you is about here." He pointed to the marker.

They nodded.

"Okay, then, that's where we'll search." Montana stood. "We've got to get the operation under way. You gentlemen stay and enjoy some breakfast. It's on me." He started to walk away, turned back. "Oh, and gentleman, please don't leave town until this little affair is sorted out."

When Montana and Darby were gone, Zack looked at his watch. "We're early for our meeting, but two thirds of us are here already. Let's wake Malden."

Malden griped and moaned, but agreed to join them.

Zack peered at Eagle Feather over his coffee. "I wonder what Sergeant Montana's gonna think when they find the blood and Dom's rifle?"

"Not good thoughts, I'd say. We better get ready to become suspects."

"Yeah, I thought of that. It shouldn't last, though. Sooner or later, they'll figure we couldn't have been responsible for all those blood spills."

Malden arrived fifteen minutes later, bleary eyed, sluggish. Zack poured him a coffee. They put in their breakfast orders.

"Something occurred to me last night," Zack said. "When Barnard first called us, he said it was Jesus who had been killed. He called later and changed the story. I got to thinking about the timing. You figure the body is discovered, the Santa Maria police are notified, they come check it out. Then, maybe someone calls Barnard." Zack glanced at his companions. "Barnard isn't directly involved, don't you see? A murder in a Santa Maria hospital belongs to the Santa Maria police department. Barnard is pretty far down the chain, just a courtesy call, really. By the time he gets a call, they should have sorted out the mistaken identity, even with the charts switched. Any nurse on that floor would recognize the dead man. So how is it Barnard thought Jesus was killed?"

"That's right," Malden said.

"You're saying Barnard knew about it before the Santa Maria police." Eagle Feather stared at Zack.

"Which couldn't have happened unless—"

"Unless whoever notified Barnard was the killer." Zack finished for Malden.

Malden let out a breath. "That's it. Whoever called Barnard must be the inside man."

"Unless Barnard himself is the inside man," Eagle Feather said.

They stared at each other.

"We have to consider every possibility," Zack said, after a moment. "From what Jesus told us, two people knew he was in the hospital. Rufus sent him there, and Jorge took him there. Did they tell anyone else about Jesus?" He picked up his phone. "I wonder who called Barnard?" He redialed Barnard's number.

"Good morning, Zack."

"Morning, George. Sorry to bother you so early."

"Eight-thirty isn't early for me," Barnard said. "What can I do for you?"

"I'm trying to establish the chain of events yesterday for my report. Who told you about the shooting in the hospital?"

There was a moment of silence. "That was a courtesy call from Chief Daniels, of the Santa Maria police."

"Both calls?"

"Both...oh, yeah. Both. His guys had the wrong ID the first time they called. Something about the med charts being switched." Barnard chuckled. "Who'd a thunk this Mex was that clever?"

"Thanks, George, I really appreciate this. One more question: how long after they called you did you call me?"

Barnard hesitated. "Zack, is something going on here?"

"I'm constructing a chronology for my report. I'm sorry to be a pain in the ass."

Barnard sounded brusque. "I was tryin' to be a nice guy by calling you. Didn't know that meant I'd be interrogated." He paused a moment. "I know—you gotta do it. You feds are sticklers for nickel and dime detail. No problem, really. I confess I didn't call you right away the first time. It might have been ten minutes before I got to you. But the second time was as soon as I learned of the mistake." He chuckled. "I didn't want you to put the wrong info in your report."

"You've been a great help, George."

Zack put away his phone, glanced at the other two men. "He says he waited ten minutes before the first call."

Malden scratched his head. "So assume the empty bed and the dead guy are discovered by the nurse, who notifies his or her supervisor, or whatever the protocol is, who then notifies the police. The police investigate, update their chief. I doubt he calls Barnard first thing—courtesy calls would come later, no matter how great buddies they are. It seems to me this mistaken identity would have been cleared up long before that."

Zack nodded.

"Why not call Rufus, see who he told?" Eagle Feather suggested. "Let's not give anyone time to think up a story."

"Good idea." Zack called Rufus. The phone rang several times, went to an answering service. Zack didn't leave a message.

The waiter came with their orders. They ate with gusto. Lack of sleep seemed to encourage a big appetite.

Zack's phone rang.

It was Rufus. "I see you called me?"

"Yes, thanks for calling back, Rufus. I know you're busy; let me cut right to the chase. Did you tell anyone you sent Jesus to the hospital?"

"Uh, no, I don't think so. My supervisor knew, of course, 'cause he took him. I...oh, wait. I did tell one of my girls, a worker, Candida. She was friendly with Jesus, asked after him a number of times. Jesus took her side after my old sup raped her, she's the reason I had the guy arrested. So, yeah, I told her to ease her mind. Why, was this a secret?"

"When did you tell her?"

"Had to be around noon, when they took their break. What's goin' on, Zack?"

"There was a shooting in the hospital. His roommate is dead."

279

"Christ."

"Exactly."

"What about Jesus. Is he okay?"

"Nobody knows. The cops think he killed his roommate, then bolted."

"Jesus? No way."

"You sound very sure."

"He just doesn't have it in him. He's a gentle guy who's had to react to everything around him. All he wants is to go home to his wife and kids."

"Maybe he has," Zack suggested.

After the call, Zack peered into his friends' curious faces. "He told one person, he says, this worker named Candida. She'd been asking about him. He told her around noon. She must have gone back to work after that, but might have had time to call someone." Zack sighed. "Now we've got four possibilities."

"Isn't Jorge the most likely leak?" Malden said. "After all, we already know he's involved with the cartel."

"He might have leaked, but he couldn't be the shooter. He knows what Jesus looks like," Eagle Feather said.

Zack nodded. "We're not much better off than we were. Jesus is the key. We need to find out what it is he knows that is so important to someone he's determined to silence him."

CHAPTER FORTY-FOUR

Jesus had never slept so well. Despite his fear and the uncertainty of the previous night, blessed blackness enveloped him the moment his head hit the pillow. He slept long; when he awoke his knee felt better. By now he was almost used to disorientation at the moment of awakening—the total darkness, air conditioner thrumming, blanket and soft sheets womb-like around him did not come as a surprise.

Jesus luxuriated for several minutes, at last hauled himself out of bed. He opened the blinds. Bright sun rushed in. A small stack of neatly folded clothing waited on the desk chair: socks, underwear, jeans, a shirt—everything for the day. In the shower warm water ran over him, cleansed his spirit along with his body. The clothing was fresh and clean, a bit tight, but would do. His knee hurt to bend; it took a while to pull on the pants.

Dressed, Jesus wondered what he should do next. The FBI agent warned him not to venture out of the room.

The bedside clock said 8 AM. He was very hungry. He remembered Señor Zack had left a card with his cell number. Jesus found it on the bedside table. As he reached for the phone, a knock sounded at the door.

Susan's voice came to him in broken Spanish. "Jesus, it's Susan. I need my clothing."

He peered out the peephole. It was Susan. He opened the door to the chain, made sure she was alone, let her in. Only then did he remember the FBI agent insisted he call his cell before he opened the door.

Susan locked the door behind, reset the chain. She smiled at Jesus. "I just need to gather a few of my things."

"*Sí*," he said, nodded his understanding. "I am hungry."

"Oh, poor man. Of course you are. I'll have some breakfast sent up." She walked to the bedside table. Before she could lift the receiver a knock came at the door.

"Room service."

Susan looked at Jesus in surprise. "Did you call room service?"

Jesus shook his head, stared from Susan to the door.

"Just a minute," Susan said. She grabbed Jesus by the arm, pulled him to the wardrobe. "Quick, get in here."

It was tight. Jesus had to scrunch. A hotel bathrobe hung from a hanger; he spread it in front of him. Susan closed the doors. A moment later he heard the sound of the room door latch. The next noise was an impact against the door, rending wood, the chain rattling, a short cry from Susan, sounds of a struggle. Men's voices spoke in low tones, muffled footsteps around the room. More talk, a groan as if lifting a heavy object, a door slam. After that, silence.

ZACA

Jesus trembled, couldn't stop himself despite the fear he'd make noise. His legs quaked from crouching. He thought the men were out there, it was a trap. He must stay in this closet, very still, for as long as it took.

CHAPTER FORTY-FIVE

After breakfast, Eagle Feather wandered off in search of a morning paper. Malden drove home to freshen up and feed Toker. He'd wait for a call. Zack dialed his own room number, where Susan now stayed.

The phone rang and rang. Zack was surprised; he knew Susan had engagements today, he didn't think her appointments were so early.

Zack returned to his room. Once there, he splashed some water on his face, scrutinized it, decided he didn't need a shave just yet. He went to Susan's room, knocked on the door. When no answer came, he gave it up, walked on to her old room to check on Jesus. He knocked, three louds and three softs, the arranged signal, and waited for his phone to ring. It didn't.

Zack felt mild frustration. Nothing seemed to work out this morning. Maybe Jesus was sleeping in; he certainly deserved it. Zack had a key. He unlocked the door, pushed it open. Another surprise—the security chain wasn't on.

Zack's frustration turned to annoyance. His instructions had been clear. The man's life depended on these security measures, after all.

"Jesus." Zack looked around the room. It was light; the drapes open wide. The covers were thrown aside, the bed empty. "Jesus," he called a bit louder. The bathroom door was open. It, too, was empty. What the hell...?

Zack surveyed the room from the bathroom door. Everything was as he left it last night. How could Jesus be so careless? Where had he gone? Had he run again? He called Eagle Feather.

"Yeah?"

"Get up here right away. Jesus is gone."

"Gone?"

"Yeah, gone. I'm standing in the room. The security chain wasn't engaged—the place is empty. The clothing I left on the chair for him is gone."

"Is he with Susan?"

"Nobody answered when I knocked on her door. I've got a key. I'll go take a look...wait. There's something written on this pad."

Zack leaned down to read it. The writing was a scrawl, words misspelled. It read: "*If U want the gurl alive don't talk to no one. Wate for call.*"

Zack breathed hard. "Eagle Feather, get here quick." He hung up, his head spun. He sat on the edge of the bed, stared at the note. This didn't make sense. Why Susan? Why had the note been left here? Where was Jesus?

Eagle Feather appeared in the door.

Zack pointed at the pad.

Eagle Feather came and read it. He grunted. His eyes widened. "Where's Jesus?"

"I don't know."

"Have you been to Susan's room?"

"No, not yet."

They left, walked down the corridor to Zack's old room. Zack knocked again, this time loud and insistent. When no one answered, he used his key to get in. The room smelled of Susan, but she wasn't there.

At the late hour their meeting adjourned last night, they were too tired to carry anything beyond necessities to their new rooms. Most things in the room belonged to Zack. They saw a change of clothes Susan had piled on the chair. The bed covers were thrown back.

"Wherever she is, she's still in her nightclothes," Eagle Feather said.

"I see no signs of a struggle." Zack walked to the door. "The chain catch isn't broken or even bent, no sign of forced entry."

"They could have used some ploy to gain entrance. If they were professional, you wouldn't expect signs of struggle."

"Damn." Zack slumped into the chair. "What's going on here?"

Eagle Feather glanced at him. "Do you think this is about Jesus, or something altogether different?"

"I'm no believer in coincidence. Jesus is gone, too. Maybe he somehow knew they were here, ran, got away."

Eagle Feather inspected the carpet near the door, shook his head. "Nothing." He glanced at Zack. "It's strange that with all your warnings last night, both of them were so careless."

Zack had other concerns. "We can't go for help with this. We can't take a chance they might hurt Susan, whoever they are. We don't know who we can trust anymore."

Eagle Feather sat down on the bed, studied Zack's face. "Only one person knows we had Jesus."

"Malden. I know, I thought of that. I just can't believe it."

"He sat with us at breakfast. What better way to keep an eye on us while his men kidnapped Susan."

Zack slapped his forehead. "I can't believe how stupid I've been. You warned me about trusting Malden."

Eagle Feather got up, walked to the window. "What I don't get, why kidnap Susan if they already have Jesus? What do they need Susan for? Jesus is the one they've been trying to kill."

Zack shook his head. "Maybe they think we still have Jesus. Whatever it is, they want something from us. Susan is their leverage." Zack stood. "Let's go back to the other room and do another look around. I'll put that note in a Ziploc, send it to our lab in Arizona. Maybe we can get a print. It's not gonna help us right now, but..."

They closed and locked the door behind them, walked back to the larger room. Zack bagged the note. They inspected the room closely this time.

Zack found a few specks of sawdust near the door. He looked up at the security chain; saw where the screws had pulled out. He gave a low whistle, showed it Eagle Feather.

"They forced the door."

"Why this room?" Zack said. "Why Susan's room? Did they come for her after all?"

He heard a sound. It came from the wardrobe. They walked softly to it. Zack stood beside the door; Eagle Feather flung it open, pulled aside the bathrobe.

Jesus crouched there, his face drained of color. He tried to rise, fell on the floor instead. Eagle Feather helped him to his feet, got him to a chair. Zack poured him a cup of water.

Jesus drank; spoke all in a rush.

Eagle Feather translated. "Susan was here. She came to get some things. Someone knocked on the door, said they were room service. She had Jesus hide in the closet. Jesus heard loud noises. He was afraid to come out, thought the men might still be here."

"They didn't search for him?"

Eagle Feather posed the question; Jesus shook his head.

"They didn't know Jesus was here," Zack said. It came to him all at once. "Otherwise, they would have looked in the closet."

"They came for Susan."

"Right. They knew we had Jesus, but didn't know where we had him." Zack gave a sudden grin. "That lets Malden off the hook. He knew Jesus was in this room."

"Then why Susan?"

"Maybe they hope to trade Susan for Jesus."

ZACA

There was nothing to do now but wait. Zack stayed in his room. He didn't think they'd use the house phone, more likely his cell. Regardless, he didn't want to chance missing the call.

The hours crawled by. Jesus kept occupied with a Spanish TV channel. Zack and Eagle Feather took turns napping; even forty-five minutes of sleep refreshed them. Zack's cellphone rang just before 2 PM. Zack grabbed it.

It was Sergeant Montana. "We found Dom." His voice was terse.

"Is he okay?" Zack tried not to sound too ingenuous.

"Not at all. The team found his fancy rifle next to a whole lot of blood. We won't know for sure if it's his blood until we get it tested. Regardless, we're treating this as murder."

"There's no body, like the others?"

"Yeah, just like the others. Like the one's you boys keep stumbling over."

Zack didn't reply.

"I want you and your friend to stay available."

"Are we suspects?"

"Of course not. You might be able to assist us, though." Montana ended the call.

Zack sent a meaningful glance at Eagle Feather.

"They found him, eh?"

"He says to stay available."

Eagle Feather grunted. "Seems we've got no choice, anyway." He lay back on the bed, supported by pillows. "They figure anything out we didn't already know?"

Zack gave a wry grin. "Even less."

His phone rang again. He looked. This time it was Malden.

"I expected to hear from you guys before this," Rick said.

"There's nothing to do right now but wait."

"Did Jesus have anything to add?"

Zack peeked at Eagle Feather as he spoke. "Still nothing to help us understand why someone wants to kill him. Right now, though, you might as well get some of your other work done. We'll call you if there's a break."

"Sure there's nothing else I can do? You want me to come interview Jesus? Maybe I'll have more luck." Malden seemed insistent.

"What Jesus needs most right now is rest. When he's more relaxed, he'll remember more. He's wound tighter than a piano string."

Malden rang off, said he'd be around if needed.

"You decided not to tell him about Susan." Eagle Feather peered at Zack.

"Not 'til I'm absolutely sure about him. I've made too many mistakes as it is." Zack climbed out of his chair, paced around the room. "We've had every call but the one we want."

Eagle Feather watched him. "Save your energy. You may need it later."

ZACA

The afternoon wore on. Around four o'clock Jesus told Eagle Feather he was hungry.

" I understand that much," Zack said, and grinned. "I forgot about lunch." He looked at Jesus. "Pizza?"

Jesus nodded his head eagerly.

Zack glanced at Eagle Feather, grinned again. "The universal language." He reached for the house phone. "I'll order some up for us."

CHAPTER FORTY-SIX

Zack walked down to the lobby to pick up the pizza. He'd ordered two full size pies. There'd be leftovers, but he wanted to be sure everyone got enough. By the time he was back in the room and they began to eat, it was after five, nearly time for dinner.

After two bites, Zack's phone chirped for a text message. He put down his pizza, picked up the phone. "Here it is, men."

He read it aloud. "Go to GPS location. Bring Jesus and your Navajo friend. Tell no one or she dies."

Everyone stared at the phone. There was no need to translate for Jesus; it was easy to see he understood.

"It's Jesus they want," Eagle Feather said.

"It's all three of us they want. They've had Susan all day. They know everything she knows by now; therefore they know everything we know. Worse, they probably believe we know more than we actually do."

"Like what Jesus knows that we don't know."

Zack nodded. "Exactly—what Jesus doesn't know he knows. When we go to this GPS location, I don't think any of us are expected to walk away."

"You have a plan, White Man?"

"Not yet." Zack did a search with his smartphone. "Let's see where these coordinates put us." He brought up the results. "Zaca Lake, it says." He held up the screen. "Right there. It says it will take us 50 minutes from here."

Eagle Feather stood. "It'll feel good to do something, even if it does put us at the wrong end of a firing range."

Zack walked to the door, turned to Eagle Feather. "I'm going to get some things from my room. When I come back, you go get what you need. Explain to Jesus what's up; tell him it's strictly voluntary."

Eagle Feather raised an eyebrow. "We can't show up without the main man, can we? They'll kill Susan."

"They plan to anyway, along with the rest of us. Once we're all gone, there's no proof of anything."

Eagle Feather shook his head. "I'd sure like to know what it is they think we know. That would be some consolation, anyway." He turned to Jesus.

Zack went to his old room, took out his backpack, loaded it up. He removed his sidearm from the bedside table drawer, checked the load. He put on the shoulder holster, holstered the gun. His worn Stetson went on his head. He was ready.

When he returned, Eagle Feather told him Jesus insisted on going along. "I hope he understands, I explained several times."

Zack glanced at Jesus. The man returned his look with a steady gaze. Zack knew he understood, nodded his appreciation.

Eagle Feather went to his room to prepare.

Zack turned to the wardrobe, looked through it. He found the clothing Jesus wore when he ran away from the hospital. Zack took it all out, dumped it on the floor. He stuffed it into the hotel laundry bag. A full size pillow and two small decorative pillows from the bed went on the floor next to it. Jesus watched with a puzzled expression.

Eagle Feather returned with a backpack. He eyed the pile in the middle of the floor. "We don't really have time to do laundry."

Zack didn't smile. "Get me the laundry bags from the other rooms."

Eagle Feather returned with two more bags, dropped them on the pile. "I see you've come up with a plan."

"A partial one, anyway." Zack gave a tight grin. "We need to get all of this down to my rental without the hotel staff seeing us. Stuff the pillows in the laundry bags. We can each carry one."

At the rental, the backpacks went into the trunk, the laundry bags in the back seat. Zack ushered Jesus into the front passenger seat. Back at the open trunk, he pulled a handgun from his pack, gave it to Eagle Feather.

Eagle Feather took it, hefted it. "What is this, a toy?"

"It's a Beretta Nano. It's five inches long, and just an inch thick, so you can hide it almost anywhere. Drop it in your shirt pocket, if you want. It's a 9mm, plenty of power, but you're gonna have to get close."

Eagle Feather snapped the magazine release button to inspect the load. "Eight plus one? How many of 'em do you expect me to take on?"

"I don't want you to run short."

He closed the trunk and they walked around to the passenger side. Eagle Feather stood at the open door as Zack knelt to talk to both men. "They're expecting to see three people in this car. That's what we're gonna show 'em. Eagle Feather—give Jesus your hat. I know, I know, you never go without it. I'm hoping they know it, too. Jesus will ride up front here, like he's you."

Eagle Feather grinned. "I'll use the clothing and pillows to build a Jesus in the back seat."

Zack nodded. "You got it. When we get close enough, I'll let you out, give you time to locate them, get close. Then wait for us. When we approach, we'll stay just far enough away so they can't see us clearly."

"And then?"

"Play it by ear."

"Sounds good."

Zack drove and Eagle Feather went to work on the decoy. He explained the plan to Jesus. "You don't do a thing," he told him. "Stay in the car. If shooting starts, get down low. As long as you don't get out, we can keep up this ruse."

Jesus' eyes glistened with excitement.

Zack watched the Mexican. He's glad to have a chance to strike first for once, he thought.

The drive took less than fifty minutes. Zack slowed to allow Eagle Feather time to finish the dummy. The silhouette in the rear view mirror looked very real.

Foxen Canyon road wound past Zaca Mesa Winery then up a steep grade and over a rise. On the downhill side, Zack turned off. A gate blocked the road. "This is the way to the lake. It's five or six miles. This access road goes along the base of that ridge over there. We'll need to get close before we let you out, Eagle Feather. You'll want to stay on the ridge side of the road until you get close to the retreat buildings."

"How many buildings?"

"I can't tell, looks like several. There's the main lodge, right on the water. Cabins are spread out around the lake beyond it."

"Caretakers, campers?"

"There's gonna be at least a caretaker, they probably disabled him." Zack went to the website, looked up the retreat schedule. "According to this, there shouldn't be any guests, but we've got to be careful, just in case."

Jesus climbed out, opened the gate for Zack to drive through. They took it slow, watched the terrain, tried to assess their progress. It was coming on twilight, light enough to see, but detail blurred at a distance. After four or five miles the road split. Zack went left, close to the ridge. He glanced in the rear view mirror. "Get ready." After another tenth mile he slowed to a crawl. "Now."

Eagle Feather pushed open the rear door, rolled out as the car moved on. Zack reached behind his seat, pulled the rear door shut as he drove. The road looped around a sweeping corner, with cliffs to their left. Then the cliffs receded and they were in a wide valley. A lake came into view. Pine trees clustered near it.

"Okay, *amigo*, the fun's about to begin," Zack said.

CHAPTER FORTY-SEVEN

Jesus was terrified. He understood few of Señor Zack's words. He did know the FBI man intended to meet with the hombres who wished him dead. He did not believe the dummy in the back seat would save their lives.

The Indian man had told him he had a choice, whether or not to go with them. In his heart, Jesus did not believe this, but he did believe these men were in danger because of his own actions. It all began with his anger with the supervisor Rafael. If he had managed to hold his temper, none of this would have happened. Therefore he saw it as his duty to face these evil people, whoever they were.

At some point during his experience in the mountains, Jesus began to believe he would never return home to Mexico. He would die here. It had made his choice to join the FBI man and the Navajo easier.

Now the car inched along the gravel road. Shadows were long and deep. They approached a large building next to the lake. Señor Zack studied it as he drove. There was no sign of life. The large glass-paneled entranceway was closed, no light shone inside. Everything was deserted. Up the slope on their left another building came into view. It too looked deserted.

They drove on. The road continued along the lake. Here and there Jesus saw cabins peek out among the pines. The road forked. One side continued along the lake, the other angled toward the mountains.

Señor Zack stopped the car. He studied both roads. He glanced at Jesus. "I'm going to flash the lights. Someone is watching us now, you can be sure. Be ready to get low the moment I tell you."

Jesus understood the get down part. He watched tensely. The FBI man flashed his lights three times. They waited. Señor Zack sat still. He seemed very calm, peaceful, even.

Jesus felt his leg muscle quiver, tried to stop it.

He saw motion up the road to the left among the pines. A pickup truck was coming. It inched toward them, stopped fifty yards away. A man climbed out the driver's side, stood behind the open door. He reached into the cab, brought out a rifle. He held it in his right hand, the barrel resting on his shoulder.

Jesus could not see the man's face well, yet something about him was familiar. The man called to them.

"*¡Hola!* Jesus. Is that you, *mi compadre?*"

Jesus gasped. *Jorge.*

Señor Zack looked at him. "Do you know him?"

"*Sí.* It is Jorge. He is *mi amigo* from Señor Reyes' rancho."

"Not your friend so much, I'm thinking. Answer him."

299

Before he could respond, Jorge called out again. "Jesus? Is it you?"

Jesus stayed in the car, called out the window. "*Si,* Jorge, it is me."

Jorge lifted the rifle from his shoulder, waved it.

"Down!" Señor Zack said.

At that moment Jesus heard a loud impact in the rear of the car. Glass flew. Jesus turned to look in time to see the hat on the dummy fly off and the pillows slump away. Then the FBI man's hand was on his shoulder pushing him down. Jesus crunched under the dash.

"Jesus?" It was Jorge.

Señor Zack looked down at him, his finger across his lips. He opened his door, stepped out, stood behind it. "You got what you came for. Now where is Dr. Apgar?"

"You are a funny man," came the reply. "You are in no position to bargain."

Jesus watched Señor Zack calmly pull his handgun from his holster and check the load, concealed behind the door. Fascinated, as with a rattler about to strike, he peeked up over the dash. He saw Jorge once again wave his rifle.

"*Adios,* FBI man."

Jesus cringed, waited. Nothing. He felt his heart pound like a hammer. He saw Jorge step around his door toward the front of the pickup, wave again. The sound of a distant rifle followed the splatter of Jorge's head, a spray of blood. His body slumped to the ground.

A man Jesus had not noticed leapt from the passenger side of the truck, sprinted back up the road. Señor Zack steadied his pistol on the top of the door: two rapid shots, a bright dart of flame for each one. The running man fell.

Señor Zack glanced down at Jesus. "Stay there and stay down." He climbed back in the car, his door left open. He drove around the pickup truck, stopped next to the man who had run away, stepped out. He raised the man by his shoulders so Jesus could see without leaving the car.

"Know him?"

The man looked Hispanic. His forehead was a stew of blood and bone. He was a stranger. Jesus shook his head.

Señor Zack climbed back in his seat, inched the car along the road. He studied both sides as he drove. He spoke without looking at Jesus. "We're not out of this yet. Stay down unless I tell you otherwise."

They broke out of the pines. Jesus saw an open area on the right, a building on the left close to the road. The shadows were deeper now, the building dark. The FBI man drove with one hand holding the door, the other steering. His pistol lay on his lap. They crept past the building. The low murmur of the car engine and the throb of the exhaust were the only sounds.

A grassy area came into view, grew larger. Another building, dark and silent, inched by. The road ended at a large cabin. One window showed light. A hundred feet away, Señor Zack stopped the car. He turned on the headlights, left them to shine on the small front porch. He waited.

A minute later, the front door opened, a large man stepped out onto the porch. He sat down on the top step, looked directly into the headlights.

Jesus gasped. He knew this man. He was the gringo who unlocked the storage unit for Jesus and the dope smugglers that night so long ago.

CHAPTER FORTY-EIGHT

Zack watched the man walk across the porch, sit on the step. A large man, he moved with a familiar grace. It was Barnard.

"Hi, Zack." Barnard spoke in normal tones. His voice came clear to Zack. "I didn't expect you to make it this far, but I suppose I shouldn't be surprised." He patted the space on the front step next to him. "Come sit with me. I am unarmed. My man has your friend Susan in the cabin. We can chat for a moment. You have time, don't you?"

Zack spoke an aside to Jesus. "Stay down." He removed his gun, put it in the seat, stepped out of the car. He studied the nearby terrain, then walked down the headlights to the porch.

Barnard looked up. "You might have turned off those annoying headlights."

Zack grinned, sat down on the step next to Barnard. He turned toward him, rested his back against the post. "It came down to either you or Malden, in my mind."

Barnard chuckled. "Poor Malden. How could you think that even for a moment? He's the most earnest man I know."

Zack eyed him. "I assume you have a proposal of some sort?"

Barnard shook his head. "No, I think it best to wait and see what happens between your Indian friend and my man. Care to place a wager?"

Zack smiled. "Eagle Feather hasn't let me down yet."

"He must have talent."

Zack shrugged. "A bit."

Barnard stared into the headlights with a slight smile. "I suppose you left those lights on so I couldn't see into the your car. The question is: is Jesus dead or alive?"

Zack shrugged again.

Barnard studied his face. "I'm gonna guess alive. I think that's why the headlights are on." He looked away. "Well, that's okay. After my man is done with your friend, he'll finish the job."

Zack raised his eyebrows. "You're very confident.

"He's the best there is. I spent a lot of money on him."

"How's Susan?"

Barnard turned to Zack. "You know, she's a charming young woman—so knowledgeable. We've spent a wonderful day together." He sighed. "I do wish we'd maintained our original charade: simply enjoy one another's company, you drift away, I go about my business."

Zack peered at Barnard. "What is your business, exactly?"

Barnard stared at Zack for a moment. "I guess there's no reason not to tell everything. Soon one or the other of us won't be around to worry about it." He smiled. "You must know that a small town police chief doesn't make much money. If the town happens to be bankrupt, like Santa Lupita, there's simply not enough to survive. You know, Zack, it's very difficult to watch your department grow smaller each year, your resources shrink, everything you need to do your job disappear. Think about my family. I run an entire police department, yet I couldn't put a meal on my own table." Barnard shook his head. "It was unacceptable." He sighed. "When Jorge came to me with an idea, I knew it was the only solution for me."

"I wish I had a nickel for every story like that I've heard."

"That's your problem, Zack. You think too small. Nickels don't add up very fast." Barnard shifted his position. "The point is I really wanted to do right by my town. I wanted the town to have all the police protection it deserved; keep the gangs out, keep the streets safe. I knew about the drug trade, I'm not blind. It was gonna go on with or without me. Part of our deal was Jorge would keep the trade out of my town." He tapped Zack's arm. "Kinda ironic, isn't it? Santa Lupita is probably the only town on the Central Coast with no gangs and no drugs."

Zack nodded slowly. "So you helped Jorge, stored his drugs, allowed his boats to land, probably got him his job with Rufus?"

"Good old Rufus. His workers comin' and goin' really confused him."

"Then a rival gang tried to move in on your operation?"

Barnard raised his hands in protest. "Not mine. I'm just an employee. The marijuana crops in the National Forest were Jorge's idea. I was opposed. It made us vulnerable. The cartel was all for it, though. By then, I didn't have much choice. That's when I recruited Dom. He was a natural. He had a flair for cruelty, and he needed money. He already worked with the rangers from time to time." Barnard laughed. "He enjoyed busting the growers. He kept an eye on their activities for me."

Zack was confused. "But the rival cartel, the assassins. Where'd they get their information?"

Barnard raised his eyebrows. "The only thing more remunerative than a payoff from one cartel is from two."

Zack stared at him. "You played one cartel off against the other. That's ballsy."

"Yeah, it was delicate. Dom helped me with that. He'd tell the one cartel where to find the grow, I'd warn the other they were coming." Barnard paused. "You know, I think Dom might have been triple dipping. Someone started killing off the killers."

They both looked up at the sound of two shots, one after the other. They came from somewhere up in the pines.

"Handguns," Zack said.

"Two different ones," Barnard agreed. "I think we'll know which man is best soon."

306

Zack stared at Barnard. "You figure you can eliminate four people—one a distinguished college professor, one a not so distinguished FBI agent, a respected Navajo hunter, and one of Rufus' workers and go on like it's business as usual?"

Barnard sighed. "Probably not. Of course, I'd make it look like a cartel hit. With Jorge and the other Mex dead—they are dead, I expect—it gives the right flavor. Realistically, though, it will likely be time to retire. I've set aside a retirement fund that should suffice."

A man stepped out of the shadow of the forest. He walked slowly toward them, a rifle in the crook of his arm, a handgun in the other. Part way, he stopped.

It was not Eagle Feather.

Zack could not see the man's face; he did not look familiar.

Barnard chuckled. "I guess I win this wager." He lifted his voice. "Señor Brown, there is a man in that car who requires your attention. While you're there, please turn off those annoying headlights."

The man stood, looked at them.

"Señor Brown, did you hear me?"

The man didn't respond. Slowly his legs buckled, he fell to his knees. The handgun and the rifle fell from his hands. He pitched forward on his face.

That same moment Zack stared into the barrel of a small gun.

"I'm sorry, I lied," Barnard said. "I was armed, in case of something like this. I'll need you to remove your gun."

Zack slid his jacket open to show the empty holster.

"Ah, a trusting man." Barnard reached across, patted Zack's jacket pockets, swept his back under the jacket. "Very well." He turned his eyes toward the headlights. "You, in the car. Turn off those headlights. Come out where I can see you, hands in the air."

They waited. The headlights went off. After their bright glare, the opaque curtain of dusk turned black. When his eyes adjusted, Zack saw a man in front of the car. He wore a wide-brimmed hat with a single lopsided feather.

Zack groaned. "I told you to stay in the car."

"*¡Me disculpe!*" It was Eagle Feather's voice.

Some sixth sense warned Barnard. He stared, whipped his gun around; fired.

Everything happened at once. A bright stab of light came from Eagle Feather's position. Barnard spun behind the balustrade. Zack dove from the porch steps. He heard the thunk of a bullet hit the top step where Barnard had been seconds before. A muzzle flare and report came from Barnard's position, the car windshield exploded. Another shot from Eagle Feather, this time from the other side of the car. The creak and snap of the screen door—Barnard was inside.

Zack scurried to the corner of the cabin, heard Eagle Feather call.

"White Man, you forgot something."

He saw movement. Something arced into the air toward him, landed two feet away with a thud. Zack reached for it, pulled it to him, his Sig-Sauer. He checked the barrel for dirt, checked the load. The sound of breaking glass came from above and behind him, a shotgun blast. Zack felt the wind of it. He dove around the corner to the other side. Glass broke out of the other window above him, the shotgun roared. This time Zack heard a sound of punched metal—the car.

Zack fired two rapid shots up at the window. He was next to the building, the angle too steep to be effective. It silenced the shotgun momentarily, anyway.

"Cover me," Zack yelled, ran away from the cabin across the grass toward the woods. He heard rapid fire from Eagle Feather's gun. He counted to five, zigged left. The shotgun roar came. He heard the shot go by. More shots sounded from Eagle Feather. Zack saw the hired killer's body just ahead. He dove, rolled behind it just as another shotgun roar sounded. The shot whistled overhead.

Zack saw what he'd come for, the rifle. He stayed low, pulled it toward him. Another shotgun blast dug up the ground in front of him, sprayed the body with dirt. He checked the load in the rifle, laid the barrel across the body, sighted the window. He saw light reflect off something metallic, centered on it, pulled the trigger. There was a groan. The window was empty. There was silence in the cabin.

He heard Barnard's voice. "I'm coming out."

The car headlights came on, flooding the cabin porch with light. The screen door pushed open. Susan came through it, her hands bound in front of her, mouth gagged. Barnard came behind, pistol to her head, holding her close. He walked to the center of the porch, stopped in the full glare of light.

"Time to negotiate," he said.

CHAPTER FORTY-NINE

The windshield burst, sagged inward. Jesus tried to squeeze deeper into the foot well; there was no more room. He covered his head with his arms, held on. A shot sounded right next to him, at the driver's door. His ears rang with it.

He heard a voice. "Stay down, amigo."

He realized it was Eagle Feather. He saw a hand reach in, take the gun from the seat, heard him yell. A loud roar came from the house, a big gun sound. He heard glass break, more shots. Something hit the car, shook it. Shots sounded from the Navajo's position. He heard another loud gun, this one more distant. Then—silence. Jesus waited, terrified.

He heard the gringo in the house call out.

Eagle Feather's arm came into the car, pulled on the headlights.

Señor Zack's voice came from somewhere, his voice strong, authoritative.

The other man's voice again, insistent.

Jesus realized Eagle Feather was gone. He raised his head, tried to peer through the windshield. It was punched inward, a thousand tiny pieces held by hair-thin cracks, a hole in the middle. Jesus couldn't see. He needed to know what was happening. Despite his fear, he crawled across the seat to the driver side, raised his head inch by inch until he could see through the crack between the open door and the car body.

The car headlights shone on the cabin porch. The man from the house held the blonde woman Susan in front of him, a gun to her head. He didn't see Eagle Feather. He heard Señor Zack's voice come from the direction of the woods. He couldn't see him either.

Jesus felt a touch from behind. Startled, he whipped his head round. He gasped in surprise. It was Tomasa, his angel. She smiled down at him. He could see her clearly, even in the dark. She seemed to glow with her own light. Her face was soft with compassion and kindness. Jesus felt relief—Santa Tomasa had come to save him once again.

"Do not fear. You will be safe." She moved past him, seemed to glide across the grass toward the cabin.

* * * * *

"You are in no position to negotiate." Zack tried to sound confident, yet he was filled with fear for Susan. Barnard must see the end was near.

"I will kill her. Drop your weapons to the ground, clear away from the car. We are going to walk to it. If you don't do as I say, I will have no choice. I have nothing to lose. I will die here rather than become a prisoner. Your friend will be the price of my death. It's your choice."

Zack knew he meant every word of it. He sighted the rifle on Barnard's head, the only part of him he could

312

see. The shot was too uncertain, a chance he couldn't take. He looked toward the car, in hopes Eagle Feather might have a better vantage, couldn't see beyond the bright headlights.

"You know I can't let you leave," Zack said.

Barnard pushed Susan ahead of him, took a shuffling step across the porch, stayed tight to her body. "Your choice," he said again.

From the corner of his eye, Zack saw movement near the car. He risked a quick glance that way. His jaw dropped in surprise.

Tomasa stood there. Where the hell did she come from? Zack could see her clearly, almost as if she was illuminated by her own glow. She moved down the slope toward the cabin.

Zack returned to his aim, kept the rifle on Barnard's head. If he moved the pistol toward Tomasa he would shoot, regardless. He heard Barnard's surprised voice.

"Who the hell are you?" Then, "Don't come any closer."

Tomasa didn't stop. She kept coming.

In one motion Barnard clutched Susan's head tight against his shoulder with his right arm, took the pistol away from her head, pointed it at Tomasa.

Zack still had no shot.

There was a blur of motion. Zack saw Eagle Feather throw himself at Tomasa just as Barnard fired. Eagle Feather gave a cry, slumped to the ground.

"Eagle Feather." Moved by sudden rage, Zack jumped to his feet, charged down the slope. Barnard pushed Susan out of his way. She stumbled, fell down the porch steps. Barnard leveled his gun at Zack.

In those seconds during his blind attack Zack's brain registered several things: Eagle Feather seemed to fall *through* Tomasa, who came on completely unaffected, Barnard's gun was on Zack at point blank range, something huge loomed behind Barnard.

* * * * *

Jesus watched Tomasa move toward the cabin. He saw the gringo register her presence, saw his surprise, heard his harsh words. The man clutched the woman Susan closer to him, turned his gun on Tomasa.

Jesus did not consider himself a brave man. He forgot that now. When the man's pistol leveled at Santa Tomasa he ran to save her. Almost immediately his foot caught on turf and he sprawled forward on his stomach. From there he saw Eagle Feather leap at her. The man's gun sounded, Eagle Feather cried out, fell to the ground. Tomasa continued on as if nothing had happened.

The man pushed the blonde woman forward out of his way. She fell. He turned, pointed his gun up the slope at Señor Zack who ran right toward him.

He saw something else. Behind the gringo stood a giant figure, a huge man, with bare chest, in breechclout and leggings. Jesus never saw him arrive. The giant reached

314

a huge hand around the gringo's face, lifted him off the ground by his head. His other hand held a knife. He sliced upward into the man's abdomen—cut him open like a watermelon with one long slash. He held the gringo, feet dangling above the ground while he glared at Señor Zack, who stopped his charge mid-step. The giant turned his head to stare at Eagle Feather where he lay on the ground, then at Jesus.

When the giant's angry red eyes came to rest on him, Jesus felt a chill that froze his heart. The gringo's body twitched in the huge Indian's grip, his intestines slithered out of the gaping wound.

Señor Zack raised the rifle in his hand, aimed it at the giant. Santa Tomasa turned to him, lifted her hand and spoke words that Jesus couldn't hear.

As the giant glared at Señor Zack, it underwent a change. Its face became scaly, lizard-like, its nose lengthened into a snout, fangs emerged, red eyes glowed, arms turned to thin muscled appendages with claws, a greenish prehensile tail twitched. Its head was large, domed, the forehead high like a human's, its neck thick. In those red eyes Jesus saw anger, hate...and intelligence.

His glimpse of this monster was momentary. The apparition changed back in an instant, once again the huge Indian. The metamorphosis was so fast Jesus wasn't sure what he had seen. He watched in shock as it slung the gringo over its shoulder, stepped off the porch, and with one long leap disappeared into the darkness beyond the cabin.

* * * * *

Zack stopped his headlong rush when Barnard turned his gun on him. He had accomplished his purpose—to draw Barnard's attention away from the others. Barnard gave a small smile of satisfaction. Eagle Feather had given up his advantage to save Tomasa, now Zack had given up his to save Eagle Feather. The odds had changed in moments.

Zack's face must have mirrored his surprise when he saw the Indian. Barnard's smile vanished; he tried to turn his head—too late. A huge hand covered his face from behind, lifted his body off the ground. With deliberate precision, the Indian opened Barnard's abdomen with a great knife, as one would butcher a hog. Barnard's gun, now an afterthought, dropped to the porch floor. His eyes stared over the hand that held him, met Zack's with a look of bewilderment.

Zack raised his rifle. When he did, the Indian changed, and Zack saw the true monster within reveal itself at the threat. In those hostile red eyes he read intent, he knew he could not defeat it.

Tomasa's voice came to him, soothing, calm. "Put down your rifle, Zack. I will not let him harm you."

Zack did as she instructed.

At her voice the reptilian humanoid creature transformed back to the giant Indian. It lifted Barnard over its shoulder like a sack of potatoes, stepped off the porch.

ZACA

In a moment it was gone. The only trace left of Barnard was a pool of blood on the wood boards of the porch.

CHAPTER FIFTY

Zack ran to Eagle Feather. Tomasa had his head in her lap. The front of Eagle Feather's shirt was red with blood.

Zack knelt next to him, opened his shirt, cut away his undershirt. A small round hole bubbled red on the left side of his chest. Eagle Feather's eyes were closed; his breathing seemed regular.

"You've ruined one of your best shirts, my friend" Zack said, in a low voice. He spoke to Tomasa. "We've got to get him to a hospital."

"He will heal," she said.

Zack looked at the rental car. A hole gaped in the radiator, fluid dripped to the grass. "We won't be going anywhere in that car." He remembered Jorge's truck. "Stay with him, please," he said to Tomasa. "I'll go get the truck."

"Your friend will heal," Tomasa said again.

Her insistent confidence soothed Zack. "I hope so." He ran across the lawn, down the drive. It was farther than he remembered. Nearly dark, the roadway had become a tunnel beneath a roof of fused atramental branches. Zack stumbled once where the drive was uneven, nearly fell. Ahead he saw the outline of the pickup truck, both doors open like wings. The key was in the ignition, the truck started without hesitation. Zack reversed the truck into a K turn, let the doors slam shut, drove around the body of the man he killed and back up the road.

He drove out of the trees, into the clearing. The cabin wasn't there. The lawn, his friends, the car were all gone. In their place was a lush green forest, well-spaced trees as in an English wood, green carpet-like grass underfoot. A well-worn dirt path led into the wood, wildflowers bloomed in bright patches, squirrels darted from tree to tree, birds sang, a doe grazed. The sun, filtered through leafy branches, was bright, the patches of sky above deep blue.

Zack stopped the truck and stepped out, his jaw slack with amazement. He stepped onto the dirt path. As he did, the truck disappeared, the forest closed in around him. It was as if he had stepped into a painting.

The deer looked up, ears alert, peered down the path. The squirrels sat up expectantly, the bird songs swelled into a chorus. A large buck came to stand by the doe. The animals all looked up the path.

Something moved among the trees, a form approached. A glow suffused it, radiated an aura around it. The figure's movement was effortless, graceful as a wild creature. The figure drew close. Zack saw an Indian maiden: young, beautiful. A bird perched in her hand, a spotted fawn followed close behind. Her chestnut hair, parted in the middle, was done in long braids that draped across her shoulders and fell to the waist of her ornamented buckskin dress.

She drew near. Zack saw her features clearly now, the soft smile, pool-like brown eyes full of kindness. This vision, this beautiful Indian maiden—was Tomasa. The animals came to her. The warmth of her countenance expressed tangible love for each of them. She raised her eyes to Zack.

"Go in peace," she said. "Leave my forest as you found it, a balance of all things, evil and good, old and new, magical and ordinary." She spread her arms wide. "This place has always been so and always will be. Evil men come. They upset the balance; the Protector restores it. It is as it should be, for the spirits of my ancestors dwell here."

Tomasa began to disappear, the forest and its creatures with her, as an old photograph fades. She raised her eyes to Zack and smiled. "Do not fear for your friend, his wound will heal." In a moment the magical forest, and all within it, was gone as if it had never been.

The cabin, the car, and his friends returned.

They placed Eagle Feather gently in the bed of the truck, on a nest of clothing. Jesus and Susan climbed in next to him, supported him. Zack drove away from Zaca Lake.

* * * * *

"I don't understand it." Dr. Benedict Peabody, the thoracic surgeon, shook his head. "When admitted, he had an open pneumothorax, difficulty breathing. We suspected pericardial tamponade—he exhibited muffled heart tones, distended veins in his neck, and hypotension. We dressed the pneumothorax wound, performed a pericardiocentesis, gave him fluids, and rushed him right into the OR. We found the bullet inside the wall of the bronchus, and bleeding wounds on the anterior and posterior walls of the left pulmonary artery. We removed the bullet, then I prepared to stitch the bleeding wounds on the pulmonary artery, but...I couldn't find them. There was no sign of damage, as if the wounds had never been there. I've never seen anything like it. Even the entry wound was partially closed, as if healed—in twenty minutes, during surgery. It's as if we'd rolled in the wrong patient. Give me a break. This doesn't happen." He shook his head again. "Does your friend have some sort of special powers?"

Zack grew impatient. "Doc, you haven't told me what I need to know yet. Will he be alright?"

"Will he be alright?" Dr. Peabody gave a humorless laugh. "He's already alright. Once he awakens, he'll need some rest, but I see no reason why he can't walk out of here in twenty-four hours."

Sergeant Montana was waiting for Zack outside the recovery room. After Zack called him from the ambulance, he sent investigators over to Zaca Lake Retreat. They found the bodies of the four Mexican nationals, but not Barnard.

Zack and Montana walked to the small waiting room nearby to talk. The sergeant turned a chair around, faced Zack. "Tell me what happened to Chief Barnard."

Zack wasn't very helpful. "He was there, he shot Eagle Feather, used Susan as a body shield, then pushed her away and went off the far side of the porch. At that moment, my attention was on Eagle Feather."

Montana looked thoughtful. Susan and Jesus had already told him versions of the same story, Zack knew. Susan told of being thrust forward down the steps. She tried to save herself with her bound hands, ended up bruised and slightly concussed. She had no idea what happened to Barnard after he pushed her. As for Jesus, he was on the ground where he had fallen. His focus was on Tomasa and Eagle Feather. He didn't see where Barnard had gone.

"Where can I find this Tomasa?"

"She's a Chumash woman. I never learned where she lived. You might inquire at the reservation."

Montana nodded. "My men will continue the search for Chief Barnard. It seems most likely he sustained a bullet wound in the exchange and ran. If he's out there, we'll find him." He inclined his head toward Zack. "From what Rick Malden had to say, it seems Barnard had a fairly sophisticated operation going on right under our noses."

Zack was surprised. "You spoke to Malden?"

It seemed Malden had gone to Montana after he had tried to reach Zack and Eagle Feather, without success. Worried they might be in danger, he told Montana that Dom had tried to kill Zack and Eagle Feather. Although reluctant to believe it, Sergeant Montana did some quick checks, including Dom's bank account. He was now ready to accept the fact that Dom had been dirty.

He listened to Zack tell the full story of the kidnapping and shootout. When Zack finished, he shook his head slowly. "I've known Barnard professionally and personally for years. He always went above and beyond in his service to the town of Santa Lupita. That town was his life. I just don't understand it."

"He told me he entered into the drug conspiracy for that exact reason; to assist his city, keep it safe during a time of crises," Zack said. "He seemed to think the end justified the means."

Montana stood. "It all got way out of hand. Next thing you know, it's kidnapping and attempted manslaughter. I just didn't think he had it in him." He began to walk away, turned back. "This investigation is far from over. I'm missing two bodies, and at least one killer. I'd like you to stay in town for the next couple of days."

Zack nodded. "I figured."

CHAPTER FIFTY-ONE

Rufus Reyes came for Jesus at the hospital. Jesus was happy to see him; the hospital did not hold pleasant memories.

The police sergeant had interviewed him, asked many questions. He didn't seem satisfied with Jesus' answers. At last he had called Señor Reyes. He told Jesus to wait in the lobby.

Jesus was surprised to find Candida waiting in Señor Reyes' truck.

"Don Rufus asked me to interpret for him," she said, and gave Jesus a bright smile. "I wanted to see you before you went home."

"Home?"

"Yes, Don Rufus has booked your flight. We are on our way to the airport now."

Señor Reyes started the truck. "I can't seem to keep you out of trouble, young man. I'm gonna take you right to the airport this time and put you on the plane myself."

Candida gestured to the back of the truck. "He has packed all your belongings. You'll be home with your wife and daughters today."

It seemed impossible to Jesus. Even now he didn't dare believe it, after all that happened. "But the policeman? He was not happy with me. He will let me go?"

ZACA

"He is satisfied," Señor Reyes said through Candida. "He does not believe you were responsible for any crimes. He spoke with Immigration. They are willing to consider this a deportation. That is how it will appear on record."

Still, Jesus did not dare to hope. He looked at Candida. "What will you do?"

She glanced at Señor Reyes before she replied. "Don Rufus has asked me to take Jorge's job as superintendent. I told him I would."

Another surprise. Jesus stared at her. "But, you are a..."

"A woman? Yes, it is unusual. Don Rufus wants to make many changes. He feels that a woman boss will be sure to look out for the safety and rights of all women."

Señor Reyes spoke. Candida interpreted. "He says he wants his farm to become a model for all farms that employ immigrant workers. He thinks when other farms see how he can help his workers and still be profitable, they will copy his methods."

"That is a wonderful thing," Jesus said. "For you as well, for you will be part of it. I am very happy for you."

They arrived at the Santa Maria Airport, parked in the lot. They all walked into the terminal together. Don Rufus helped him check his bag. He explained to Jesus he would change planes in Los Angeles, again in Mexico City. He handed him his ticket.

Only now did Jesus believe that he was truly on his way home.

325

They walked together to security. Candida gave him a long hug. When she stepped back, Señor Reyes gave Jesus a small satchel.

"For the trip," he said. He patted Jesus on the shoulder.

Jesus watched them walk away.

In the plane, Jesus stowed the satchel under the seat in front of him. When the seatbelt sign was off, he picked it up, looked in it. He found a clean shirt and pants. There was a small cosmetic bag with toothpaste and toothbrush, deodorant, and items he could use to clean up during the layover at Los Angeles. There was a check. Jesus stared at it. It was for more money than he had ever had at one time. When converted to pesos, it would last him and his family for several years, maybe even more, if he invested wisely.

Jesus watched the golden hills crawl by far below. What an amazing, magical land, this America.

CHAPTER FIFTY-TWO

Thirty-six hours later Eagle Feather felt well enough to join Zack and Susan for a visit with Paula Sanchez at the Chumash Reservation. Dr. Peabody had released Eagle Feather from the hospital the day after surgery. By then the entrance wound looked like the two-year-old bullet wound scar on Zack's shoulder.

"I heal quickly," was Eagle Feather's only comment.

Zack had a different vehicle, a Jeep this time. Luke Forrester, his boss back in Tuba City was not happy to see the size of the repair bill the rental company had presented him. The Jeep came from the FBI fleet in Santa Maria where they did their own repairs.

Paula told Zack on the phone to come on down her road, now that he knew the way. Rebecca, it seemed, was having a busy day in the public relations office. When they arrived, Paula invited them into the house and steered them to her living room. She had iced tea and a plate of cookies for them.

When introductions were complete and everyone had their drink, Paula waved them to chairs. She cocked an eyebrow at Zack. "Well, Cowboy, you certainly did stir things up."

Zack gave her an embarrassed grin.

"Don't get me wrong, I'm mighty pleased. Now that the conspiracy between the chief and the drug cartels is destroyed, we look forward to less crime and more peace in those forests." She looked at Zack with admiration. "You held on like a pit bull on a bear to get it done. Congratulations."

Zack chuckled. "I had to, Eagle Feather was on my case the whole time."

"White Man here needs a nudge to get him goin'."

Paula turned to Eagle Feather. "How's that wound? From what I heard, you shouldn't even be out of bed yet."

"Just fine."

Zack turned to Paula. "That brings up a subject we'd like to discuss with you. We feel some spiritual influence might have effected Eagle Feather's healing."

"How so?"

"Well, we think..." Zack interrupted himself, his eye on the wall opposite him, above Paula's head. He stood, walked over for a closer look at a photograph hanging there. It was a group of people in an impromptu portrait at an outing of some sort. It might have been a family, a mix of ages and genders. He pointed to the photo. "What is this?"

Paula's eyebrows arched in surprise. "Why, that's my sister's family on a picnic at Lake Cachuma."

"When was it taken?"

"Oh, maybe twenty years ago now." Paula studied Zack. "Why?"

"Who is that?"

Paula rose from her chair for a better look. "That's my niece. She died a year after that picture was taken, in an automobile accident." Paula shook her head. "A real tomboy, that one. Always roaming the woods, from the time she was a little girl. Loved it." Paula's eyes filmed over. "Now you've gone and done it, Cowboy. Why on earth did you ask about her?"

"What's her name?"

"Why, her name is Tomasa, but we all called her Tommy, 'cause she was such a tomboy."

There was stunned silence in the room.

Paula looked around in surprise. "What?"

"Paula, when we last met you thought it wise to send someone with me to represent the tribe while I was in the mountains. Who did you send?"

"To be honest, Cowboy, I forgot to send anyone."

Zack took Paula gently by the arm, led her back to her seat. "Sit down. We've got a story to tell you."

For the next hour Zack, Susan and Eagle Feather told all that had happened to them. Each contributed to the fabric of the tale from his or her particular perspective, right up to Eagle Feather's miraculous healing. Eagle Feather even opened his shirt to show the angry pucker of the entry wound in his chest.

Paula sat back in her chair through it all, overwhelmed. "I always felt there was truth to the legends. I just never thought..." She lapsed into silence.

"You just never thought your niece might end up as part of the legend," Susan said gently.

Paula nodded.

"She may be a reincarnation of the original," Eagle Feather suggested.

Susan was excited. "We know the girl of the legend died, or I should say was sent to the Upper World at a young age. It may be that each reincarnation of her spirit is destined to repeat the experience."

"She seems trapped between the Middle World and the Upper World," Eagle Feather said.

"It's a good thing." Zack glanced at Paula. "She balances the hostility of the other character out there with her gentleness."

"Tell me more about that one," Paula said. "You call him the Protector?"

"That's what Tommy called him. We called him the Hunter, because of the way he hunts and dresses out his prey."

"He kills, you say. Spirits don't generally kill."

"He's no spirit," Susan said.

"I don't understand."

"We believe he's another species of human, but he appears as a spirit." Zack saw the puzzlement on Paula's face. "I know this is a lot all at once. You accept the legend of the Indian maiden, so you're half way there."

Susan held up a hand. "Let me try to explain. As an anthropologist, I've known that Homo sapiens is not the only member of our species. There have been many others in the past, but most became extinct. We scientists think we have it all worked out, and then we discover new bones that tell a different story. Until recently, we thought Neanderthals were similar but not connected to Homo sapiens. We now know that they probably lived and bred together." Susan looked at Paula. "Still with me?"

"Yes, yes, go on."

"Okay. Now consider *Homo floresiensis*. Although discourse continues, there is no doubt in my mind that this was a member of the genus Homo, shared a common ancestor with modern humans, but split from the modern human lineage and followed a distinct evolutionary path. *Floresiensis* lived from 100,000 up to 12,000 years ago, almost yesterday in anthropological terms. But these people were just one meter in height with a brain volume smaller than a Chimpanzee. Because they lived on islands, separated from other humans, they evolved differently."

Susan paused, sipped her drink. "I...we have become aware of another mutation of Homo sapiens, one that is not only recent, but current. This species of human evolved differently yet parallel to Homo sapiens. My theory is they were outnumbered by our ancestors; chased out of the light into the deep woods where they hid away. Without fire, they necessarily evolved with different skills. They are fiercely predatory. They are bipedal yet have maintained prehensile feet and a tail, which allows them to travel like our ape ancestors through the trees. They have tremendous strength and agility, as one might expect. They have demonstrated another intriguing mutation: the ability to change their form to that of other creatures, including humans."

331

"Shapeshifters," Eagle Feather said.

"Yes. You see, that capability would have become necessary when the deep woodlands, their habitat, diminished, and contact with humans became more frequent. It is that capability that has allowed them to hide in plain sight."

"Their predatory instincts remain," Zack said.

"Exactly. They do not coexist peacefully with us."

Paula gazed intently at Susan. "You think this Protector, or Hunter, is one of these."

"Yes."

Paula glanced at the others. Eagle Feather and Zack nodded in agreement.

"I saw his metamorphosis," Zack said.

Susan and Eagle Feather peered at him in surprise.

"You didn't tell us that," Susan said.

Zack shrugged. "Thought I'd wait until the time was right."

"Wait a minute, now." Paula rose to her feet, surveyed her three guests. "What will be done about this creature? We can't leave him to roam the woods hunting people."

"It does seem a moral dilemma," Zack said.

Eagle Feather shook his head. "Paula, just as everyone here in this room is different yet similar, so it is with these creatures. This particular one seems to have bought into the legend. He's taken on a Protector role. He appears to attack only those who kill people out there. We don't know how long these creatures live, this one may have been in those mountains a very long time."

"He seems to have a relationship with Tommy...or rather the Indian maiden," Zack said. "He responds to her. She herself remarked that together they maintain a balance."

Paula slumped into her chair. "That's a relief...I guess. I honestly don't know what to think about all of this yet."

Susan took a sip of tea, jingled ice cubes in her glass. "Come to one of my lectures, I'll tell you all about it." She pulled her glasses down on her nose to look professorial.

The others laughed.

Paula surveyed them one by one. "Only the three of you know of the existence of these creatures?"

"Four of us," Zack said. "My wife Libby knows."

"Have you told your FBI buddies about them?"

Zack laughed. "That's a good way to get assigned to the North Pole."

Paula turned to Eagle Feather. "Do your people know of them?"

"The Old Ones do. We have the legends; we know the shamans talk of seeing them. But the young modern Navajo have other things on their minds. They are less inclined to believe."

Paula looked at Susan. "You actually lecture about them."

Susan smiled. "Not specifically. As a university professor, I need to maintain credibility—if I want to keep my job, anyway." She looked at Zack. "No, what I do is preach the possibility that a parallel race could exist. Zack, here, adds reality from time to time."

"What happens if you learn of one of those creatures running amuck?"

Zack nodded toward Eagle Feather. "I call my friend here and we go deal with it. It's not a frequent thing, nor readily identifiable. It's difficult to determine whether you've got a serial killer or one of these creatures." Zack gave a wry grin. "Humans are a predatory species too, you know."

* * * * *

They met Malden at Zaca Mesa Winery. He had been out at Zaca Lake with Sergeant Montana. The winery was a convenient location for both parties to meet.

They brought their wine glasses to a picnic table out on the veranda. Toker curled up in the sun next to the table. Malden looked at the three of them, shook his head, spread his hands wide, and said, "Jesus."

They laughed.

"That about sums it up," Zack said.

"I think its pronounced *Jesus*," Eagle Feather said with a grin.

"Poor guy. Whatever happened to him?"

"He finally got to go home, thanks to Rufus," Zack said.

Susan put her hand over Malden's on the table. "How are you dealing with all this? Your friends working with the cartels and all that?"

"I'll manage just fine. I haven't been kidnapped, anyway." Malden looked at Zack. "I do feel bad you couldn't trust me."

Zack started to say something, Malden held up a hand. "I know, I know. I'd have done the same thing. You couldn't take the risk of telling me. I get it."

Zack nodded.

"Montana says we still got a killer loose in those mountains. We haven't found this guy who preys on the cartel assassins." He peered at Zack. "Are you involved in that?"

"Oh, no. As soon as Montana gives me the OK, I'm going home. My boss is getting tired of doing my job. Plus, I've got a wife and kid I haven't seen in a long time."

Malden twirled his glass. "I keep feeling there's something you aren't telling me."

Eagle Feather eyed Malden. "I'll tell you now. You know those spirits the Chumash say are in those mountains? The ones whose presence you feel once in a while when you're out there alone? They're real."

Malden gazed at Zack and then at Eagle Feather. "I'll take that under advisement."

Other Zack Tolliver FBI Novels by
R Lawson Gamble

THE OTHER

"The hunters noticed the circling birds against the rose-tinted sky above the rim rock and saw where the flat rays of the early morning sun glinted on something that didn't belong there and the three of them walked that way."

What they find sends FBI Agent Zack Tolliver and his friend Eagle Feather in pursuit of a dangerous and powerful killer.

MESTACLOCAN

Dawn in San Francisco finds the body of a young woman crumpled against a concrete bunker like yesterday's newspaper, her throat slashed. She is the third female victim, each with the same injury, all nine days apart. With a serial killer in the city, Homicide Detective Marty O'Bannon is in over his head; he calls on old friend, FBI Agent Zack Tolliver.